illicit

[a novel]

JUNE GRAY

Cover design by June Gray.

ISBN-13: 978-1532890000
ISBN-10: 1532890001

ACKNOWLEDGEMENTS

Thank you to my "ride or die" ladies, my awesome beta team: Lara, Beth, Gillian, Shannon, Kerry, and Danielle. You've been with me from the beginning and I can't tell you enough how much that means to me!

To Mary at Clean Leaf Editing: Thank you for all you do.

To my family: I love you guys so much! Thank you for your patience and understanding.

Most importantly I want to thank you, Reader. Thank you for loving the written word.

June Gray

[part one]

jocelyn

June Gray

[one]

I never meant for it to happen, to fall in love with a man who wasn't mine.

I was just reading on my bed one Sunday morning, completely lost in a different world, when my mom came into my room and said, "I want you to meet someone, Joss."

I looked up from my book so fast, I almost got whiplash. "Who?"

"Jake Mitchell."

"And who is this mysterious Jake Mitchell?" I set the open book on my chest, my interest fully piqued. My mom was a serial dater, so busy with work travel that she didn't have time for anything more than dinner or drinks. And she certainly never had time to bring them home.

She bit her lower lip, a move that made her look younger than her forty-one years. "Just someone I've been seeing."

"You've been seeing someone? And you want me to meet him?"

"Don't sound so surprised."

"Well, I am," I said, scrambling off the bed and following her down the hall. "This is the first guy you've brought home since that Joe Incident."

Nine months after the divorce with my dad was finalized, my mom had gone on a date with a man named Joe. The date had gone well so Mom invited him over to our house in Pembroke Pines, Florida, for a nightcap. I had had the unfortunate luck to walk in on them making out in the kitchen and, apparently still secretly hoping my parents would get back together, had freaked the hell out. As a result, Mom no longer brought men home and only ever mentioned them in passing, never even giving them a name.

Until today.

I didn't know what I was expecting when I turned that corner; maybe someone with a Jersey accent who looked suspiciously like Bob Hoskins in Mario Brothers. Or maybe a debonair, silver-haired fox in a suit. But this Jake Mitchell took me completely by surprise. He was really a looker, with his short brown hair, square jaw, and the bluest eyes I'd ever seen. Nor was he wearing red overalls or a pin-striped suit. No, he was just casually put together in his dark jeans and blue button-up shirt. And he was tall, fit, and... quite a bit younger than my mom.

"Hi. You must be Jocelyn," he said, getting up from the couch and offering his hand.

I shook it, trying to hide my surprise at the roughness of his palm. "Nice to meet you."

He flashed me a smile that lit up his face and crinkled the corners of his eyes. "You are the spitting image of your mom."

"Thank you. I hear that a lot." Ever since I could remember I'd been told that I looked just like my mother. Tall and lithe, with natural honey-blonde hair and bright green eyes, Amanda Blake was the kind of effortless beauty that garnered jealousy from women and attention from men. When out together, people always assumed we were sisters rather than a woman and her twenty-year old daughter.

I glanced at Mom but her gaze was fixed firmly on her new man. I couldn't really blame her; this guy was seriously handsome in an easygoing kind of way.

My eyes gravitated back in his direction. "Where did you two meet?"

"Blind date," he said in his deep, slightly coarse voice, his warm gaze directed at my mother. "Our mutual friend set us up, we hit it off, and now here we are."

"And you've been together how long?"

"Almost three months."

My eyebrows shot up.

Mom noticed the look on my face and burst out laughing. "Well, don't look so shocked. I *am* capable of a relationship." She walked over to Jake and slipped her arm around his waist. "I just had to find the right man first."

I grinned as I contemplated the pairing. Her pale skin and blonde hair was a nice contrast to his tan skin and dark features. They looked so good together I felt almost envious. *Someday*, I told myself, *I'll find a guy like that*.

"Well, I need to get going." Jake tucked some hair behind Mom's ear then pressed a soft kiss on her lips. "I'll be back tonight."

She beamed up at him—I swear I've never seen her look

9

this happy—then she uttered the words that sealed the deal, proving once and for all she was dead serious about this Jake guy: "I'm cooking steak and vegetables."

"But you don't cook!" I blurted out.

My mom laughed. "I will for the right man."

He chuckled, pressing a kiss to her temple before heading to the door. "Nice to meet you, Jocelyn."

After he left, I stared at Mom in bewilderment. To her credit, she managed to keep a straight face for a whole three seconds before the joy exploded all over her face.

"He's a keeper, I take it?" I asked, her smile infecting me as well.

"I think so."

"But how old is he? Like, twenty seven?"

She bit her lips together. "Thirty."

"You cradle-robber!" I teased, pinching her side. "He's only ten years older than me."

She giggled—yes, my mom actually *giggled*—and ruffled my hair. "Honey, sometimes age is only a number, not a state of mind." She wrapped an arm around my shoulder and leaned her head on mine. "Besides, Jake makes me feel young again."

"Are you happy?" I asked, but one look at her gave me the answer. Her entire face glowed, her eyes bright and cheeks flushed.

She let out a sigh and squeezed me. "I am, Joss."

I hugged her. Goodness knew, after an ugly divorce and struggling as a single parent for seven years, she deserved a little bit of happiness. "I'm happy for you, Mom."

———————

Jake came back for dinner that night bearing a bouquet of roses for my mother and a smaller bouquet of daisies for me.

"You didn't have to get me anything," I said, lifting the flowers up to my nose anyway. I mean, daisies weren't really all that fragrant, but it seemed like the thing to do. "Thanks. Now, can you educate the guys at my school on how to treat a woman?"

"I don't think they'd listen to an old geezer like me," he said with a good-natured chuckle.

I flashed him a mischievous smile over the flowers. "I wouldn't call you old. Geezer maybe, but not old."

He chuckled, and it was then I noticed the corners of his eyes crinkle when he's happy.

We went out to the back patio to start setting up for dinner. Mom and I rarely dined outside as we found South Florida weather to be too humid for comfort, but I guess tonight was a special exception, frizzy hair be damned.

"So what's your major?" he asked, following me with the plate of raw steaks.

I bent down to turn on the gas and start the grill. "Undeclared."

Mom joined us a few moments later with the vegetables. "If it was possible to major in reading, Joss would have a PhD by now."

"What kind of books do you like to read?" Jake asked. "Twilight? Hunger Games?"

I shrugged. "Those were entertaining, but I go through phases. Lately I've been reading biographies."

One dark eyebrow rose. "Oh?"

"Right now I'm reading about Margaret Thatcher."

"Really." He held out his hand, asking for the spatula. "May I?"

I handed it over and stepped aside. "Uh, sure." I watched as he set the steaks on the grill, his entire demeanor one of self-assurance. It wasn't his finest moment, to be sure.

"I think grilling is in every man's DNA, don't you agree?" he asked, glancing at me.

I almost snorted. "I read an article recently about caveman instincts that still linger today," I said in a forced nonchalant manner. "How even the most progressive men still display latent alpha male tendencies, especially around females who are more than capable of taking care of themselves."

He stilled, studying me for the longest time. I waited for him to back down, to apologize for taking over, but he surprised me by lifting an eyebrow. "I guess we're not as evolved as we think. Our instincts still dictate our actions." He held up the spatula, amusement in his eyes. "Now, how do you like your steak?"

Regular dinner at the Blake house usually consisted of me eating ramen noodles or mac and cheese in my room while mom worked. But we had a longstanding date every Sunday, when we'd go to a restaurant and spend hours catching up over dinner. I always looked forward to that time together, talking about our week, chatting away like girlfriends, and ordering way more dessert than we could ever eat. It wasn't a traditional kind of family setup, but it was our way and we made it work.

So to have all three of us sitting together that Sunday, using the wrought iron dining set that we'd only used a handful of times, was unusual and slightly awkward.

"Jocelyn, we have something to tell you," Mom said during the meal.

My ears perked up. She rarely ever called me by my real name. Unless… "Is everything okay?"

Jake reached for my mom's hand across the table and nodded for her to continue.

My heart started to thump hard in my chest. "Are you getting married?"

"No," he said with a nervous laugh. "Nothing that monumental."

"I've asked Jake to move in with us," Mom said.

An incredulous laugh escaped from my mouth. "And that's not monumental?"

"Joss," Mom began. "I know it's a bit of a surprise, but—"

"A bit! I just met him today," I said, trying to keep my voice a few octaves below hysterics. "You just met him three months ago."

The news worked like acid; the longer it seeped in, the more it burned. Here they were, holding hands at the table, addressing me like parents explaining something complicated to a child.

I turned to my mom with hurt in my eyes. Used to be it was the two of us against the world. Now I was the outsider, and my opinion was no longer needed when it came to life-changing decisions.

"Joss, say something," Mom said.

I took a long sip of water, swallowing down the angry words that were threatening to spew out. I stood up, the iron chair scraping loudly against the brick patio. "I need to do my homework," I said and left.

I heard them come in the house a half hour later, talking in hushed, muted tones. And not too long after, someone knocked on my door.

"Can I come in?" asked a deep voice that was definitely not my mother's.

I wiped at my cheeks with the sheet and sat up. "Fine."

The door cracked open and Jake's concerned face peered in. He entered cautiously, casting a long look around. "Nice room."

"I haven't had a chance to clean it up," I said, wishing I'd at least taken the time to put my dirty clothes in the hamper instead of throwing them in the corner of the room.

He walked over to the books piled in front of the overfilled, sagging bookshelf. I'd long ago run out of room for my books and had taken to stacking them on the floor. I was at seven teetering towers and counting.

He pulled out a book from the bookshelf and held it out. "Everyone says their favorite book is To Kill a Mockingbird, but I don't know."

"What? You didn't like it?" I asked, momentarily setting aside my resentment to talk books.

"I did. It's a good story, just not my favorite," he said with a shrug. "In fact, I can't really choose one favorite."

"You like to read as well?"

He slid the book back in place and stuck his hands in his pockets. "I believe *voracious* is the word," he replied. "So what's your favorite?"

"If we base favorite on how many times I've read it, I'd say Jane Eyre."

"Ah, the classic young girl falling for the older man."

I smiled, thinking that maybe Jake had some redeeming qualities after all. At the very least, he knew a little about the classics. "So are you going to do it, then? Are you moving in with us?"

He sat on the end of my bed, oceans of blanket between us. "That depends."

"On?"

"You."

We locked eyes across the bed, his gaze so direct that I found myself first to look away. "Do you *want* to move in?"

"Yes."

"Do you love my mom?"

He didn't even blink. "Yes. I know three months doesn't seem all that long, but this feels right."

I picked at a loose thread on my blanket, at a loss for what to say.

"Jocelyn, I just want you to know, I have no plans of acting like the Big Man of the house," he said. "I'm just here to share a life with the woman I really care about. And maybe with her daughter, if she'll let me."

I studied his face, looking for telltale signs of insincerity. "All right, you can move in," I said when I saw none. "But don't think you can leave hair all over the bathroom sink or anything."

His eyes crinkled at the corners. "No problem."

"You can't hang a singing fish or anything with antlers on the wall either."

His lips twitched. "Wouldn't dream of it."

"And you have to keep your books sequestered."

He laughed, deep and rich. "Of course. Can't have our books fraternizing."

"It would be chaos."

"Pandemonium."

Once again, our eyes locked across the room, but this time there were no expectations or disappointments between us, only the first sprouts of a growing friendship.

[two]

Jake started moving in the next week. I was home alone when he showed up at the front door with a huge brown box and his very own set of keys.

"Sorry. I didn't know you'd be here," he said as soon as he saw me doing homework on the couch. He walked over and placed the box down by the living room wall.

I set aside my laptop. "I have the day off from work and don't have to be in class till two."

"Oh. Where do you work?"

"At the bookstore at Pembroke Gardens."

"Huh," he said, regarding me with curious eyes. "That sounds kind of perfect for you."

I jumped up from the couch, only belatedly realizing that I must look like a hot mess in my cutoff shorts and a ratty old tank top. I hadn't even bothered to tie my long blonde hair up properly, instead just twisted it in a knot at the top of my head.

"I should go take a shower."

"Wait," he said. "Would you mind giving me a hand first? I have a few more things to unload."

"Um, sure." Barefoot, I followed him out to the driveway where his pickup truck occupied my mom's space. "I don't recommend parking there," I said with my hands on my hips.

He jumped onto the truck bed. "What? Here?"

"Yeah. That's Mom's space, and she's very territorial."

He turned to me with a dimpled grin and handed over a box. "Duly noted."

I set the box down on the ground and was immediately handed another one. Only then did I notice the several power tools—*machines* was a more accurate word—that sat near the front of the truck bed. "We're unloading those?"

"Do you mind? They're not very heavy."

"Somehow I don't believe that."

"Okay, they're a little heavy." He surveyed the contents of truck then turned to me. "Tell you what. You come up here and just slide them over to the edge and I'll lower them." He jumped off the truck, landing neatly on his running shoes.

I put my hands on the tailgate, getting ready to clamber up when I felt large hands go around my waist and lift me with ease. I swallowed hard and tried to ignore the sudden awkward tension. "Um, thanks. So… which one first?"

"Let's start with the table saw."

I made my way over to what was essentially a small table with a serrated half-circle sticking up in the center. "This?" When he nodded, I started to slide it over, finding it lighter than I expected. "Looks like one of those deli meat slicers."

"When you're not careful, it becomes a literal meat slicer."

I winced at the gruesome visual. "Have you ever cut your meat?" Our eyes flicked to each other and we burst into laughter.

"Can't say I have," he said, still chuckling. "Though I did accidentally slice off the tip of my thumb a while ago." He held out his right hand, showing me the blunt edge of his thumb. It was then I noticed the rest of his large, manly hand and the strong forearm connected to it, dusted with hair.

"All right," I said, shaking off the strange feeling that had come over me. "What do you want me to hand you next?"

That night, Mom cornered me in the hallway, glancing in the living room to make sure Jake was staying put. "Are you really okay with him moving in?" she asked in a hushed voice.

"Sure." What I really wanted to tell her was that it was a little too late for that question when the guy's stuff was already all over the house. But I knew this meant a lot to her and I wanted to make the transition as painless as possible.

"I'm glad." She kissed the side of my head. "I think it'll be good, having him here. At the very least there's someone else in the house whenever I leave town."

"Mom, I told you I was fine. I can take care of myself."

"Yeah, but that doesn't keep me from worrying whenever I leave you. I'm your mom, it's my job to worry."

I studied her, seeing a happier reflection of myself. "You think you're going to marry him?"

"I don't know about that," she said with a nervous laugh. "One step at a time."

"You know some people get married first before moving in together."

She gave me a withering look. "Are you sure you're not the mother in this relationship?"

"Sometimes I really wonder."

She laughed and pinched my nose. "I love you, you little brat."

"Love you too, Mom."

———————

The first night with Jake was not as uncomfortable as I'd expected. Still, eating together at the dinner table like a regular family might take some getting used to.

"You don't have to work tonight?" I asked Mom.

She shook her head, her mouth too full of spaghetti to speak.

Jake drank from his glass of water, his Adam's apple bobbing up and down. "How many hours a day do you work, Amanda?"

"During tax season? Twelve to fifteen."

He frowned. "That seems like a lot."

"Thank you! That's what I've been telling her," I said. I leaned forward conspiratorially. "Maybe between the two of us, we can convince her to slow down and take on fewer accounts."

He grinned. "Deal." He turned to my mom. "I hope you know Joss and I are going to come down hard on you. We won't relent until you slow down."

Mom flashed a tight-lipped smile at the two of us. "Okay. Okay."

"To my new daddy," I joked, lifting my glass for a toast. "Already laying down the law."

Mom choked on her garlic bread while Jake just chuckled. "Call me daddy again and you'll be grounded for a month," he said with a mock stern face.

It was my turn to laugh. "Yeah. Good luck with that."

Afterward, Jake insisted on washing the dishes even though it was my chore.

"I got it," he said, shooing me away with the flower-shaped scrubber, his hands encased in bright pink rubber gloves.

Mom and I backed off, biting back our smiles as we watched him scrub food off the plates. "Alpha male tendencies indeed," I whispered.

"You ladies can stop giggling now," he growled with his back to us.

Mom sidled up to Jake and hugged him, pressing her cheek to his back. She let out a long, contented sigh. "We're just glad to have you around."

He picked up her hand and dropped a kiss on her knuckles. "Happy to be here."

I stood there, watching the exchange, feeling like I was intruding on an intimate moment. I edged out of the room to give them their privacy.

"Jocelyn," Jake called before I could turn the corner.

"Yeah?"

Mom was still wrapped around his back when he said, "I left some books out on the coffee table. You're welcome to borrow them."

I brightened. "Thanks." I hurried to the living room and found five books, each with a beautiful embossed-leather cover. I gave each one due attention, skimming the pads of my fingers along the aged covers, opening each book and holding my nose between its pages. They smelled old, musty. Divine.

When I looked up I found Jake sitting on the arm of the couch, watching me with a smile tugging at his lips. "I love it too. The smell." He sank down beside me and took a book, opening it to the inside flap to show me the handwritten name inside: *John Jacob Mitchell*. "These belonged to my grandfather."

"So the nerd runs in the family?"

"That it definitely does." He shut the book gently and handed it back to me.

"I'll take good care of them," I said, feeling a little like a child who'd been trusted with something important.

He nodded, making a noise of approval from the back of his throat. "I'm sure you will." He pushed up off his knees and stood. "Well, goodnight."

"Night." I watched him walk away with a light, buoyant feeling in my chest. "Hey, Jake?"

He stopped and looked over his shoulder. "Yeah?"

"Welcome home." After he left the room, I hugged the books to my chest and let out a happy sigh.

[three]

After a long shift at work I came home one day and found Jake rearranging his tools in the garage. I meant to go straight inside the house and veg in front of the T.V., but found myself stopping in the middle of the garage to watch him instead.

"How was work?" he asked, muscles straining as he pulled a large metal drill press across the concrete floor.

"Oh, you know, customers trying to return books they'd obviously already read, people spilling their macchiatos on shelves. The usual. I swear, if I didn't have to deal with customers, it'd be the perfect job."

He dusted his hands on his shorts and grinned. "You mean if you could just be alone in that entire place, surrounded by coffee and books?"

"Exactly," I said with an unexpected laugh. The guy definitely understood me. "So what's going on here?"

Jake wiped at his forehead with the hem of his shirt,

allowing me a quick peek at his abs. Apparently he works out. "I need to get this space sorted out so I can get back to work."

"What do you do?"

"I'm a furniture maker." He leaned against the table saw. "I work mostly by commission, but I also have a few stores that display and sell my work for me." He flashed a rueful smile. "I used to have a huge detached shed to work in, but the owner of the house I was renting decided to sell."

"Oh."

"But I want to make it clear your mom asked me to move in long before I even knew I was getting kicked out."

"I wasn't even thinking it."

"I know. I just want to clear any misconceptions before they arise."

"Okay. I'm going to go change then I'll come out and help you," I said to change the subject because, yes, I actually had been thinking it.

After an hour of moving things around, he was finally satisfied with the layout. "I think this will work." He swiped at his forehead. "Damn, it's humid out today."

"Hang on, I'll be right back," I said and disappeared inside the house. A few minutes later I came out with a tray with two glasses and a pitcher of ice-cold lemonade.

His face brightened. "Oh, perfect." He took the tray and carried it to the open bed of his truck. "Did you make this?" he asked, pouring out two glasses.

"Mom made it last night." I jumped into the truck and sat down, my legs dangling over the edge of the open gate. I took a long pull of the lemonade and sighed in relief. He wasn't kidding—it was as hot as Satan's balls out here.

He followed suit and we sat for a few moments in comfortable silence.

"So what's your story, Jake?" I asked after some time.

He turned those blue eyes on me. "Well, I was born and raised in Boston. Studied industrial design and furniture design in college."

"What brings you to South Florida?"

"Employment, mainly. After college I moved to Orlando to work at an amusement park."

I sucked in my cheeks to keep from smiling. "Please tell me you played a prince at Disney World. That would make my day."

He chuckled, shaking his head. "Actually, I worked behind the scenes. Building and maintaining sets, that kind of thing."

I sagged, sticking out my lower lip. "That's nowhere near as fun."

He raised an eyebrow. "Not as embarrassing either."

"So is your family back in Boston?"

"Mostly, but my brother's living it up in Miami. He came for spring break one year and never left," he said. "Tristan's a big fan of women, the lifestyle, and the weather, in that order."

"What about you?"

He shrugged. "Not really my scene."

We were quiet for a time. A question burned on my tongue, but after some thought I realized I already knew the answer: Relationships with older women was clearly his *scene*.

To fill up the silence I pointed to the house directly across the street. "The Lombarts live there. Two kids, one handicapped. To the right is a young couple, Pepper and Mark.

He's a firefighter and their garage is fixed up like a fancy gym. Next door is a family from India. Their daughter is thirteen and apparently loves Taylor Swift and One Direction, based on what I hear blasting from her bedroom."

I pointed to the elderly man a few doors down who was busy watering his flowers with a leaky hose. His dog yapped around his feet, chasing around the wayward streams of water from the hose. "That's Mr. Jackson. Those are his wife's flowers. She used to be out there everyday, gardening."

"What happened to her?"

"She died. Heart attack," I said, remembering the night last year when Mom and I had awoken to the sirens and had peeked through the curtains to find flashing lights across the street. "Since then he's been coming out here every day, making sure her garden is still as beautiful as the day she died."

Jake took in the story quietly, his eyebrows drawn as he gazed across the street. Without warning he jumped from the truck and ran inside the garage to rummage through his boxes. A few seconds later, he jogged across the street with a hose looped around his arm and a brand new nozzle in his hand. He approached Mr. Jackson and introduced himself before offering the hose. The older man nodded and pointed to the faucet, watching as Jake attached the new hose and nozzle.

After testing the hose, the two men shook hands, and Jake bent down to scratch the dog behind his ears before making his way back to our driveway.

"That was nice of you."

He shrugged. "I wasn't using it."

"You always such a Boy Scout?"

He flashed me a playful grin. "Not always." He took a drink of his lemonade, completely emptying the glass before pouring another. "So tell me about yourself, Jocelyn."

I lifted my hair away from my neck to keep cool. "What do you want to know?"

"Everything."

"Okay... I've lived in this house my whole life. My parents divorced when I was thirteen and Dad moved up to Tampa." I chewed on my lip. "That's about it. There's nothing remarkable about me or my life."

"I doubt that," he said. "So what about boys? Should I expect any gentlemen callers coming around to woo you?"

"What am I? Seventy-five?" I laughed, leaning back on my hands and swinging my feet until my flip-flops fell off. "But no."

"No?"

I turned and looked at him. "Nope. Nobody coming around, breaking down my door."

"I find that hard to believe."

It was my turn to shrug. "There is this one guy in my Econ class—Eli—who sits next to me. He's asked me a few times if I wanted to 'hang out,'" I said, making air quotes.

"And, what, you're not into him?"

"I don't know. He's cute and he's fun to talk to. But I don't know. I'd rather stay home and hang out with my book boyfriends. At least they keep me satisfied." My face flamed when I realized what I'd inferred. "Not in *that* way."

He laughed, chucking me in the arm. "You get embarrassed easily. I knew what you meant."

"I just…" I took in a deep breath and decided to be blunt. The last thing we needed in this situation was a misunderstanding. "I don't want you to think I'm flirting with you. We have an unusual situation here, so I want to make sure the lines are drawn and clear."

A smile tugged at his lips as he nodded. "Agreed."

"But don't go acting like my dad either."

"Ha! I wouldn't dream of it." He held out a hand. "How about friends then?"

I took his hand, surprised by its warmth as his fingers folded around mine. "I think that will work."

One corner of his mouth tipped up. "But if you need me to pull the dad card, just say so. I'll do the whole cleaning my shotgun thing should you want a guy chased off."

"Don't worry, I don't think that will be a problem."

"Why not?"

"If they're not put off by my big nose and butt chin, I'm sure my introvertedness will do it."

He let out an incredulous laugh. "First of all, your nose is not big. Not by a long shot. And second—" He reached out and pressed his thumb to the shallow cleft in my chin. "This gives you character. It makes you unique."

I snorted and pulled away, my chin still tingling from his touch.

He gave me a reproachful look. "I know I'm not your dad, but if I had come into your life sooner I would have told you every day that you're beautiful."

I stared at him, caught between admiration and adoration. I shook off the strange feelings before they took hold. "I'm more than my looks. That's what having a mom taught me."

He nodded. "You certainly are." Finally he cleared his throat and looked down at his watch. "When does Amanda get home today?"

"In thirty minutes. I'd better go get ready," I said, jumping off the truck and slipping back into my flip-flops.

"Where are you going?"

"Out."

"By yourself?"

"With my friend, Ashley."

"Dancing?"

"Yes."

"Drinking?"

I folded my arms over my chest and raised an eyebrow. "These questions are seriously bordering on parental."

He grinned and held up his palms. "Okay. Got it. But if you need a ride home, just call."

I waved him away. "No need. I'm the DD."

It turned out I was a terrible designated driver. Buoyed by the fact that we made it inside the club without getting carded, Ashley managed to talk me into ordering a drink. "Surprise me," I'd told the bartender and had received a tall glass of Long Island Ice Tea. Halfway into the drink, I realized I was not going to be getting behind the wheel anytime soon.

I called my mom's phone, not sure how she would take the news that her only daughter—underage, no less—was drunk. After a few rings, she picked up.

"Mom?" I shouted into the phone as the music thumped all around me.

"Joss?"

"Can you come pick us up?" I asked, trying to temper my voice in hopes that my inebriation wouldn't be as obvious.

"You don't have to shout, sweetheart."

I covered my mouth, giggling. "Sorry, I thought I was whispering."

"Are you drunk?" she asked with amusement in her voice.

Filled with a mixture of guilt and giddiness, I said, "Not entirely drunk. Just... tipsy. I didn't mean to even get this far. I think the bartender put too much alcohol in my drink."

"Don't worry, Joss," she said. "You're an adult."

I let out a humorless laugh. "Right. An adult who needs her mom to come pick her up."

"Jake will come get you."

"Jake?" I asked, panicked by the idea that he would see me acting like some young, out-of-control kid. "Can't you do it?"

"I'm sorry, Joss, but I've had a few drinks myself. You're not the only drunk Blake girl tonight," she said with a chuckle. "So sit tight. He'll be there in a bit."

I hung up and turned to Ashley, who still swayed to the music with her eyes closed and her hands waving in the air. I poked her stomach to get her attention. "Jake's picking us up."

"Who?" she asked, her mouth shaped into an O while she kept swaying.

"My mom's boyfriend. And our new roommate."

That got Ashley's attention; she stopped and gaped. "I didn't even know she had a boyfriend, let alone one serious enough to move in!"

"Neither did I." I leaned against the wall, trying to keep from wobbling in my mom's eight hundred dollar Jimmy

Choos. In hindsight I probably shouldn't have borrowed the shoes, and I definitely shouldn't have told Ashley about Jake. But alcohol, I found out, has a way of screwing with one's decision-making. "You should see him, Ash. He's so hot."

Her eyes got big. "Are you crushing on him?"

"No!" I cried, slightly horrified that she was a little bit right. "Okay, maybe a little. But he's off limits. To me, to you, to anybody but my mom."

She grabbed my hand and dragged me to the exit. "Okay, let's go. I need to see this guy."

Jake's truck pulled up to the curb ten minutes later. He jumped out to open the passenger door for us. "Ladies." He smiled as he held the door open, looking so damn good in his jeans and a V-neck shirt that molded to his body.

Ashley pinched my side and whispered, "Holy shit."

I turned to her with wide, agreeing eyes. "Right?" I mouthed then turned back to Jake. "Thanks for coming to get us."

He climbed back into the driver seat and started the truck.

"Sorry to get you out of bed," Ashley said, still eyeballing him.

I heard the ding of an incoming text and checked my phone. *I bet he was naked when you called.* When I looked up, Ashley was biting back a smile.

Stop that! He's right beside me! I wrote back.

"It's no problem," Jake said, keeping his eyes on the road. "I was in the garage anyway."

"Oh? What were you doing?" Ashley asked.

"Just some woodworking."

He was working with his wood, Ashley text me.

I snickered.

I don't know how you can stand living with him.

I glanced up at Jake and thumbed my phone. *What do you mean? He's a nice guy.*

Yeah, that's what I mean. He's nice and he's HOT. I wouldn't be able to sleep with him right down the hall from me.

I sleep fine. Now shut up.

If I were you, I'd drill some holes in the wall so you can watch him take a shower.

I put my phone away and jabbed an elbow into her side, letting her know enough was enough.

After we dropped Ashley off at her apartment, Jake turned to me with dimples drawn. "What were you two texting about me?"

"What? We weren't," I said, averting my gaze.

He chuckled and pulled away from the curb. "Okay, but make small holes if you're going to drill holes in the wall. Don't want your mom finding them too quickly."

I sank into the seat, my face no doubt flushing scarlet. "For the record, I didn't write that."

He laughed and gave a light smack on my knee. "I'm just kidding, Jocelyn."

I leaned my head back and closed my eyes, intending to sleep the rest of the way home, but I couldn't shake the visual of Jake naked and wet, maybe even playing with himself...

I opened my eyes, my face hot with shame.

Still, if there was ever an acceptable time to entertain dirty thoughts about my mom's boyfriend, it was now. Like I said, alcohol messed with one's ability to make decisions, good or—in this case—very, very bad.

June Gray

[four]

"So how do you like Jake?" Mom asked me that Sunday as we ate at Brimstone, a restaurant close to where I worked. She had decided to keep our longstanding Sunday dates just between the two of us, a symbolic gesture to let me know that a man would never come between us.

"He's nice. But he uses up all the hot water when he showers."

Mom laughed, taking a sweet potato fry from her plate and offering it to me. "So you've noticed too. We're planning on getting a new hot water heater soon. The one we have is just too small for three adults." She leaned back in her seat, eyeing me quietly.

I squirmed, wondering if she could read minds because, if so, I was in trouble. I still couldn't get the image of a naked Jake out of my mind; in fact, my imagination had filled in details, like the v on his hips or the vein running down his swollen biceps, amongst other swollen things. The image had also infiltrated other parts of my life so that every time I read a fiction novel, my brain automatically cast Jake as the male protagonist. Needless to say I'd gone back to reading non-fiction. "He also leaves his running shoes everywhere."

Mom clapped her hands to her cheeks with a mock shocked face. "No!"

I couldn't help but laugh. "And he doesn't screw the cap on the orange juice all the way before putting it back in the fridge."

"The monster!"

"Do you know how many times I've shaken the bottle only to have juice come out all over the place?" I asked. "It's annoying."

Mom tempered her smile. "I'll talk to him about that."

"What prompted these questions anyway?"

"I just want to make sure you're okay with him. So if you have anything else you want to get off your chest, now's the time."

I said nothing.

"He's not making you uncomfortable, is he?" she asked, concern wrinkling her forehead. "I know it's strange to have a man in the house and all."

"No, he's fine," I said quickly. "Not uncomfortable."

"I know you two have many things in common. I'm glad you two get along so well."

"Yeah. Me too."

"So," Mom said, wiggling her eyebrows. "Let's talk about your twenty-first birthday. I was thinking a party. A big, crazy shindig where everybody gets drunk and pukes in the hedges."

Illicit

"I'd rather not have a party. You know I hate being the center of attention. A quiet dinner is more my speed."

Mom eyed me thoughtfully, her beautiful green eyes blinking at me while she probably wondered if there'd been a mix-up at the hospital the day I was born and she'd gone home with someone else's baby.

"I'm pretty sure I'm your offspring. We look exactly the same."

"That's not what I was thinking."

"Then what?"

She let out a soft sigh. "I was making a wish for you. That you'll find love soon. The bone-deep, borderline obsession kind of love that rips your heart out and shreds you to pieces."

"Gee, thanks," I said, even if a part of me wanted it too.

"But see, that kind of love also have the ability to transform you. You don't know who you truly are until you put yourself back together."

"So let me get this straight: You want your only daughter to be ripped apart by love?"

"Yes."

"Very malicious of you, Mother," I said, sarcasm dripping from my voice.

She laughed into her drink.

I chewed on her words. "And have you? Fallen in love like that?"

She nodded gently, setting her glass down. "Your dad. He was the love of my life, at least I thought so at the time. And as you can see, I came out better than ever. I only hope that your love doesn't end in a messy divorce."

I chewed on my lip before shaking my head. "Nope, I'm good.

37

I don't need that kind of bullshit. I'm good with my unbroken self."

She lifted her glass of white wine. "Sorry, can't undo it. You're stuck with my wish."

"And if it doesn't come true?"

Her eyes sparkled and I found myself actually believing her. "It will. Give it time."

———————

I'm not easily intimidated; at least, I didn't think I was. But when I came home from school one afternoon and Jake greeted me with a grin and a blindfold, I about had a heart attack.

I remained just inside the front door, too unnerved to go further. "What... what's that for?"

He held up the folded black handkerchief. "I have a surprise for you."

"What kind of surprise?"

"It won't be a surprise if I tell you." He took hold of my book bag and set it on the floor, then took a step closer so that his mouth was inches away from my forehead. "Now close your eyes while I tie this on."

"Can't you just cover them with your hands? We don't need this Fifty Shades business."

He laughed heartily, shaking his head. "I hate that I understood that reference." He reached around to the back of my head, the dip at the base of his throat the last thing I saw before the blindfold stole my vision. But whereas my eyesight was gone, my other senses were heightened. His scent was all around me, a mixture of cool cologne and a unique scent that

I'd become familiar with over the past several weeks. I was very aware of my heartbeat thumping a jungle beat in my ears.

"I'm not crazy about surprises," I said with a shaky laugh. I jumped when he took hold of my shoulders and began to steer me through the house. We walked and walked, circling through the house, until he led me back to where we began.

"Are we back in the living room?" I asked.

He laughed. "Well that didn't work. I was trying to confuse you."

"I grew up in this house, remember?"

"I guess that's true." I felt him behind me as he untied the blindfold. "I know it's not your birthday yet, but I got done early."

It took my eyes a few seconds to adjust to the light then another second to understand what I was looking at. Blinking, I took a step back to take it all in, nearly bumping into Jake.

"It's a bookcase," I said. The entire thing was made of solid wood, stained dark, and spanned the entire wall.

He walked over to the end and touched a ladder that was attached to a metal rail. "And the best part," he said and slid it over to me.

I barely contained my squeal. "It's beautiful!" I ran my palm along the ladder's smooth rungs. "You made this for my birthday?"

He tried to act nonchalant, shrugging like building me a freaking bookcase was no big deal, but the crinkle at the corner of his eyes gave him away.

"Thank you." I shook my head, my gaze drawn back to the molding up top, giving the whole thing a built-in look. "This is too much."

"It's really not. Come on. I'll help you move your books."

It took several trips to my room but we finally managed to transfer all my books into the bookcase, arranged by genre and alphabetized by author name. But even with as many books as I had, the bookcase was only halfway filled.

We stood back and assessed our work. "It looks wrong. Uneven," I said.

He frowned. "It does?" His eyes flew to the shelves, automatically searching for flaws in his work.

"I mean, it just needs more books." I turned to him with a look then headed to the master bedroom, where his books still sat inside packing boxes.

"What about the no fraternization rule?" he asked after I came back with a box.

"Screw the rules." I opened the box and was immediately overcome with excitement at the sight of new-to-me books. I took the first paperback, a mystery, glanced at the generic cover then began to read the blurb.

Jake crouched beside me, grabbing several out of the box. "This is going to take all week if you read each one first."

I smiled at him and lay down on the carpet. "I got time."

He shook his head, chuckling softly, and went back to shelving.

That night, Jake and my mom went out on a fancy date. Mom looked glamorous in a slinky black dress that accentuated her slim figure, her hair pulled back in a chignon.

But it was her date that really took me by surprise. Jake was good looking on any given day, but tonight, with his freshly-shaved face, pressed slacks, and button down shirt, he looked like a bona fide movie star.

"Damn, you clean up nice," I told him as he waited for my mom to finish applying lipstick.

He grinned, deploying the dimples. "Because I usually look like crap?"

I couldn't take my eyes off him if I tried. Which I didn't. "Something like that."

When Mom came out of the bathroom and took her place beside Jake, I felt a strange tickle in my chest. Only after they left did I recognize envy for what it was. In an attempt to subdue the green monster that was trying to claw its way out, I sent a text to the guy from my class, the one who was always asking me to hang out.

Hey, Eli. How are you?

A few minutes went by before he finally replied. *Hey. Hi! What's up?*

I was... I paused, my thumbs hovering over the glass surface of the phone. I took a deep breath and continued. *I was wondering if you wanted to maybe see a movie tomorrow afternoon?*

Sure.

And with that one short word, I had a date.

I didn't know if it was a good idea to start something with Eli, but hell, I might as well be adventurous for once. For all I knew, Eli might be the great love that my mom had wished for. It didn't seem likely, but what the hell did I know? Sometimes love isn't obvious; it sneaks up on you and whacks you upside the head with a frying pan and you find yourself laid out on your back, wondering what the hell just happened.

June Gray

[five]

The date with Eli went by without a hitch. He picked me up, met Jake and my mom, then took me to the movie theater where we watched the newest superhero flick. During the movie he leaned over and whispered things that the director had changed from the comic books. Our hands bumped in the popcorn bucket a few times and we shared a package of Twizzlers. Even with our arms pressed together on the armrest, he waited until twenty minutes into the movie to finally work up the nerve to hold my hand.

We had dinner at a Cuban restaurant right after. We talked, we laughed, we experienced no awkward lulls in the conversation. It was all so pleasant, so easy.

"I had a great time," Eli said as he walked me to my front door like a gentleman. "I'm glad we finally did this."

"Yeah, me too." And I meant it. He was laid-back and funny and wasn't bad to look at either. He had definite second date potential.

He blinked down at me for a few seconds before finally leaning down and pressing his lips to mine. I tilted my head back and returned the kiss. It felt natural to open up and deepen the connection.

My entire body tingled when we pulled away. "Goodnight, Eli. I'll see you in class," I said, biting my lips.

He licked his lower lip, looking like maybe he wanted to kiss me again. "I'll call you."

"Okay," I said, waving before going inside.

The house was completely dark save for the soft glow down the hall coming from my mom's office. I made my way through the darkness, skimming my fingers along the walls to find my way like I'd done since I was a child.

A few feet from her office I heard a noise that froze me where I stood. And then it came again, another moan that sounded suspiciously like a man about to reach climax.

I pressed my back to the wall, my heart racing. I should just go to my room and bury my head under a pillow, but I couldn't make my body move. Instead I waited for the exact moment when Jake let out a drawn-out, almost pained groan. I arched my back at the same time, my entire body catching fire as desire surged through my veins. If I'd had the guts to touch myself right then, I'm sure I would have exploded in two seconds flat.

Then it stopped and all I could hear were the sounds of two people trying to catch their breaths.

"Come take a shower with me," Jake said in a low whisper.

Mom sighed. "I can't. I still have more work."

Guilt and shame set in right then, making me feel dirty for getting turned on. Because as exciting as it was to listen to Jake, the other person he was screwing was still my mom.

Before I could push away from the wall, a figure emerged from the doorway and the naked form of Jake passed by, completely oblivious to my presence. I watched him walk down the hall, completely enthralled by the sight of his wide back, muscular thighs, and that ass until he disappeared into the bedroom.

As quietly as possible, I hurried to my room and locked the door.

The next morning I shuffled out of my room in my pajamas, rubbing my tired eyes as I made my way to the kitchen. I hadn't slept. I'd lain awake most of the night, wondering how the hell listening to Jake orgasm had done more to my body than the awesome kiss with Eli. It didn't make any damn sense.

I finally got up, made some chai tea, and headed to the living room to read and hopefully take my mind off my issues. But the sight of Jake sitting on the couch stopped me short, visions of his naked, firm rear immediately bombarding my brain.

I shook my head to clear my thoughts. "What are you doing?"

He looked up from the hardback he was reading and just about knocked me off my feet. Wearing black-framed glasses and day-old scruff, he was the epitome of sexy to a book nerd like me. Hell, the way he looked right then with his dimples barely showing, the thin material of his tee shirt accentuating his muscles, he was the epitome of sexy to anyone.

"You've got to be kidding me," I found myself saying. He wasn't real. He couldn't possibly be. First with the face, then with the body, and now with the reading. Ugh, this guy.

He took off his glasses as his dark eyebrows drew together. "What?"

"You're in my spot," I said, agitation setting in. Who had given him permission to look this good? It was seriously pissing me off.

He chuckled as he picked up his cup of coffee and moved to the opposite end. "I see Amanda isn't the only territorial one around here."

I sank down into the cushions and set my tea on the side table. "You've made an indentation," I grumbled even as I snuggled into its warmth.

He studied me for long moments. "You're grumpy this morning. What are you doing up so early anyway?"

"Same thing as you."

"You get up early on a Saturday to read?" he asked incredulously.

"Do you?"

"Touché." He set his glasses back on his nose and turned his attention back to the book, taking intermittent sips of his coffee.

I tried to do the same but couldn't help but sneak glances his way, now knowing what he looked like under his clothes. I told myself I wasn't coveting my mom's boyfriend, that I was just admiring a man who reads, but deep down I knew what I was feeling was less innocent. What began as admiration was fast becoming something more complicated and forbidden. It was turning into full-blown infatuation.

I forced my attention back to the book, trying to ignore the warning bells. But my eyes, for whatever reason, kept getting pulled his direction. Finally I shut the book with a sigh. "So where's Mom?" I asked to remind myself why this crush needed to be, well, *crushed*.

"Still asleep." He set aside his book. "How was your date last night? I didn't even hear you come in."

"Fine. Great. Perfect," I said, angry all over again that his sexual noises had managed to eclipse a very real and very good kiss with my date. "He's a good kisser."

"You going to go out with him again?"

"Definitely. I really want to see where this goes," I said, somehow finding the need to aggrandize.

He gazed at me for a few heartbeats, his eyes so blue even behind the glasses. Finally, his lips curved into a smile. "I'm glad." He pushed up off the couch. "I'm going to make some bacon and eggs. You want some?"

I shook my head, burying my face inside the book. "No thanks. I'm good."

———————

On Monday morning I woke up feeling like microwaved roadkill. My throat felt like sandpaper and my entire body was on fire. Even the act of reaching over to my nightstand to turn off the alarm on my phone was a monumental feat. I barely managed to snuggle deeper into the blanket and close my eyes.

I dreamed many things, most nonsensical and stupid. A

few times Jake's face showed up in there but it was jumbled up with lions and old books and huge bottles of orange juice.

The sound of a chime roused me from sleep, and I opened my eyes to realize I was still holding the phone in my hand. I glanced at it and realized I'd received a text message from Eli.

Missed you in class today.

Flu was all I managed to type before the phone slipped from my trembling fingers and landed on the floor. I groaned, deciding that it would just have to stay there for the rest of the day.

I turned onto my back and closed my eyes, but falling asleep was hard with a throat as dry as the desert. All of a sudden I was tormented with the idea of a refreshing glass of orange juice. I tried to convince myself that it wouldn't be worth the effort to get the juice, but the more I thought it the more I wanted it. I was so obsessed I could almost feel the cool, sweet liquid sliding down my throat.

With a resigned groan I rolled my aching body out of bed. I started to shiver the moment the air hit my body; I didn't think I'd ever been so cold, so hot, and so weak all at the same time.

I shuffled into the hallway, sweating and shaking. I used the wall for support as I stumbled toward the kitchen and struggled to pull open the fridge. But there it was—the gold at the end of the freezing rainbow. I grabbed the jug and, even though my hands felt like oven mitts, I uncapped it with ease and brought it up to my lips.

The relief was heaven, the taste divine. This Minute Maid orange juice was truly the nectar of the gods. I almost felt stronger. That was, until it slipped from my fingers. The plastic jug hit the tile floor with a loud thunk, sending juice spilling all over my feet. I tried to jump out of the way but failed, instead ended up slipping on the wet tile and falling hard on my ass.

"*Ow*," I said, writhing on the floor sure that I'd broken my coccyx or some other bone in my butt.

"What—" Jake appeared in the doorway with a concerned look on his face, a towel on his hips and nothing much else. Even in my pained stupor I noticed his hair was wet, his wide chest glistening with water. He made his way over, stopping outside the juice splatter perimeter. "Are you okay? What happened?" His hair-covered legs stopped in my line of vision.

"I was drinking juice and I fell," I said, covering my face with my hands.

He grabbed the roll of paper towels from the counter and got down on his knees to sop up the mess. With every ounce of energy I had left, I pushed myself up to a sitting position then immediately lay back down. "Why's the room spinning?" I mumbled, pressing my cheek to the cool tile and closing my eyes.

I don't know how much time passed, but I found myself in Jake's arms being carried back to my room. He gently lowered me to the bed then stood back with his hands on his hips. "Your shorts are wet."

"Your abs are nice," I croaked.

"Do you want to change your shorts or just leave it?"

I lifted an arm, thinking it was possible to touch his body from several feet away. "You work out a lot, don't you?"

I wasn't sure; I thought I saw his lips tip up. But then Serious Jake took over. "You're delirious." When he came forward to touch his hand to my forehead, I hooked a finger into the towel and pulled.

I don't know why I did it. Well, yes, I did it because I was curious to see if the front matched the back. But when that towel fell off his hips and his bare crotch came into view only inches from my face, I immediately realized I'd done something inappropriate.

"Joss!" He grabbed the towel and quickly wrapped it back around his waist. "What the hell?"

I couldn't help it; I covered my mouth and giggled.

A flush rose from his neck up to his face. "Yep, just what a guy wants to hear when a girl sees his dick."

"No, it's nice," I said quickly. "Nice and thick and... wait, why was it hard?"

He closed his eyes and pinched the bridge of his nose, taking in deep breaths. Without another word he turned on a heel and marched out of the room.

Another giggle bubbled up from my throat before I lost consciousness.

I slept for a long time. I sweated and shivered. I huddled under the blanket and then threw it off in cycles. After what felt like days of sleeping, I finally surfaced. As soon as I opened my eyes I saw a glass of orange juice on my nightstand that I was almost sure hadn't been there before.

I sat up with a groan, feeling weak but at least coherent. My legs were sticky and my hair was glued together in stiff, sweet-smelling clumps. Then it all came back to me: The spilling of the juice, the hot guy in the towel, and the removal of said towel.

My face flamed at the thought of what I'd done. I had no clue what the hell had come over me, which was not to say I regretted the outcome.

Feeling grungy as hell, I shuffled to the bathroom in hopes a hot shower would make me feel human again. Maybe then I could come up with an acceptable reason for doing what I did. If nothing else, I could blame the flu.

Twenty minutes later I finally pulled myself out of the shower when the hot water threatened to run out. Before exiting the bathroom, I stuck my head out the door and listened out for Jake. Hearing only silence, I headed to the kitchen but froze when I saw him at the cabinet, grabbing a bowl.

Before I could do an about-face, he saw me and said, "Hey." He moved to a take-out sack on the counter, keeping his back to me. "How do you feel?"

"Fine, I guess." With no way to make an obvious exit, I sat down at the table and decided to just tackle the subject head on, so to speak. "I'm so, so sorry."

He turned and placed a bowl of chicken noodle soup in front of me. "Don't worry about it. It didn't take too long to clean up."

I filled my mouth with soup, wondering if I needed to go further. I mean, it was possible I'd just dreamed the whole thing up.

Jake leaned against the counter and folded his arms over his chest. "Although if you're apologizing for yanking my towel…"

My face burned like I was spiking a fever again. I kept my eyes glued to the carrots in the soup, wondering if I could convincingly fake fainting to get out of this conversation.

"Sorry," I mumbled around the spoon. "I don't know what I was thinking."

"You weren't," he said with something like amusement in his voice. "You were delirious, not quite yourself. Right?"

The tone in his voice made me look up. He gave me a meaningful look and began to slowly nod his head.

"Right," I said. We stared at each other for a long time. Finally, I asked, "You're not going to tell Mom, are you?"

"What? That her only daughter is a pervert who wants to see my junk?"

"I'm not—!"

He pushed off the counter and grabbed a beer from the fridge. "I mean, not that I blame you for wanting a peek."

"That's not—!" But I didn't get a chance to plead my case. He raised his beer bottle with a dimpled grin and left.

[six]

I tried to keep busy. I stayed at school longer to study for finals and took on extra hours at work. Weeks had passed since Towelgate, but it was still awkward around Jake and, more importantly, Mom. Despite the guilt, every now and then the image of his penis would flash through my mind, giving me instant hot flashes of embarrassment or excitement or both.

One time I emerged from my room, ready to head to school, and found him shirtless in the living room, doing pushups. The sight of him glistening with sweat, his muscles bulging from exertion, froze me in place. I couldn't have moved or even averted my eyes if I'd tried. That was the day I finally admitted to myself that the little sprout of a crush had grown into something wild and unwieldy.

Having him around, knowing what he looked like naked, didn't help. It was so wrong to be this infatuated with my mother's boyfriend, but I couldn't help it. How could I when

I'd dream about him, when I'd see his face before I even opened my eyes in the morning?

Each night, as he and my mom headed off to bed together, I felt a stab in my gut. I'd never envied my mother before, not truly anyway, but suddenly I found myself wanting to take her place, wanting to be the one Jake made love to at night. To even think it felt like a betrayal of the worst kind, but I no longer had control of my desires. Every night I felt myself winding tighter and tighter until I had no choice but to focus all my sexual frustration on Eli.

"Joss, wait," he said, pulling away after another epic makeout session at his apartment. When I tried to lean in for another kiss, he held me away by the shoulders. "Stop. Hold on."

"What's wrong?"

He fell back on the bed. "I need to catch my breath."

"Catch your breath?" I stretched out at his side, running my hands on his chest. "What for?"

He fixed his eyes on the ceiling. "I have to calm down a bit before it's too late to stop."

"What if I don't want to stop this time?"

His head swiveled around to me, his eyes weary. "That's what you said last time."

"I'm allowed to change my mind," I said, sitting up.

"I know you are. It's just… I'm a little frustrated here."

I blew out a breath. "I am too."

"Then what's the problem? You told me you're not a virgin. And clearly you're horny. But you always change your mind at the last minute."

I turned back to him. It was true—I *was* horny as hell—but each time we had moved past kissing, I'd locked up. When it came down to it, Eli wasn't the guy I was lusting after.

"I'm sorry," I said, placing a palm on his stomach. He was a good guy; he deserved the truth. "I'm just... I'm confused about someone else."

He shot up. "Who is it?"

"You wouldn't know him."

"So what... you're sleeping with him?"

"No."

"Then what?" He watched my face then nodded in understanding. "You want to."

I bit my lips together, the non-denial speaking louder than words.

But Eli didn't seem angry or jealous. Instead he scooted closer, slinging an arm over my shoulder. "You could pretend I'm him," he whispered, nuzzling into my neck.

I gaped at him, not sure if he was a sleazeball or just a really understanding guy. Maybe, like all of us, he fell somewhere in between. Me, of all people, had no right to judge.

So I kissed him and, this time, we didn't stop.

I tried to hide in my room that night, hoping to avoid Jake altogether, but eventually hunger won out.

"Oh, hey," Jake said as soon as I ventured into the kitchen.

I froze in the doorway. "I didn't know you were here."

He shrugged, grabbing the box of Cheerios in the pantry. "Didn't have anywhere else to be." After he poured himself a bowl, he ate leaning against the counter. "Something's different with you," he said, watching me intently.

"I'm hungry," I said. My stomach chose that second to grumble. "See?" Finally I entered the kitchen, heading to the fridge to grab my leftover burger.

He chuckled. "No, I mean, you look different. More relaxed. Something with your hair maybe?" He pointed his spoon at me. "I got it. Botox, right?"

"Haha," I said, realizing I needed a plate in order to heat up my burger and that the plates were in the cabinet right behind Jake's head. Venturing closer, I tried to reach behind him without making physical contact.

Jake had other ideas. He reached up and poked my cheek with a finger. "Okay, maybe not Botox."

I reached out to give him a playful smack on the arm but he was faster and grabbed my wrist. The moment our skin made contact, I felt the desire spreading over my body like liquid sun, the tightness returning to my core. I didn't know if he felt it too, but the intense look in his eyes made me wonder if he didn't want this as much as I.

"It must have been the sex," I said just to see his reaction.

"What?" He let go of my arm as the skin between his eyebrows creased.

"I had sex with Eli."

His face remained impassive but beneath the cool exterior, I could sense he was struggling to conceal his real feelings. Or maybe I was just hoping for it.

"Do you love him?" he asked after some time.

I whirled away, putting my burger in the microwave. "No. Why?"

"If I were your parent, I would hope that I'd raised you to

know that sex is not something you do with someone you don't care about."

"Really, Jake? Slut shaming?" I asked, taking a step back. All of a sudden, the sheen of Jake was tarnished. "Don't give me that double-standard bullshit. It's okay for a guy to have meaningless sex but the moment a woman does it, she's labeled a slut? That's complete bull."

"No double standards here." He shook his head. "I believe that sex is an intimate act, that you give something of yourself away with each person you share it with. I live by that rule."

"You?" I asked in disbelief.

"What? Is it impossible that a man only wants to have sex with someone he loves?"

"Yes! Especially one that looks like you."

He stared at me for a long, charged moment until I squirmed.

"You're a hot guy," I said to ease some tension. "You can have a different girl every night. If you want to, anyway."

"You know what I want?" he asked closing the space between us. "I want the next guy you have sex with to be someone you actually really care for. Maybe even someone you love."

"Me too." Tears sprung to my eyes but I blinked them back and lifted my chin. "But, really, you don't have to worry about me."

"I still do."

"Why?"

"Because..." His eyebrows drew together as he looked at me like I had the answers written on my face. "I can't help it. I just do."

He reached up and brushed a lock of hair from my cheek, tucking it gently behind my ear. His finger lingered there for a moment before lightly tracing down the line of my jaw. I couldn't breathe, couldn't think past the possibility of his kissing me.

Just then the front door opened. Jake and I flew apart as Mom entered the kitchen with a smile. She hugged me first, giving me a peck on the cheek. "Joss," she said, giving me an extra hard squeeze. "I feel like I haven't seen you in forever."

"Just been busy, I guess," I said, fighting like hell to keep my eyes from straying to the man beside her.

"You joining us for dinner?" she asked, turning and giving Jake a quick peck.

"I ordered pizza," he said, tucking Mom in to his side even while giving me a dark, perplexed look.

I dove for the microwave. "No, thanks. I'll just eat my burger. Still need to study." My heart thumped a million miles a minute as I barricaded myself in my room once again, afraid and exhilarated from how close we'd come to disaster.

———

"Finals are finally over, I take it?"

I looked up from my novel to find Jake standing over me with a book and a beer in hand. "I didn't know you were home."

"Just got back from delivery." He sat down on the other end of the couch. "How'd you do on your finals?"

"Okay, I guess. I don't have the results yet." I wasn't expecting my grades to be anything spectacular because, even though I'd spent a lot of time studying, in the end I hadn't been able to concentrate during the exams.

"So does that mean you're done avoiding me?"

My mouth fell open. "Um, that's very presumptuous of you."

"Am I wrong?" He raised an eyebrow, daring me to lie.

Choosing instead to ignore him, I held the book open in front of my face. He's a reader, he should understand the universal symbol for "leave me alone, I'm reading."

He got the message. From the corner of my eye I spied him shake his head then crack open his own book. I tried to refocus on the words before me but his smug presence made me jittery, made me want to leave the room. Damn if I'd let him chase me out of my favorite reading spot. I'd hidden from him for weeks now; it was time I stopped running.

Hell, I can do uncomfortable too.

I scooted closer until I was right beside him. "See? I'm not avoiding you."

He narrowed his eyes in suspicion but didn't move away. He simply turned back to his book like having me pressed against his side was no big deal.

I faked a big yawn. "Do you mind if I lay my head on your lap?"

The suspicious look returned. "What for?"

I gave an exaggerated shrug. "I usually stretch out on the couch while I'm reading but you're taking up the space." Before he could refuse, I curled down on my side and laid my head on his thigh.

His muscles remained frozen for a few heartbeats but he finally relaxed when I opened my book to let him know I wasn't going anywhere. He sat back with a resigned sigh and took a long pull from his beer before going back to reading.

And I, surprisingly, was finally able to concentrate. Being close to Jake had a soothing effect on my nerves, as if his nearness settled the turmoil inside me.

Then he slid his fingers through my hair and the internal swirling of emotion returned tenfold. He had to know how his fingertips rubbing my scalp would affect me, but he just went about reading his book as if nothing was amiss.

I tried to ignore the pleasant tingling all over my body and focus on my book, but after the fifth time of reading the same sentence I gave up. "I can't concentrate. That feels too good."

"You like that, huh?" he asked, glancing at me from under his book. He added more pressure with his fingers, massaging my scalp in earnest.

My eyes fluttered closed and toes curled at the added sensation. I couldn't help but imagine those fingers working somewhere lower and wetter, curling in to me and massaging that spot. My core clenched just as a moan escaped my lips.

Jake's hand stopped and his thigh hardened against my cheek.

"Why did you stop?" I flipped onto my back to look up at him, but my cheek accidentally made contact with something hard and long.

His eyes widened. His Adam's apple bobbed up and down. "Sorry. That wasn't... I didn't mean to do that."

To see him flustered was a nice change, spurring me to take bigger risks. Keeping my eyes fixed on his, I turned my face a fraction and nuzzled into the rigid length in his pants.

Jake leapt up off the couch, very nearly throwing me to the floor in his haste. "Joss!" he cried, glaring down at me.

I waited, my heart thumping wildly, trying not to stare at the very clear outline on his pants. I opened my mouth to apologize but he just held up a hand and, without saying another word, stomped out of the room.

I lay on the couch for a long time trying to calm my nerves, shame and excitement roiling through me. From across the room my mom's framed photo smiled out at me, reminding me of what I stood to lose.

"I'm sorry, Mom," I whispered to her image. "It won't happen again."

June Gray

[s e v e n]

If I thought that Jake would somehow wake up with selective amnesia, I was so, so wrong. The very next morning, while Mom was in the shower, he knocked on my bedroom door.

"Jocelyn?" he asked, peering inside.

I pulled the blanket up to my chin, suddenly very aware that I was only wearing a thin white tank top and panties. "Privacy please!"

He shook his head and entered, closing the door soundly behind him. "We really need to talk."

I avoided his gaze, my face on fire. "It was an accident. I'm sorry."

"That—" He cleared his throat, taking a step closer. "That was no accident."

My throat closed up. What could I say? *Yes, I meant to rub my face on your huge dick?*

Jake walked to the side of my bed, standing tall and imposing with his hands on his waist. He probably thought he looked fatherly when, in reality, he reminded me more of a Dom about to issue a command. "Joss, I know you're probably curious about me, but you need to understand that this can't happen again," he said in a stern voice. "There are plenty of other guys out there you can do this with."

"I know!" I threw my hands up. "Don't you think I know it's wrong to covet what my mom has? But I do, and it's eating me up inside."

He sat on the edge of my bed, the mattress sinking under his weight. "It could never work between us. You're still so young."

I sat up, making no move to stop the blanket from falling away from my chest. I arched my back, sure that my nipples were visible through the thin white fabric. His jaw clenched as he visibly fought to keep his eyes fixed on my face. I challenged him with a look, raising an eyebrow in question. "Am I?"

Feeling crazy and reckless, I took hold of his wrist and brought his hand up to the center of my chest, to where my heart was trying to pound right through.

"Joss…" he said in warning. "Don't."

I slid his hand lower and to the side. I sighed when his palm closed around my breast. "Am I?" I repeated.

I felt the moment he gave in, when he let out a ragged breath as his thumb began to trace the outline of my hardened nipple. "No, you're not," he whispered.

I leaned into his touch, craving his hands all over me. God, it was so wrong but felt so right. The guilt fed the desire that fed the guilt.

I whimpered when he let go of my breast and trailed a finger along my collarbone, up my neck, and traced the outline of my lips. "I've tried my best to overlook the fact that you're a young woman blooming right before my eyes."

"But I turn you on." I parted my lips and drew his finger in, sucking on it.

He swallowed. Hard. The vein in his neck pulsed rapidly, his chest rising and falling like he'd just come back from a run.

"Jake..." But I didn't know how to finish the sentence, didn't know how to say out loud that I wanted him to take me right then, that it didn't matter if my mom found us, I had to have him inside me or I would die.

But I couldn't say the words. To admit it would light the fuse that would blow apart our lives as we knew it.

He blinked a few times and withdrew his hand. "We can't," he said, rising to his feet. Still, his eyes burned into me. "This has to end. Now."

I lifted my chin, my entire body starting to tremble. "Then say it like you really mean it."

He walked over to the door but, at the last minute, turned around. "Do you want to hurt your mom?"

"Of course not."

He took in a deep breath, collecting his wits, something I was currently failing at doing. "Then this can't happen again. Agreed?"

Our gazes locked across the room, reminding me of that first night when he'd asked my permission to move in. If I'd only known then how much that one decision would affect our lives.

"Okay," I finally said. "For Mom."

————————

It was Jake's turn to play hide-and-seek. For the next few days, he made himself scarce, spending a lot of time at the gym or in the garage or basically anywhere but in my presence. And frankly, that was okay with me.

I scoured the internet for available apartments, knowing the only solution was to take myself out of the equation. Maybe the crazy hormonal reactions wouldn't be so bad if I didn't have to see him everyday.

"You okay, sweetheart?" Mom asked one night as she stood at my bedroom door. "You've been so withdrawn lately."

I kept my back to her and finished tying my hair back into a ponytail, feeling like a vine was wrapping around my chest. "Have I?"

She sighed. "I've been so busy at work. I feel like I haven't seen you in forever."

I faced her, finding it hard to breathe. "You don't have to feel guilty," I said and wrapped my arms around her. I squeezed her hard, hoping it would help ease the tightness in my own chest. No dice. "It's my fault. I've been busy with school and work."

"And boyfriends," she said with a laugh. She pulled back with bright, curious eyes. "How is Eli, anyway?"

I forced a smile. "Eli's not my boyfriend."

"Yet."

"I don't know. He's a good guy but..." I shrugged. "I don't know."

"Sounds like there's a juicy story there," she said with a knowing wink.

"Maybe another time. Maybe over Sunday dinner." I bit my lip, carefully choosing my next words. "Mom, I have to talk to you about something."

She sat at my desk, her worried mom-face on. "What is it?"

I took a deep breath. "I need to move out." Guilt stabbed me in the gut at the hurt in her eyes, but I knew I could hurt her ten times worse if I stayed. "I think it's time."

"Is something wrong? Did something happen?" she asked.

"No, nothing like that," I said quickly. "It's just... we always talked about me moving out when I turned twenty-one. And with Jake here, I figured you'd be okay without me."

She stood up, a pained expression on her face as she reached for my hand. "I'll never be okay without you."

I smiled even as tears pricked my eyes. "I'm not getting any younger," I said, trying to lighten the mood.

That got a chuckle out of her. "Yeah, you're so old." She squeezed my fingers. "But if you really want to go, I'll support it."

I nodded. "I do."

"Fine," she said, wiping at her cheek. "Just give me a few weeks to get used to it first."

I swallowed. I didn't know if we had that kind of time before shit hit the fan, but what could I do? "Okay."

"Let's talk about your birthday party instead."

"Not that again."

She let out a watery laugh, hugging me. "I'm just talking about dinner reservations. No big parties. Promise. Just you, me, Jake, and if you want, Eli."

As luck would have it, Mom had to leave for a two-day trip the day of my birthday, leaving me with Jake and Eli at the Blue Moon Fish Restaurant in Fort Lauderdale. At least the place had a trendy, rowdy atmosphere to mask my anxiety that verged on outright panic. How the hell was I going to get through dinner, sandwiched between the guy I was sleeping with and the guy I wanted to sleep with?

"Nice view," Eli said, admiring our waterfront table on the patio.

Jake looked over at me across the candlelit table, looking so good in a dark blue button-down shirt that highlighted the color of his eyes. "It's a pity your mom can't be here."

"Yeah. She's already texted me ten times, apologizing."

"Why did you come?" Eli asked him. "I mean, you're her mom's boyfriend, so you technically don't need to be here."

Jake raised an eyebrow, sensing the challenge in Eli's tone. "Because I promised I'd be here." His eyes met mine across the way. "And because I care about Jocelyn."

Eli scooted his chair closer to me and slung an arm across the back of my chair. "That's why I'm here."

I fought the urge to roll my eyes. Still, I'd be lying if I said a part of me wasn't enjoying the testosterone slinging just a little.

Luckily the waiter chose that moment to deposit a bright blue drink in front of me. Blue again, the color of Jake's intense gaze.

"Um, this isn't mine." I attempted to give it back, even if the drink looked appealing.

Jake sat up. "It's from me. Your mom asked me to get you twenty one drinks."

My eyes widened as I eyed the drink. He chuckled at my reaction. "I figured I'd start with one and see where you go from there."

"Well, thanks." I took a sip and immediately went in for another. It was delicious and was definitely needed. Before I knew it I'd downed more than half the drink and, because of my empty stomach, quickly felt a buzz.

"I'm ready for number two," I told Jake, then snickered. "The drink, I mean."

Jake's eyebrows drew together. "So soon?"

"Can we get another?" Eli said to the waiter, pointing to my empty glass.

It took exactly two of those blue concoctions to make dinner bearable. Still, it didn't make me less aware of Jake's disapproving glare as Eli became more and more affectionate with me. I played it up, nuzzling into Eli's neck, giving him pecks on the mouth, knowing a pair of blue eyes watched my every move. It was childish to want to make Jake jealous, but hell, it was my birthday and I could do whatever the hell I wanted.

After dinner, as we stood waiting for the valet to retrieve the cars, I decided I wasn't ready to go home just yet. "My birthday celebration can't possibly end at eleven o'clock!"

"Okay, where do you want to go?" Jake asked.

"You can go home," Eli said, taking hold of my elbow. "I can take her wherever she wants to go."

Jake frowned, looking me over. "She's had a lot to drink."

"Don't worry. I'm driving." Eli turned to me. "So where to, Babe?"

I ran a hand through my hair, feeling unusually good. Sexy even. "I don't know. To a club. I want to dance."

Jake pulled me aside and asked in a low voice, "Are you okay? You're not drunk, are you?"

"No. But I do have a nice buzz." I flashed him a bright smile. "And I'm fine. Eli's a good guy."

He threw an uncertain glance over my shoulder. "You want me to go with you?"

I pinched his cheek. "Jake, you're cute, but no. Don't wait up. I might stay over at Eli's."

His face remained carefully impassive, but I saw a muscle in his jaw tick. Still, he stepped aside and allowed me to leave with my date.

Eli took me to Aerostorm, a two-story club at the shores of Fort Lauderdale. It was loud and flashy and just the right place. Eli offered to buy me another drink but I waved him off, dragging him instead to the dance floor.

We danced for several songs, Eli getting closer and closer until he had his hand under my top while grinding his crotch into my ass. People stared at us—some with looks of disgust, others with envy—but I was beyond caring at that point. I closed my eyes and pretended it was someone else behind me, holding me freely.

"Let's get out of here," I whispered in his ear.

Eli was quick to grant my wish, whisking us out of the club before I could blink. The next thing I knew he had me pressed against the side of his car, his thigh wedged between my legs and tongue inside my mouth. The whole time I thought of Jake, of how it would be like to kiss him, to grind on him.

"That's enough."

Jake's voice pierced through the fantasy and, in my alcohol-induced stupor, I almost expected him to throw Eli aside and take over with the kissing and the leg humping. That would have been the best birthday surprise ever.

Instead Eli pulled away from me. "I thought you went home?" he asked.

"I'm glad I didn't," Jake said, standing a few feet from us with his arms folded across his chest.

Eli turned to face him. "She's fine. I'm taking good care of her."

Jake looked absolutely murderous. "I'm taking her home."

"Look man, you're crossing the line. You're not her dad."

Jake angry gaze turned to me. "No, but I'm her guardian."

"You are acting way more possessive than her guardian. If I didn't know any better—" Eli stopped, his head whipping back around to me. "Is this the guy?" he demanded, jabbing a thumb towards Jake. "He's the one you want to sleep with?"

My eyes flew between the two men, unable to form a denial. How could I when I couldn't even tear my eyes away from the huffing, sexy guy that was completely forbidden to me?

Eli gave a humorless laugh. "Oh, that's fucked up, Joss."

With palms up, he started to back away. "I don't want any part of this situation."

"You're an asshole," I said in Jake's truck a few minutes later. "What the hell were you thinking making a scene like that?"

He glared at me before starting the truck. "I was thinking I had to save your dignity."

"My dignity was intact, thank you."

"Not from where I was standing." He pulled out of the parking lot, taking the turn so hard I almost fell sideways. "Besides, your mom would kill me if I let that asshole molest you like that."

"It was by choice. We weren't doing anything I didn't want to!" I wanted to beat my head into the dashboard. "That was just foreplay. We weren't going to do anything until we got back to his place."

Jake was quiet for a long, charged moment. "Really, Joss?" he finally asked. "What do you see in that guy?"

"He's nice to me. And he's one of those rare guys who likes going down on a woman."

He let out a huff. "Not so rare," I thought I heard him say under his breath.

I turned away. "Well, you've just robbed me of an orgasm."

"Sorry," he said, sounding anything but.

I kept my eyes fixed on the window, thinking about Eli and the way he'd looked at me when he figured out my secret. Who was he to judge?

"Maybe he's right," I whispered. "I am fucked up."

Jake glanced at me. "Nothing an aspirin and water won't fix."

"No." I turned my entire body towards him. "I mean I'm fucked up. I want something I can't have."

"Joss..." he said on a sigh.

"I know. I get it. You don't want me!" I said, throwing my hands up. "It's just... for the first time in my whole life, I feel this *need*, this craving. Like, I lie awake at night physically needing you. To do—I don't know. Everything. Make love to me then cuddle with me. Talk to me until we can't keep our eyes open anymore."

He refused to look at me. "You know why that can't happen."

"I know. I'm a terrible person and the worst daughter, to even think those thoughts about you. I love my mom so much. She deserves an honest man, someone who'll love her and take care of her." I swallowed down a sob. "But... it's my birthday, and I kind of think I deserve someone like that too."

"You do," he said, turning to me. "Someday he'll come along and sweep you off your feet. And then you'll see that you're just projecting a fantasy onto me. At most, it's nothing but a tiny, insignificant crush."

"A tiny, insignificant crush," I echoed with a humorless laugh. Somehow I didn't think this was that. At all. "But I'm moving out soon, so I won't have to see you as much."

He pulled over on the side of the road and killed the engine. "You're moving out?" he demanded.

"Didn't Mom tell you?"

"No." He leaned back in the seat, lost in his thoughts for a moment. Then he asked, "Because of me?"

I shook my head. I had just bared my soul but somehow it seemed important that he know I wasn't running from him. "Because it's time. I should have moved out a long time ago."

"Joss..." he began. "That's really not necessary. I can move out if it's too uncomfortable."

"No. I need this. I need to just... go."

He was quiet for a long time, his blue eyes flying all over my face. Finally, he reached over and retrieved something from the glove box. "Here," he said and held out a small gift-wrapped package.

"What's this? You already made me the bookcase for my birthday."

He set it on the seat between us. "Just open it."

I ripped the packaging and found a small wood box with intricate swirly silver inlay. "It's beautiful." I flipped the lid open and found a wooden heart inside.

"It's carved out of African Blackwood, one of the strongest in the world." He lifted out the heart and placed it on the center of my palm. "One day, Joss, you'll find the right guy who actually deserves you. Until that day comes, you keep your heart protected in this box."

"What if I've already found him?" I asked, holding his gaze.

He shook his head. "It's not me. And it's definitely not Eli."

"And what if I give it to the wrong guy?"

He didn't have an answer for that. I suspected he was wondering the same.

"Thank you," I told Jake as we entered the dark house twenty minutes later.

His eyes pierced even in the dark. "You're welcome. Happy birthday."

It hurt to turn away, to walk off knowing this was definitely the end between us.

Then he grabbed my elbow and spun me around.

We collided in a jumble of limbs and chests, our lips meeting in a blistering kiss. I stood on my toes and opened up to him; he wrapped his arms around my back and pulled me closer, deepening the connection. His hands moved up to cup my face as he slowed down the kiss, his tongue dancing with mine as he let out a soft groan that I felt down to my core.

When we pulled away, my hands flew up to my tingling lips. "What was that for?" I breathed.

"That was for your birthday." He paused to lick his lips, my face still cradled in his hands. "And this," he rasped, moving closer, "is for closure." He kissed me again, more deliberately this time, as if trying to memorize every touch, taste, sound. And I fell into him as swiftly as I was falling for him.

He said it was for closure, but I knew that it wasn't the end. A kiss like that—the kind that made me feel as if fireworks were exploding, simultaneously glowing and scorching me inside—could never be mistaken for a goodbye.

June Gray

[eight]

I awoke the next morning with a stupid smile on my face after a deep, peaceful night's sleep. I jumped out of bed and took a shower, humming to myself as I started the coffee maker.

I felt, rather than heard, Jake enter the kitchen. He shuffled in, saw me, and immediately turned to leave.

"Coffee?" I asked, holding out a freshly-filled mug to thwart his escape. If he thought he could get away with not talking about last night, he was dead wrong.

His wide shoulders rose and fell in defeat. "Thanks," he said, turning around and taking my offer. He leaned against the counter and took a sip.

I did the same, eyeing him over my mug as he ran a hand through his bedhead then yawned. Even with the dark circles under his eyes, he still looked adorably exhausted. "Did you get any sleep?" I asked.

His eyes drew up to me. "No."

"Why not?"

"Why not?" he echoed sarcastically. He drew up to his full height, his mood significantly different. He glared at me, nostrils flaring, and finally said, "Because I couldn't stop thinking about you."

"You were thinking about me?"

"You know I was! You made sure of that." He stalked over to where I stood and slammed his mug into the granite counter behind me. "I haven't slept in two weeks, Joss. Because I can't fucking stop thinking about you."

"What… what were you thinking about?"

He was quiet for a long time, blue eyes appraising me as he figured out what to say.

I lifted my hand and pressed it against his bare chest. "Tell me. Please."

He looked down at our point of contact. "I've been thinking of ways this could work."

"This?"

He gave me a weary look. "You and me."

The breath hitched in my throat. My mouth turned into a desert.

He slanted closer, forcing me to lean back. "I want you so much, Joss, and it's driving me crazy." He swallowed. "Last night… that kiss… it wasn't supposed to happen. But I couldn't hold back anymore."

"Then don't."

And he didn't. With his gaze holding me captive, he pressed his warm hand to my stomach and slowly slid it down the front of my shorts. "You're not the only one who lies awake at night, craving something forbidden," he whispered.

My lips fell open when his fingers found my wetness, and one pained word spilled out between my lips. "Please…"

"What? Tell me what you want."

"I want—" I couldn't form a coherent thought, not when my entire body was a live grenade.

"This?" He curled his middle finger and slid it into me. I gasped the same moment my back arched. "Or this?" He pierced me with another finger, making my sex clench.

My breath escaped in a trembling moan. "Jake…"

He kissed me then, a hard kiss that ended as quickly as it began. "I haven't been able to get the taste of you out of my mind," he rasped, dropping kisses along the column of my neck. "I shouldn't have kissed you last night. I thought it was just sexual tension that I could excise with one kiss. I was so wrong."

My back arched as the orgasm stole through me, the sensations traveling through me like a tidal wave. I could only moan as his fingers continued to move, continued to draw out the longest, most intense orgasm of my life until I was left breathless and quivering.

Jake watched me the entire time, his face colored with desire. After I gave a final shudder, his body bowed and he pressed his forehead to my chest. "I'm not strong enough to resist this, Joss. I can't pretend anymore."

I wove my fingers through his hair, hugging him to my chest. "Then don't."

His expression was one of relief as he stood up. "I need to call your mom."

"What for?" I asked in a panic, grabbing his wrist.

He took hold of my hand and squeezed. "To break up with her. I don't want to deceive her any more than I already have."

I sucked in a breath. "You'd risk your relationship, your place to live and work, for sex? With me?"

"Not for sex with you." He shook his head as he wound his fingers behind my neck. "For you."

Our eyes locked, a thousand words passing between us in that silent moment. Finally he gave a short nod, the question in his eyes. "Okay?"

"What will you do—" The words came out on a whisper. "If I agree?"

He gripped my hair and pulled, his breath low and raspy. "I'm not going to lie, Jocelyn. I'm going to fuck you all the ways I've been imagining. All the ways you want to be fucked. I'll make you come until you're screaming and then I'll hold you afterward, talk to you until we can no longer keep our eyes open."

A shiver raced down my spine, culminating in my core. I wanted everything he was offering, so much that I found myself whispering, "Yes."

He took a step back, heading down the hallway. "I'll be right back."

I stood there, the thread of my thoughts unraveling into several different directions. We were going to have sex. He was going to call my mom. They were going to break up so he and I could be together. He wanted me. Mom would hate him.

Mom would hate me.

I shot out of the kitchen and ran down the hall, finding Jake sitting on the bed with the phone at his ear. His eyes flicked up as I entered, jaw clenched and eyebrows knitted as he watched me approach. "She's not answering."

I took hold of the phone and turned it off. "Don't."

His nostrils flared as he hooked his hands behind my thighs and pulled me between his legs. "You don't want this to happen?"

"I can't do this to her." But even as I talked, my hands went to his shoulders and clutched at him. I knew I needed to move away, that to be this close was asking for trouble, but he didn't seem to want to let me go. And I didn't want him to.

His hands slid up my legs until they wrapped around my ass. "And I can't not have you. Not now."

"I'm scared," I said with a quivering voice. "I don't want to hurt her."

He looked up at me and waited patiently while I made my decision. "Whether you choose this or not, I have to break up with Amanda. I can't be with her anymore. Not when I want to be with someone else."

I choked back a sob even as I felt the urge to laugh. Despair and exhilaration battled inside me, conscience and body going to war. My legs finally made the decision, carrying me onto the bed and settling me on Jake's lap. My spine took over then, bending me forward until my mouth touched his.

"You sure?" Jake whispered against my lips.

I let out a soft laugh. "No."

His hands slid up my ass, my back, finally resting at the base of my neck. With his cheek pressed to mine he whispered, "It's okay, Jocelyn. You can say no."

"I... I can't."

My fingers shook as I threaded them through his hair but any lingering doubt was forgotten the moment our lips met, when we finally gave in to the incredible pull between us. It was an intoxicating, surreal feeling to submit to this force after fighting it for so long. It seemed more like a dream than reality.

Afraid I'd wake up at any moment, I ground my hips into the hard length in his pants, letting out a soft gasp when it hit just the right spot. I moved faster, wanting more, searching for relief.

Jake's hands went to my hips and stilled me. "Slow down," he said. "We have time."

I shook my head, my nerves buzzing with tension. "I need... I need..." I slid off his lap and onto the floor, immediately reaching for the waistband of his pants. Despite his protests, he lifted his hips and allowed me to pull his clothes down, stripping him completely bare.

I sat back on my legs, dazed as I took him in. I wasn't prepared for the sight of him leaning back on his hands, muscles straining against his skin, cock standing at attention.

"You okay?" Judging by the hint of a smile on his face, he knew the answer to that question.

I set my hands on his thighs when he tried to move. "Stay there." And with my eyes fixed on his face, I leaned down and traced the tip of my tongue from the root of his length to the tip.

"Damn," he said on a hiss. He opened his legs wider. "Do that again."

I wrapped my hands around his cock, squeezing a little. Thick and hard and warm, it pulsed in my palm. I wrapped my lips around the head and slowly took him deeper in my mouth, stopping only when he hit the back of my throat. I formed a tight vacuum around his shaft and began to bob my head.

His leg twitched each time I sucked him in, his shaft growing even harder in my mouth. Unable to stand it any longer, I pulled away and undressed, emboldened by the blaze in Jake's eyes.

"God, you're beautiful." He sat up and reached for my hips but I pushed his hands away and climbed on his lap. "I want to taste you," he said.

"No time." I reached between us and positioned him at my entrance. "If I don't have you inside me right now, I'm going to die."

"I need to get a cond—" He gave a shout when I sank onto him without waiting. "Fuuuck!"

I squeezed my eyes shut. My entire body shook, trying to adjust to this sweet invasion. I had never been with anyone so big, so thick.

Sensing my discomfort, he wrapped his arms around me and pulled me against his chest. "You feel so good," he rasped, his fingers gripping my hair. He brought our mouths together for a kiss before dipping his head and taking a nipple in his mouth. "But we can go slow."

I shook my head, scared that slowing down would give my conscience a chance to catch up with me. "I need you. Fast. Hard." I lifted my hips and then slammed back down, gasping as he hit my core. I did it again and again, each time harder than the last. When my muscles tired I changed to a swaying motion, desperation coloring my need.

From a faraway place I heard him say my name, but my thoughts were much too scattered to comprehend. Finally, he took hold of my face and forced me to focus. "Jocelyn," he said in a soft rasp.

I bowed my head, gasping for air.

"Look at me," he said, angling my head up so that I had nowhere else to look but into his blue eyes. "Are you all right?"

Tears stung my eyes. Somehow I knew it would never be all right again. "I'm fine. I just want—I want—"

He brushed hair away from my face. "What?"

I wrapped my arms around his neck and brought our foreheads together. "You. Without strings. Without guilt. Just you."

He moved with speed, lifting me and laying me on my back without dislodging himself. With his arms under my knees, he opened me further and settled between my legs. "You have me," he said, drawing out slowly and sliding back in. He rolled his hips, making love to me with his mouth and his cock as if we had all the time in the world.

I was helpless underneath him, pinned down by his weight and his will until I gave in and accepted what he was giving. I kissed him, biting at his lower lip before spreading kisses all over his stubbled jaw. I'd dreamed of this moment for so long and I'd almost rushed right through it.

When he reached between us and massaged my clit, I fell completely apart. I cried out, my back arching up off the bed as bolts of pleasure raced through my veins. Jake kept moving until his hands and hips wrenched another smaller orgasm from me. I cried out his name as my body shook and trembled around him. Then he pulled out, his body bowing over me as he groaned one last time. With his eyes fixed on mine, he came, his warm seed spurting all over my stomach.

We didn't speak for a long moment, gasping and staring at each other.

After he recovered, he climbed off the bed and headed to the bathroom. Through tired eyes, I watched his muscular body moving around fluidly without any hints of self-consciousness. His body really was a thing of beauty and strength.

When he came back, he stretched out beside me and wiped my stomach with a wet towel before pulling the blanket over us.

"You okay?" he asked so gently it broke the dam inside me.

I nodded even as the tears leaked out the sides of my eyes.

"Don't regret this," he said, lifting a stray tear from the bridge of my nose. "We'll make it right with your mom."

"I don't regret it," I said with a teary smile. "You know, last night I made a birthday wish."

"What was it?"

"I can't tell you."

He tickled my side. "And did it come true?"

"Yes."

He looked at me with something like reverence in his eyes. "I don't know why I tried so hard to ignore this thing between us. Since the first day I've felt something, this pull towards you."

"I felt it too." I put my hand on his chest and he picked it up, pressing a kiss to my knuckles.

"Now here you are," he said.

"I've always been here."

His mouth curved up into a lazy smile as his eyes drifted shut. His arms tightened around me, tucking me under his chin and letting out a long, happy sigh. "Maybe now I can finally get some damn sleep," he murmured. I snuggled into him, pressing a smile into his bare chest.

And then I heard a sound that made my heart stop.

"Joss? Jake?" came the muted voice of my mom. The front door slammed shut behind her. "Anyone home?"

Jake's eyes flew open, our gazes colliding as we both came to the realization that we'd been so preoccupied with each other we'd all but forgotten about my mom's return.

I couldn't breathe. "What now?"

[part two]

June Gray

[nine]

Jocelyn moved like lightning, jumping off the bed and grabbing her clothes off the floor in one swift movement. She pulled a shirt over her head and hissed, "I didn't know she was coming home so early!"

I didn't move. I knew, even if I hadn't gone about it the right way, that I had made the right decision. Just the warmth in my chest at the sight of Jocelyn was proof enough.

"What are you doing?" she asked, smacking my foot under the blanket. "Get up!"

I steeled myself for what was to come. "Your mother needs to find out about us."

"No!" Jocelyn gaped at me, her face a picture of panic. "Not yet. I'm not ready. Please?" She spun around when Amanda's voice floated down the hall. Joss had only enough time to fold her body in the space between the wall and the dresser before the bedroom door opened.

Amanda walked in, one eyebrow raised as she appraised me on the bed. "You're only now getting up?"

I glanced at the clock on the nightstand. It was one in the afternoon. "Had a late night," I said, sitting up and searching for my pants. She approached, bending over me for a quick kiss. "Where's Joss?" she asked, turning back for the door.

I glanced across the room to where her daughter was peeking around the dresser, shaking her head. She looked so young in that moment, so unlike her usual self. "She's around somewhere," I said with a noncommittal shrug. I hated having to deceive Amanda but I had to trust that Joss had a plan.

Amanda sighed and turned back to me with soft eyes. "So did you think about it? What we discussed before I left?"

I ran a hand through my hair, sighing. We'd had the serious conversation only three days ago but already it felt like a million years had passed. I wasn't even sure I was the same man she left behind. "A little." I walked over and rubbed her arm, hoping to lead her out of the room for this conversation.

She stopped, looked around, and sniffed the air.

I rubbed the back of my head, trying to play off the distinct musk of sex in the room. "I was, you know," I said, holding a fist in front of my crotch and making a crude gesture.

Amanda cracked a smile and pressed her body to mine. "You missed me?" she asked, gazing up at me with eyes that looked too much like her daughter's for comfort. I tried not to cringe from self-loathing when she stood on her toes and kissed the side of my neck.

I was conscious of Joss's gaze on my back, keenly aware of how it must feel to watch your lover kiss someone else. No doubt Joss was seething right now, either hurting or jealous or both. My mind spun with ideas on how to refuse Amanda's advances without suspicion, but thankfully, she pulled away first.

"I should go greet Joss happy birthday though," she said, her face filled with regret. "We can do this later."

————————

"Enjoy it!" My younger brother, Tristan, clinked his beer bottle to mine as we sat at a bar the next day. "You, Big Bro, are living the life!"

I glared at him, taking a long pull from my beer. "It's not like that."

He shook his head, chuckling. "You know what the next logical step is, don't you?"

I let out an impatient huff. "Don't even go there." I gave him a warning look. "I swear if you say threesome, I'm gonna break this bottle on your face."

Tristan threw his head back and laughed. "Isn't that every man's ultimate fantasy? To bag the mom *and* her daughter?"

I smacked the back of his head. "You need to stop watching so much porn." I held the bottle up to my lips, drained my drink, and got off the stool. "Why am I even talking to you about this? It's not like you have a conscience."

Not that I could talk.

Tristan clutched at his chest. "Ouch. That almost hurt," he said then held up his palms. "Okay, okay. I'll be serious. Just sit your ass back down, you drama queen."

"You can't tell anyone about this," I said, acquiescing.

"You know I won't."

And he wouldn't. Since we were kids, Tristan and I had been close. He was my cocky little prick of a brother who liked to pick fights with the bigger boys at the playground, and I was the protective tough guy who made sure he didn't get his ass handed to him. Now that we were bigger and older, Tristan no longer needed me to fight his battles, which wasn't to say he was no longer a cocky little prick. But prick or not, I trusted him with my life.

"So is the daughter your girlfriend now?"

"No. Amanda is still, technically, my girlfriend." I shook my head. I should have broken up with Amanda the moment she walked in the door. How had this all gotten so out of hand?

"So let me get this straight: You're cheating on Amanda with her own daughter?"

I dropped my head to the bar. I was a cheater. I had become the very thing I reviled. "But this isn't the same as what Eleanor did to me," I insisted.

Eleanor Moreau, the woman to whom I'd given my grandmother's wedding ring only to discover she had been cheating on me the entire length of our two-year relationship. It had taken well over three years and a few failed attempts at relationships to get over the betrayal, to let go of the emotional baggage. And now that I had, I realized I'd become her.

Tristan eyed me steadily. "It's not?"

I screwed my lips shut. Cheating was cheating. Any way I put it, I was the bastard in this scenario.

Fuck.

I jumped up and threw a few bills on the bar. "Talk to you later. I have some business to take care of."

I headed straight for the bookstore in Pembroke Gardens,

knowing that Joss would be working tonight. I stalked into the store, on a mission, but the moment I spotted her talking to a customer from behind the help desk, my brain emptied of all rational thought. All I could think in that moment was the slide of her hair through my fingers and the warmth of her lips around my cock.

I ducked into a deserted aisle and rearranged my pants. My reaction to Jocelyn was unsettling, so immediate and reckless. In my thirty years, a woman had never thrown me quite like this.

Her green eyes widened when she saw me approach. "What are you doing here?"

"We need to talk."

She glanced around, then down at her watch. "I'll meet you at the café. I have a break coming up in ten minutes."

I waited at a table in the café for nearly seven minutes before I stood up and headed over to the back of the store, toward the hallway that led to the bathrooms and the Employee Only entrance. I leaned against the wall beside the water fountain and waited.

Finally the employee door opened and Joss emerged, looking surprised to see me. "I thought—"

I pushed away from the wall, my body buzzing at the sight of her. "I couldn't wait." And before I could stop myself, I rushed forward and dove for her lips. My momentum drove us to the other side of the hallway, and I pressed her back into the wall as I tilted her head up and deepened the kiss. I groaned when her hands wrapped around my waist and pulled me flush to her body.

We pulled away only when a man cleared his throat on his way to the bathroom. We turned our heads away from the stranger, our faces still only inches apart.

"Hi," I whispered, swiping at the moisture around her lips with my thumb.

She smiled at me, her cheeks red. "Hi."

I dipped my head and pressed a kiss on her jaw. "It's taking all of my self-control not to screw you right here, right now," I whispered, my lips grazing the shell of her ear. It wasn't exactly what I'd planned on saying, but it was the truth nonetheless.

She let out a shaky breath as her hands went up to my chest. "You said you needed to talk to me about something." She pushed, creating about a foot of distance between us.

I wiped a palm down my face, sobering. "I guess I did."

She bit back a smile. "Well?"

I stared at her, the words stuck in my throat. In truth I was unnerved by the thought of losing her so soon, but if I had to be a loathsome, deceitful man just to be with her, then maybe we were better off apart.

Jocelyn's face clouded over. "Please don't break up with her yet."

"Joss..."

"I'm not ready."

I held her shoulders, bending down to look into her face. "Not ready to be with me?" I asked gently.

She shook her head, eyes glistening with unshed tears. "I know it's probably too late, but... I'm not ready to destroy my relationship with my mother."

I wrapped my arms around her, fitting her inside the crook of my body. More than anything, I wanted to make it all better, make it so that nobody got hurt. That wasn't possible—not at this point, anyway—but maybe I could prolong the inevitable.

June Gray

[ten]

Despite my recent actions, I liked to consider myself a man of honor. But when Amanda crawled into bed with me that night, her lips soft and hands seeking, I found myself faced with a decision.

"Jake," she breathed by my ear, curling her warm body around my back. Her hands slid around to my front, trailing over my abs and down to my crotch.

I took hold of her wrist before she went too far. "What about work?"

"I'm done for the night." She nibbled on my earlobe and my cock twitched. Hell, I'm only human. "I thought you and I could spend some time together," she added in a voice filled with sultry promise.

"What about Joss?"

"What about her?" she murmured, nuzzling into my neck. "She's probably asleep by now." She pushed me on my back and sat astride me, rubbing her warmth into my rapidly swelling cock.

Not gonna lie, it felt damn good. But I held her hips and forced her to stop. "Not tonight."

Her face fell. "Jake, what's wrong?"

I sighed, running my hand through her hair. "Nothing. I'm just tired."

She leaned down, setting her chin on her hands. "Really? There's nothing more?"

The confession rose like bile in my throat, but I swallowed it down. "We're fine, Amanda," I said, touching her cheek.

"What about the thing we talked about?" she asked, blinking like she was trying to fight back tears. When I didn't answer, she pushed up off my chest and climbed off. "Okay. I get it."

"Hey," I said, capturing her hand before she was beyond reach. "That wasn't a no." It occurred to me that I could just give her the honest answer now and put her out of her misery, but the truth was that I wasn't the honorable man I thought myself to be. When it came down to it, I was chickenshit.

She gave me a sad smile and bent down to give me a quick kiss on the lips. "I'm not trying to pressure you."

"I know you're not." I gave her a reassuring smile. "I promise, I'll have an answer soon."

I couldn't sleep that night, my brain trying its best to wrap around the situation. I couldn't figure out how to resolve the problem without hurting anyone. Was it even possible to be with Jocelyn without destroying her relationship with her mother? Did I even want to put that bond to the test? Did Joss?

The answers wouldn't come. I finally slipped out of bed around two-thirty in the morning and went to the garage to check on some wood pieces I'd stained.

"Couldn't sleep either?"

I spun around and found Joss standing just inside the garage, closing the door quietly behind her. She looked so sexy with her hair down in messy waves around her face, wearing an oversized shirt that was falling off one shoulder. I let out a sharp breath at the sight of her.

"Couldn't turn my brain off." I swiped a palm down my face, trying to rub the lust from my eyes.

"What were you thinking about?" she asked with a raised eyebrow.

"About everything."

She cocked her head and bit her lip. "Like?"

I tried to fight it, but denying my need for Jocelyn was like swimming against a tidal wave. With a wretched grunt, I stalked over, circled my hands around her waist, and lifted her up onto the edge of the workbench. "Take a guess," I said, pulling apart her thighs and fitting myself in the space between. She hooked her heels around my ass and drew me closer until my erection was nestled in the junction of her legs.

I lifted the hem of her shirt and ogled her black cotton underwear. "Just panties?" I trailed a finger up the center of her warm crotch, then traced it up her belly and into her shirt. The breath hitched in her throat when I closed my palm around the soft weight of her breast, rolling her nipple between my fingers until it pebbled.

"So tell me," she breathed. "Tell me what other thoughts are keeping you up tonight."

I curled a hand over the loose collar of her shirt and tugged it down, exposing her breast. "I was thinking of this," I said, flicking her nipple. I tugged the shirt lower and freed the other breast. "And this." Dipping my head, I alternated suckling from both mounds, nipping at her nipples before laving each one with my tongue.

She leaned back on her hands and arched her back, allowing me more access. "What else?"

I grinned. So the girl wanted dirty talk. "I was thinking," I began, kissing my way up her neck to her ear. "About how much I wanted to taste you. To open you up and run my tongue through your folds, up and down then in circles, tasting your wetness. I want to devour you until you're squirming, until you can't stand it anymore and you break apart. I want to taste your come, feel your insides trembling around my tongue."

She let out a ragged breath.

I kept my word and proceeded to do just what I'd described. Joss grabbed handfuls of my hair, unable to decide whether to pull me away or to hold me closer. Eventually, she resorted to grinding her crotch into my face, gasping softly as the legs around my shoulders wound tighter and tighter.

"Jake!" she gasped as she climaxed. I slid two fingers inside her and continued to work her clit with my tongue, hell bent on making her come again.

And come she did. She was deathly silent but her entire body convulsed for a good thirty seconds, her inner walls quivering around my finger.

I couldn't stand it anymore; I stood up and shoved my tongue inside her mouth, wishing like hell I could screw her like I desperately wanted. She clutched at my hips but I held back. I'd taken a risk once not using a condom; I couldn't take it again. One mistake was all it would take to ruin her future, a future I wasn't even sure I'd be a part of.

Her eyebrows knitted as she waited for me. "Why—?"

I sighed. "I didn't bring any condoms."

"I'm on the pill. I thought you knew?"

"Since when? Since Eli?" The name slipped out without thought. I hadn't meant to sound like a jealous twat.

She bit back a smile. "I've been on it since I was sixteen. My mom wanted to make sure I didn't accidentally get pregnant, even though it took another two years before I even lost my virginity."

My mood darkened at the idea of someone taking her virginity. Someone not me. "Who was it?"

"Does it matter? You won't even know him."

"Yes. Everything about you matters."

She let out an impatient sigh. "His name was Harry Nicholls. We dated on and off in high school. My first time was with him on prom night." She set her hands on my shoulders. "There, you happy? My love life is a cliché."

"Who else?" I suddenly felt the need to know every single person she'd been with, unheeding of the fact that this conversation had never benefitted a relationship in the history of ever.

"Really? Right now?" She looked pointedly down between us. "You want me to talk about my ex-boyfriends while I'm exposed and throbbing?"

I brought her hand down to my erection. "You're not the only one throbbing. But I need to know."

Her nostrils flared and her eyebrows drew together, but she answered anyway. "After Francis, there was this guy, Dylan. We dated for three months. Then there was Joey. He was an art major and, I guess, my most serious relationship at six months."

"Did you love any of them?"

She fixed her green eyes on me and I was sure she could see right through me. Instead of answering, she tugged my pants down and pulled me out, positioning me at her entrance. "I'm not answering that question until you give me something in return. Tit for tat."

So I squeezed her tit.

She chuckled and scooted closer to the edge of the bench. "Now for the tat." She pulled on my hip, slowly drawing me into her warmth.

I sucked in a ragged breath and pushed in the rest of the way. "Damn, you feel amazing."

"So move."

"Answer the question first."

She sighed. "No, I didn't love any of them. I thought I maybe loved Joey, but whatever it was, it didn't last long."

I cupped her jaw in my hand and held her gaze as I drew out and slid back in. "Thank you," I said, kissing her lips. "For being so open with me." I swayed up and knew I'd hit the right spot when she gasped. But if I thought I could get away with not talking about my past relationships, I was wrong.

"Tell me about yours," Joss said, her body undulating with mine, meeting me thrust for thrust.

"You want me to talk about other women right now?" I gritted through my teeth.

102

She paused for a moment, studying me. Then she said, "I guess not."

But before she closed her eyes and dipped her head into my neck, I saw the momentary flash of sadness in her eyes.

Still moving, I held her face in my hands and made her look at me. "I have loved in my lifetime," I said, thrusting in slow and deep. "But you... you've consumed me heart and body, Jocelyn. I've never—*never*—felt this way about anybody before."

Her lips quivered as she lunged forward and kissed me. A moment later, she sucked in a breath. Her entire body tensed then broke apart, fingers clutching at my shoulders as she rode through the tremors.

I came right after, driving deep as I pumped my seed into her. With her face cradled in the palm of my hands, I leaned my forehead on hers and tried to catch my breath, trying to make sense of the inconceivable notion that I'd fallen for her at this time in my life.

"I wish I'd met you before you met my mom," she whispered, her hands covering mine.

"Me too." For a long time I'd tried telling myself that it was Amanda I wanted, but I'd only been fooling myself.

"You said before that you give a piece of yourself each time you have sex," Joss began, her eyes a brilliant green. "What piece did you give me?"

An unfamiliar feeling clanked around in my chest, sending my heart racing. I wasn't usually a sappy, emotional kind of guy but when it came to her, I wanted to spill every flowery thought that came to mind. "Everything," I said, my voice rough with emotion. "When I'm with you, I lay it all bare and give you everything."

She kissed me, deep and passionate, letting me know that she was giving me a part of herself too. But however much she gifted me, it was more than I deserved.

"Joss, we have to tell Amanda."

She recoiled, the haze of desire dissolving from her face. "I thought we agreed—"

"Joss!" I said, forcing her to look at me. "Your mom... she wants to get married."

[e l e v e n]

"What?" Joss pushed me away and jumped off the bench, snatching her panties off the floor.

"Before she left for Atlanta, she sat me down and discussed marriage. She said she wanted to make this official, make us a real family," I said, righting my pants. Somehow it felt wrong to have my cock and balls swinging around for this conversation.

"What did you tell her?" she asked, folding her arms across her chest.

"I said I'd think about it. But that was before your birthday, before any of this—" I motioned to the space between us. "—happened."

Lines etched into her forehead. "You'd be my stepfather."

"I'm not going to marry her. Obviously. How could you even think that about me?"

"I don't know!" she cried, throwing her hands up in

frustration. "I don't know what's happening here, Jake," she added in a more hushed, but no less biting, tone.

"I don't either." I dug my fingers into my hair. "I'm so out of my depth here. My first instinct is to simplify, to make it as straightforward as possible for all parties."

"Except straightforward means hurting my mom."

"What do you want more, Jocelyn? Your happiness or your mom's?"

She looked at me for a long time, her chest heaving, her eyes ringed red. Finally she gave me the answer I'd expected, which was not to say it hurt any less. "My mom. She has to come first."

"And what? I go back and pretend that nothing ever happened? Act like the good little boyfriend?"

She took in a deep breath and nodded. It didn't escape my notice that she was blinking back tears. "And I'll move out," she whispered. "Give you two some room."

I shook my head, slashing the air with my hands. "No. That's not going to happen."

"If you care about me even a little, you'll do it."

"I'm sorry, but no."

"You have to."

My feet carried me over to her. I tucked her disheveled hair behind her ears and lifted her face to meet mine. "Lately I've done so many things I'm not proud of. I need to do the right thing now."

She looked up at me, her chin trembling. "If you tell her, you'll lose us both."

From the center of my chest came a radiating kind of pain, the thought of hurting Amanda and losing Joss in one fell swoop causing me instant heartburn. "I can't do it," I told her gently. "I have to tell her."

She closed her eyes, a tear leaking out and streaking down her cheek. Her hands came up to cover my own. "Okay," she said on a whisper.

"Tomorrow."

She nodded and took in a shuddering breath. "Things are going to change."

I kissed her forehead. "Don't worry. We'll figure this out."

I slipped back into bed just as the sun began to peek through the curtains. I watched Amanda sleep for a time, contemplating what to say, knowing there was absolutely nothing I could do that would ease the sting of betrayal. How could I even begin to explain that not only had I cheated on her, but I'd done it with her own daughter?

I turned away, disgusted with myself.

When I opened my eyes the next morning, the space beside me was empty. I sat up, looking at the clock on the wall.

Ten a.m.

My eye caught on the pink sticky note on Amanda's pillow, the words written on it filling me with dread and anxiety.

We have to talk. Tonight. xo

———

I spent most of the day delivering and consulting with clients, caught between making the hours fly by and putting off the inevitable.

With a bouquet of flowers in hand, I came home and found mother and daughter at the dining table. Unseen, I hovered at the doorway and watched as they talked and laughed. It struck me then that I was coming between these two amazing women. I only hoped their relationship was strong enough to withstand what I was about to do.

"Hey, how long have you been standing there?" Amanda asked.

"A few minutes." I pushed away from the doorjamb and joined them at the table. "I didn't want to interrupt."

"You're not interrupting. I was just telling her about my day," she said, smiling at her daughter.

Joss flashed me a quick look, and in that one second managed to infuse it with warmth, regret, and dread. I reached over and plucked one red rose from the bouquet and handed it to her.

"Thank you," Amanda said when I handed her the rest.

"Yeah, thanks," Joss echoed in a soft voice.

I smiled, watching Joss's carefully emotionless face as she lifted the rose up to her nose. The very sight of her steeled my nerves and gave me courage.

"Amanda, can we talk? In private?"

Jocelyn's green eyes flicked up to mine, a look of panic spreading across her face.

"Actually," Amanda said. "I think Joss should be around for this."

"For what?" Goosebumps rose on my arms, dread snaking up my spine.

Amanda turned to her daughter, reaching across the table for her hand.

"What is it, Mom?"

"I've asked Jake to marry me."

Joss's eyes widened, doing her best impersonation of shock. "You did?"

Amanda nodded then turned to me. "I know this seems like we're moving fast but, in this case, I think it's warranted considering the situation."

A cold sweat broke out over my forehead. "What situation?"

Amanda took a deep breath. "Jake, you're going to be a dad."

June Gray

[twelve]

Joss reacted first. "What?" she asked, jumping to her feet. "You're pregnant?"

Amanda nodded with a tentative smile. Her eyes never left my face as I tried my best to keep from freaking out.

I swallowed hard and opened my mouth, but nothing came out.

Joss's gaze swung around to me, eyes glistening. "You're going to be a dad," she breathed.

"Jake?"

It took me a few moments to realize that both women were calling my name.

"Well?" Amanda asked, her eyebrows lifting up in hope.

I looked around the room, still at a loss. A few seconds passed, then thirty, and then it was too late.

Amanda stood up, her eyes red. "I thought you two would be happy."

"Of course I am," Joss said, belatedly throwing her arms around her mom's shoulders. "I'm sorry. I'm just shocked."

"Not more shocked than Jake," Amanda said, looking at me through tear-filled eyes.

I felt bad for her—really, I did—and later I might even feel some joy in the prospect of becoming a father, but right then, faced with the woman I wanted and the woman I'd impregnated, I couldn't think past the thought that I was well and truly fucked.

"I… I need some time." And without another word, I got up and left the room. My feet carried me through the living room and through the front door, and I got in my truck and drove away.

To leave right then was a dick move, but at that moment I was at a total loss.

"This is some screwed-up drama llama you've got yourself into, big brother," Tristan said as soon as I'd finished telling him the reason why I was crashing his pad at ten at night. He handed me a beer and dropped onto the couch beside me.

"Shut up," I said, nearly draining the bottle. I knew the answer to my problems wasn't at the bottom of a bottle, but I hoped for it anyway. When I'd drained that one, I tried another.

"So what are you gonna do?"

"Would I be here, crashing on your couch, if I knew?"

"Are you gonna split?"

"No," I said quickly. I couldn't. As much as I didn't want to marry Amanda, I knew I couldn't very well leave her now. She'd been a single parent once before; I wouldn't do that to her again.

Thinking was impossible when my little brother wouldn't stop yapping. "So you'll do the honorable thing and marry her. Meanwhile, you're secretly pining for her daughter, who will be the big sister to your kid?" He shook his head, chuckling softly. "This is some Days of Our Lives shit."

I punched his arm. "Shut your face." I reached for the remote control, hoping to be distracted for a little while.

After a few minutes, Tristan slammed his bottle on the coffee table and stood up. "Come on. Let's go out."

"It's Tuesday night."

"So?" He slipped his feet into a pair of boots. "Let's get wasted."

"And what would that solve?"

"Nothing. Everything. Hell, you never know, you might get some perspective." He grabbed my hand and pulled me up. "Come on. I'll get the first round."

Several hours later we stumbled back in to his apartment, way past the point of cheery inebriation. As soon as he opened the front door I made a beeline for the balcony, barely making it in time before I threw up over the railing.

Some time later, Tristan stuck his head out the sliding door. "You okay?"

From my perch on the cement floor, I gave him a thumbs-up sign.

"You coming in?"

I set my arms on my knees and hung my head between my legs. "Not until I'm done horking."

"You know I have a toilet, right?"

I waved him away. "Just go."

I sat out there on my ass for a long time that night, staring up at the barely visible stars in the sky. The balmy, almost musty night air didn't help with my nausea, but I needed to be alone for a while, needed to pick through the debris of my thoughts, pluck out what was most important, and discard the rest.

I took out my phone and pulled up a picture of Joss, taken when she was reading one of my books on the floor. Her blonde hair was spread out like a halo around her head, her eyes bright as she smiled up at me. Jocelyn Blake was beautiful, smart, and kind-hearted, the kind of woman any guy would be lucky to find. She deserved so much more in her young life.

I flipped back through my photos, finally finding the last photo I'd taken of Amanda during one of our dates. She had been looking off into the distance, a wistful expression on her face. This morning she was the woman I was going to break up with; now she was the mother of my child. How quickly that curveball comes your way.

By the time the sun started its rise over the horizon, I had chosen my fate. And even though it was going to hurt like hell for more than one person involved, I felt certain I was making the right decision.

As soon as I was sober enough to drive, I got in my truck and went back. I walked through the dark house, heading to the master bedroom. I found Amanda in the bathroom, sitting on the edge of the tub with a crumpled tissue in her hand. She looked up when I entered the room but said nothing.

"I'm sorry," I said, sitting beside her. It felt like all I'd done lately was apologize. "I was… I was in shock."

She nodded, blowing her nose.

A time machine would have come in handy right about then. But then, I realized I didn't know how far back I'd go. Would I go back to the moment she told me about the baby so I could change my reaction or would I go as far back as the day I kissed Jocelyn? "I wish you'd told me in private," I said.

"I know. I kind of ambushed you." She dabbed at her eyes, giving me a rueful smile. "I was excited."

"When… how… did you find out?"

"I realized a few days ago that I haven't had my period in three weeks."

I took a deep breath and held her hand. "We're going to be parents," I said, my voice steady even as my insides rioted.

Amanda looked up at me. "You scared?"

I had woken up this morning thinking my life would change. And, oh boy, was I ever right. "A little. Yeah."

She squeezed my hand. "Me too." She looked down at our intertwined fingers. "Jake, about the marriage proposal—I'm taking it off the table. For now."

"You are?" Despite myself, a little knot loosened in the tangled mess in my chest.

"I figured we should probably deal with the baby first. Take it one step at a time." She chewed on her lower lip, watching for my reaction. It hurt to see this normally confident woman looking so insecure.

I bent down and kissed her forehead. "I know I left before, but I'm here now, Amanda. I'm not going anywhere."

"Are you sure?" she asked. "Because I've raised a kid on my own before. I can do it again if I have to."

"You won't have to," I said, shaking my head, my resolve growing stronger the longer we talked. "I'm staying right here. This baby is not growing up without a father."

[thirteen]

When I went to the kitchen the next morning, I found Joss sitting at the table staring into a bowl and spinning a spoon over and over between her fingers.

"Morning," I said, realizing too late how flippant it sounded, as if our chances of being together hadn't just blown up in our collective face.

"Mom told me," she said, her gaze still on the soggy cereal.

"Joss…"

"It's okay." Finally she looked up, allowing me a view of the bags under her eyes, the utter exhaustion and resignation in her face. "I think you're doing the right thing."

I kept to my side of the room even if all I wanted was to wrap my arms around her. "I'm sorry, Joss. I wish things were different."

She swiped a hand over her cheek. "My mom's happy. That's what's important."

"I wish you could be happy too," I whispered.

She tried a smile but we both knew it was only for show. "I'm going to have a brother or sister. I'm happy about that." She stood up with the bowl in hand but stopped halfway across the room when she realized she'd have to come near me to get to the sink.

I held out my hand, taking the bowl from her. She recoiled when our fingers touched.

"Joss, I want to explain—"

"You don't have to explain. You chose the right woman."

I took a step toward her but she retreated, her eyes flashing. It was the first sign of life I'd seen from her all morning.

"Don't touch me, Jake. I can't take that right now."

"I'm sorry. I'll try to keep my distance." But even if I meant every word, I felt deep down the futility of that promise. I would try to stay away from Joss, which is not to say I would succeed.

"What about you, Jake? Are you happy?"

"What do you think?"

We stared at each other, the longing and the regret passing between us like currents. More than anything I wanted to hold her, but more than everything she was forbidden. "How the hell am I going to do this with you around?"

I didn't realize I'd said the words aloud until Joss said, "I'm moving out soon, so you won't have to deal with me for very long."

"Then tell me," I began in a broken voice, "how the hell am I going to do this without you?"

———————

The next few days were not easy. Joss and I lived in each other's periphery, maintaining a cautious distance at all times.

But each time we found ourselves in the same room, Joss talked about apartment prospects. Turned out finding an apartment wasn't as easy as she thought. Or rather, not as affordable, especially here in South Florida where everything had a higher price tag.

But that didn't stop her from looking. One morning, I found her in the living room with her mom, discussing an apartment listing that she'd seen online.

"You're not moving to Hialeah." I took a sip of my coffee. "It's not safe there." Hialeah was one of Miami's more notorious neighborhoods, infamous for its violent streets.

"Not really your say, Jake." Joss looked up from the couch, throwing me a black look that took me aback. True the last few days had been uncomfortable but she had never shown me any hostility until today.

I planted myself in front of the couch, making myself as formidable as possible. "Oh, I get a say."

Amanda's eyes flicked between her daughter and me, no doubt noticing the palpable tension in the room. "I agree with Jake," she told her daughter. "I really don't feel comfortable with you living anywhere in South Florida on your own, to be honest."

"Then I'll get a roommate." Her eyes flicked up to meet mine, sparking with challenge. "Maybe I'll move in with Eli."

"You think he'll take you back after what happened?" I asked, unable to keep the smug smile off my face.

Amanda turned to Joss with a frown. "Yeah, what happened? You never told me why he just ditched you at your own birthday celebration."

Joss's nose flared as she narrowed her eyes at me. I almost laughed out loud. So sue me, but I was starting to enjoy her discomfort. "Actually, Jake scared him away."

"I didn't trust him," I said simply. "And it seemed my suspicions were on the nose when I saw him trying to dry hump you out in the parking lot."

Amanda's jaw dropped. "Ja—" She stopped and turned to her daughter. "Why didn't you tell me?"

Joss flipped the laptop shut and stood up, choosing to flee again instead of fight. "Because we were just kissing. Everyone does it." She turned to me with fury and hurt in her eyes. "So thanks to you, I lost the most significant man in my life."

"Maybe he wasn't that significant if he's so quick to walk away."

"Most men are like that, Jake," Joss said with more bitterness in her voice than I'd like. "You just give them one push and they're gone."

I held her gaze. "Not all men. Some men choose to stick around."

Joss fought to keep her face from betraying her emotions, but the pain simmering right under the surface was clear as day. It wasn't my usual M.O. to be so cruel but the petty part of me wanted her to share in my suffering. If nothing else, at least we could share that.

"What's going on? Why are you antagonizing her?" Amanda asked after Joss stalked out of the room.

I shrugged. "Hialeah is not safe." I stared into my coffee mug, my mood as dark as the liquid inside. "Maybe I should go, Amanda. I don't want Joss to feel like she has to move out because of me."

She shook her head. "No, that's not necessary. She's wanted to do this for a while now. I just haven't let her." She sighed. "I just don't want her to feel like I don't need her in my life anymore now that I have you and the baby."

"I'm sure that's not what she's thinking. She knows we're doing the right thing."

Amanda squeezed my leg and stood up. "I'm glad you stayed. I don't know what I would do without you."

I forced a smile, even if her words felt like bullets piercing my chest.

June Gray

[fourteen]

I didn't see Joss again for a few days. It didn't seem possible to avoid someone for this long when you occupy the same one-thousand-something square foot area, but she was good at evasion. For all I saw of her, she might as well have moved out already.

I guess I, too, had gotten adept at avoidance. I simply stayed in the garage, working long after Amanda went to bed to steer clear of any form of intimacy. In the mornings, I took extra long showers to relieve the tension that accumulated overnight. It was the only time I allowed myself to think of Joss anymore, to remember the searing heat that had passed between us.

It was during one of those mornings, when I had one hand on the tile wall and one of my dick, fantasizing about Joss while water sluiced down my body, that I heard the shower door open. Amanda pressed her naked body to my back and reached around, taking hold of my shaft.

"Let me take care of that," she whispered by my ear and stroked me from root to tip.

And I let her. I simply dropped my head and closed my eyes, imagining someone else's hands around my cock. But the guilt and shame washed over me in waves, softening my resolve.

"What's the matter?" Amanda whispered, trying her best to rub me back to life with no luck.

I turned and held her in my arms, pressing a kiss of apology to her hair. "I just have a lot on my mind."

"You've had a lot on your mind lately," she says, rubbing her breasts against me.

Boy, wasn't that the truth.

She looked up at me, longing in her eyes. "I miss you, Jake."

Unable to return the sentiment, I simply pressed my lips to hers. And with a heart blanketed with many layers of guilt, I reached down between her legs and returned the favor.

Amanda and I emerged from the bedroom half an hour later, loose-limbed and relaxed. She held my hand and led me down the hall, chatting about the busy day she had ahead.

"I'm late for work," she said, grabbing her purse. She turned to me and pressed a kiss to my lips, smiling. "But maybe I should be late with you every morning."

Out of the corner of my eye, I noticed movement across the living room. I pulled away from Amanda and found Joss on the couch, snuggled under the blanket with a book in her hand.

"Hey!" Amanda said, walking over and kissing her on the top of her head. "I didn't know you were already up."

Joss's smile was tight. "Yep. Been up for a while now."

Amanda laughed nervously, her cheeks turning red. "Sorry. I hope we didn't wake you up."

Judging from the look on her face, Joss had heard her mom's loud moans, but she shook her head and lied. "No. I was too engrossed in my book. I didn't even notice you guys standing there."

"Thank God," Amanda said. "I'd need therapy if I ever heard my parents having sex."

I cringed inwardly. Joss hid her face behind the book.

After Amanda left for work, I remained in the living room, staring at the woman on the couch. The awkwardness in the room was suffocating, but I stayed, needing to get some things off my chest.

"Joss…"

She threw aside the blanket and got up, ignoring me.

I followed close behind, watching her hips sway as she stalked off to hide in her room. "I'm talking to you," I said, grabbing her elbow.

She jerked her arm away, keeping her back to me. "What?" she spit out.

"I didn't have sex with her."

Slowly she turned, studying my face. "Sure looks like you did."

I took a step closer. "We didn't," I said gently, hoping I wouldn't have to elaborate. "I haven't had sex with her since…" I let out a breath. "You have no idea how hard it's been trying to avoid her night after night. This morning she just caught me by surprise."

Joss cocked a hip and an attitude. "It must be so hard rejecting the advances of a beautiful woman."

"It is," I bit out between my teeth, trying to keep my emotions in check. She was making my blood boil, and there was a very thin line between anger and lust. "Not that any of this matters because you and I are not together. I'm with your mom and I shouldn't have to feel guilty every time I do something with her."

She wrapped her arms around her middle. "I know," she whispered, her lips trembling. "But it hurts. Like physically hurts to know that you're not…"

I closed the space between us. "Not what?"

Her shoulders sagged as she leaned into me, but stopped short of touching. When she looked up, the skin under her eyes were wet with tears. "Not with me."

I reached out and wiped at her tears. I couldn't *not* touch her anymore. "I'm sorry, Joss. I wish I could make this hurt less."

In that moment, seeing the pain etched in her features, I felt a pang of the physical pain she was talking about. It hurt like a bitch, but we couldn't veer from the paths we'd already set for ourselves. "We have to move past this. We have to find a way to move on."

"It's that easy for you, isn't it?" she asked, bitterness lacing her voice. "Moving on?"

I ground my teeth. "It has to be." And even though I really didn't want to, I turned my back on her and walked away.

―――――――

"What about Landon for a boy and Larissa for a girl?"

"What?" I blinked up, not realizing that Amanda had joined me out in the backyard. I took a sip of beer and continued to enjoy the balmy afternoon in the backyard. I had only hedge bushes and the lawn to look at, but I wasn't out here for the scenery anyway.

"Baby names." Amanda sat on my lap and showed me a blue book with a chubby baby on the cover. She flipped through the dog-eared pages. "I like the name Liam too."

"What about Joss?"

Amanda bit back a smile. "I think that name's already taken."

"I mean, have you asked her?"

Her smile dissolved. "I wanted to consult with the baby's father first." She pulled away, studying me. "What's with you lately? Is it Joss?"

I tried to retain my cool; Amanda's gaze was more searing than the Florida sun. "What do you mean?"

"You two haven't been getting along." I opened my mouth but she quickly covered it with her hand. "Don't even deny it. You can't stand to be in the same room together and when you do happen to be, you're always arguing."

I shook my head and looked away. Amanda wasn't stupid. Of course she noticed.

Her fingers threaded into my hair. "So what is it? It's not about the baby, is it?"

I looked into her open face, wanting so badly to confess.

I had an affair with your daughter.

Seven little words that meant nothing apart, but when put together had the power to destroy everything.

We both turned our heads when the glass door opened. My ears burned as Joss walked out to the backyard wearing a shirt and those damn cutoff shorts. But the heat that spiked my temperature was quickly doused when I saw who followed her out.

"Hey," Joss said, pointedly avoiding looking at me. She turned to the person beside her. "Mom, this is my boyfriend, Eli."

My hand squeezed around the beer bottle, trying its best to shatter glass.

Amanda got up from my lap and shook Douchebag's hand. "It's nice to finally meet you. I'm glad you and Joss were able to work things out."

Eli's eyes flicked towards me a few times but he refused to address me. I had no idea what Joss had told him about me but it must have been convincing because he didn't seem too surprised to see me with her mom. "Yeah, Joss and I..." He took hold of her hand, the asshole. "We're good together."

Yeah, like eyeballs and chili peppers. "So where are you lovebirds headed?" I asked, tipping my beer his way.

"We're just going to the pool," Joss said.

Eli gave her a full body look, undressing her with his eyes. It took everything in me not to jump up and deliver a roundhouse kick to his smug face.

My mood went downhill from there. After they left, Amanda resumed her seat on my lap.

"You two are at odds about Eli, aren't you?" she asked.

"Can we just drop it?"

Amanda nodded, acting like she was well aware of what was going on in my head. God, if she only knew. "I know you don't like him, but give him a chance. Give *her* a chance. I didn't raise her to be a meek doormat. She may seem introverted and quiet but my Joss has a strong will."

"Yeah, I noticed." I took a deep breath but felt like I wasn't getting enough air in my lungs. I eased her off my lap and stood up. "I'm going for a run."

June Gray

[fifteen]

I still couldn't sleep at night, couldn't turn off my brain long enough to get some rest. These days I was more adept at shutting out thoughts of Joss, forcing myself instead to focus on my impending fatherhood. It worked, most times.

One night, after tossing and turning in bed for two hours, I went into the garage to grab a beer and my sketchbook. I went out to the driveway and sat on the open bed of my truck, sketching out ideas for a piece of furniture that would change my life. I knew there were safety standards that needed to be upheld, like the width of the gaps between slats, but I wanted to add my own style to the piece.

After twenty minutes of sketching and erasing, I sat back and admired the final drawing of the crib, imagining the child that it would hold and protect. I could almost see Amanda standing over it, smiling down at the baby, and me...

I let out a breath. No matter how hard I tried, I couldn't

imagine myself as part of the cozy family scene.

Before I could change my mind, I grabbed the pencil from behind my ear and began drawing on a fresh page. At first the strokes were long and exploratory but all too soon the drawing took the shape of a face with long, wavy hair, haunting eyes, and chin with a tiny indentation. So it didn't turn out looking exactly like Joss—hell, I had never been that great at portrait drawing—but this was all I was allowed to have of her.

I didn't know how long I stared at that face out there in the dark, with the mosquitoes feasting on my legs, but for once, I felt a little bit of peace. And for the first time in a long time, I was able to get a few hours of solid sleep that night.

———————

"I'll be there," I told Amanda over the phone. I looked down at my watch even if I knew I had plenty of time to make it to our first OBGYN appointment. "I just need to stop at the store first."

"Don't be late," Amanda said, her voice edged with anxiety. I suspected she still didn't think I'd want anything to do with the baby, which made me all the more determined to prove her wrong.

"Just relax. All this worrying is probably not good for the baby."

Amanda sighed. "You're right. Okay, I'll see you at three."

I hung up and headed to the laundry room to get my shirt out of the dryer. On the way there, the front door opened and Joss walked in. She stopped, the panic evident in her face, even as her eyes took in my shirtless form.

"Hi." I jabbed a thumb over my shoulder. "I was just leaving."

"Without a shirt?" she asked.

I sighed through my nose. "No. Just getting it out of the dryer then I'm headed to the doctor's appointment with your mom."

Her lips thinned but she nodded. "Oh right, that's today."

"Do you want to come?" The words were out of my mouth before I could stop them, but I figured Joss would want to be present to lend her mom moral support.

Her eyes widened. "No, I can't. I'm actually expecting someone."

I bristled. "Eli?"

She blinked, looking away. "Yeah."

"Do you think that's appropriate? Having him over without me or your mom at home?"

She raised an eyebrow. "I'm twenty-one years old. I think I can have a boy over alone if I want."

I ground my teeth together, both angered and turned on by her defiance. "Yeah, not gonna happen."

"At the risk of sounding like a petulant child... I don't have to do what you say. You're not my father."

"I can still bend you over my lap and spank you."

Joss's eyes widened. The air crackled around us with unspent energy.

I shook my head, laughing nervously. "Sorry. That was... inappropriate."

"And if I want you to spank me?"

I stared at her for a long time, my dick hard as steel in my pants. She was taunting me, forcing me to break character, but I wouldn't give her that satisfaction. "No, Joss," I said with finality in my voice.

She shrugged, challenge glittering in her eyes. "Fine. Then I guess Eli would have to spank me until my ass is red and I'm squirming in his lap."

I squeezed my hands into fists, afraid that if I moved, I'd lose control of myself completely. "Stop it. I'm trying to be the good guy here."

"A good guy wouldn't keep me from trying to move on with my life."

My shoulders sagged, all the hot air leaking out of me. She was absolutely right, of course. I was being selfish, as usual. "I'm sorry." She nodded and tried to step around me, but my hand shot out and pressed itself to her stomach. "I just can't stand the thought of his hands on you," I said and immediately regretted it.

"Just Eli or everyone else?"

Fuck, I was screwed ten ways till Sunday. I needed to stop before I made an even bigger mess of things. I shook my head and backed off. "It doesn't matter. Do what you want, Joss. I'm out."

"You made it," Amanda said as soon as I walked into the clinic thirty minutes later.

I handed over the bouquet of flowers, too exhausted to even crack a smile, and took a seat.

"Thank you," Amanda said. "I already went in and for the urine and blood test. They should be calling us here shortly."

"Okay." I hunched over, setting my elbows on my knees,

staring down at the marble floor between my feet.

Amanda's warm hand pressed into my back. "Hey, you okay? Are you nervous?"

My stomach trembled and I couldn't stop my leg from jiggling if I tried. "Yeah." I felt as if I was standing on a precipice, about to jump into the dark abyss without a clue what was waiting for me below.

The feeling intensified when the nurse led us back into one of the exam rooms. Somehow I knew that when we came back out, our world would never be the same.

But before Amanda could even undress and put on the gown, a different nurse came charging in wearing blue scrubs and a frown on his face. "Mrs. Blake?"

Amanda stood up, not bothering to correct him. "Yes. What's wrong?" Sensing her tense demeanor, I took her hand and squeezed it.

The nurse looked at his clipboard. "You're here for your first prenatal visit, correct?"

"Yes," Amanda said slowly. "Is something wrong?"

"Your hCG levels are really low, Mrs. Blake."

Amanda's hand flew up to her mouth. "I had a miscarriage?"

The nurse shook his head, the frown on his face getting deeper. "No. After a miscarriage, the hCG levels in your blood should still be slightly elevated. But you have a level of three."

"What the hell does that mean?" I asked, done with all the medical mumbo jumbo.

The nurse looked at me for the first time. "It means your wife never even conceived."

June Gray

[sixteen]

Amanda wasn't pregnant. She never was.

The relief that washed over me was like a tsunami, sweeping away everything else in its path. But when the water ebbed, all that was left was guilt and sadness.

"You must hate me," Amanda said at the parking lot of the clinic.

I looked up, noticing the dark clouds that had gathered in the sky. "Why would I hate you?" I asked, wiping away the tears on her cheeks. But they kept coming, kept rolling down in rivulets.

She stared up at me with her woeful green eyes, her head shaking side to side. "Because you don't want to be with me, Jake," she said softly. "We both know the baby is—was—the only thing keeping you here."

My breath hitched in my throat. I hadn't realized how transparent I'd been. "Amanda, I—"

"Who is she?" she cut in.

I opened my mouth to speak but a booming crack of thunder intervened. I looked up in time to see light streaking down from the sky followed by another loud thunderclap a few seconds later.

Amanda ignored the weather, instead choosing to focus on the storm that was our relationship. "Her name, Jake," Amanda said.

"Whose?"

"The woman you're in love with." She let out a humorless laugh when I couldn't answer. "Come on, Jake. We've been through some shit. The least you could do is be honest with me. I can tell you haven't been with me, emotionally anyway, for a while now."

The air left my body, leaving me deflated. "It doesn't matter who she is," I said.

Amanda's lips trembled. "But she does exist."

I unlocked her car and held the door open. "Let's not talk about this here. It's about to rain."

But Amanda wouldn't let up. "This explains so much. Why you've been so distant, why you keep turning me down for sex," she said, ignoring the open door. "You fell in love with someone else but stayed with me out of honor."

I couldn't look her in the eye, couldn't say anything. As much as I tried to do the right thing, honor had been in short supply the past few weeks.

A raindrop fell on her cheek and joined the rest of the tears trickling down her face. "Well, you're free to be with her now." Her voice broke at the last word and she turned away and slid into the car just as the rain began to fall.

"Are you saying it's over between us?" I asked, leaning down and setting my hands on the car.

She wouldn't look at me as she started the car. "That's what you want, isn't it? You go your own way and I go mine."

"Let's talk about this, Amanda."

Finally, she looked up. "I need to go away for a few days. To think." She set the car to Drive. "Take care of Joss, will you?"

My ears burned at the mention of the name. Once again I came so close to telling her about the affair. Instead I stepped back and watched her drive away, getting soaked to the bone.

The rain had become a blinding rainstorm by the time I made it home. Amanda's car was absent from its usual parking space, but there were two cars in the driveway.

Fucking Eli.

With long, furious steps, I went into the house and left wet boot prints all over the floor on the way to Joss's room. Without bothering to knock, I threw open the door. "Joss, we need to t—" I froze at the sight of Eli sitting on the edge of the bed, his hands at his open fly.

Joss spun around to me, her face flushing red. "What the hell?" She lunged across the room and pushed against my chest to force me out the door. "Haven't you ever heard of privacy?"

I didn't give an inch. I stood immobile, glaring holes into Eli's forehead. But instead of being embarrassed, the punk just casually stood up with a smug look on his face. "Try knocking next time, man. We were kind of in the middle of something."

In my thirty years I'd only completely lost my shit a handful of times. Once in middle school when my brother had taken my brand new bike for a ride and scraped the paint off, and another time when an older kid at school was bullying said younger brother. But the one that stuck out most in my mind was the day I had come home early from work and found Eleanor kissing another man in the driveway. I had lost my temper then and was ashamed to say I'd resorted to violence.

This time, however, there was no shame. I charged Eli and swung, my fist glancing off his jaw when he managed to twist out of the way at the last minute. He was lucky. The rage that propelled that punch probably would have unhinged his pretty boy jaw.

He took a shot at me and missed; I may be bigger, but I'm also faster. In two moves I was behind him with my arm around his neck, holding his arm locked at his back. "I think you forget I'm the man around here and I will not be disrespected in my home."

Dimly I could hear Joss shouting at me to stop, but I was in that dark place and couldn't think past my rage. I dragged the asshole out of Joss's room, down the hall, and literally launched him out the front door into the full-blown rainstorm outside.

He landed on the soggy lawn, slipping a few times before getting back to his feet. "You're crazy!" he shouted while buckling his belt. "You're not her dad, you asshole! You're just a piece of shit lowlife freerider who's using her mom!"

I stood in front of the house with my hands clenched into fists, my chest swelling with each ragged breath. "You'd better get out of here," I said in a calm voice that belied the storm roiling inside. "Before I rearrange your face."

Eli looked behind me. "I'll call you later," he called out to Joss.

I stepped in his line of vision, folding my arms across my chest. "Like hell you will."

He ran a hand through his wet hair and stomped back to his car. Without another word, he got in and pealed out. Once his car disappeared around the corner, I spun on a heel and went back inside the house.

"You had no right to do that!" Joss cried, following me to the laundry room.

I ripped off my soaked shirt and threw it into the washing machine. "No right?" I straightened to my full height, intimidating her with my size. "I had every right."

She pushed at me but I would not be moved. Not now. "No, you don't! We're not together, remember? If I want to fuck someone, I can."

"Watch your language," I said between my teeth.

"I don't have to watch my language," she said, rising to her toes to get in my face. She poked a finger in my chest. "Because you're nothing to me, Jake."

I gnashed my teeth, sure I was about to grind my molars into dust. "That may be true, but I'll be damned if I let anyone else fuck you." I stepped away and ripped off my belt, instinct taking over. I pulled my dick out, not at all surprised to find it hard as granite.

Her eyes flew down to watch me stroke myself then back up to my face, her breathing ragged, her entire body trembling. Before I could blink, she lunged for me, her hands grasping the back of my head as she dragged me down to meet her lips. I sank into the kiss with a groan, pouring into it every moment of torture I'd been through without her.

My hand slid down her body, tugging wildly at her cutoff shorts.

"What are we doing?" Joss asked, gripping my wrists. But I kept going until her panties and shorts were down around her ankles. I spun her around and bent her over the washer, jerking her hips back. "This isn't... we shouldn't..."

"We can," I said, guiding the head of my cock to her warmth. And God, was she warm and so wet. "Your mom and I are over." The guilt tried its best to steal its way back in but I shut it out, determined to have this moment. Guilt be damned, this was about me and Joss and nobody else.

Joss gasped, looking over her shoulder. "You are?"

I bent down and kissed her shoulder, breathing her in. "Yes," I whispered against her freckled skin.

"I should go find her."

She tried to twist around but I held steady. "No. She's gone, Joss. She left."

"But she probably needs me."

"Joss!" I wound my fingers through her hair and tugged until she was looking at me. "*I* need you."

It was possibly the most selfish thing I'd ever said, but it was also the truest. I had just lost Amanda and the baby. If Joss left me now, I didn't know how I'd cope.

The fear was clear in her eyes, but beneath that I could see the yearning. She burned for me; I could see it all over her face, could feel it radiating from her skin. Her lips parted and, with a stuttered breath, she arched her back and sank halfway down my length.

I let out a low groan against her ear. My fingers dug into her hips and I tugged her to me, her warmth enveloping me completely. I let out the breath I didn't realize I'd been holding.

I molded myself to her back, holding her tight, trying to get as close as humanly possible. Here, like this, was the rightest place to be, the only place free of any doubts.

"I'm here," she said on a sigh. "You have me."

I turned her around and set her up on the machine, needing to look into her eyes. I floated my fingers across the soft lines of her face, lightheaded and completely intoxicated with this being in my arms.

"I love you, Joss." I hadn't planned on saying those words, but once they came out, I found I didn't want to take them back. I loved her, had loved her for a long time now. It was about time she finally knew.

She sucked in a breath and looked up. "What did you say?"

"I love you," I repeated, holding her face in my hands. "I'm so fucking helplessly in love with you."

She closed her eyes and nodded, absorbing my words. As I watched her, a tentative smile curved her lips upward, releasing the knots in my stomach. She wrapped her legs around me and guided me back into her warmth, her entire face glowing as we locked back together. "My wooden heart has always been yours, Jake."

I took my time rocking into her, kissing her with equal parts tenderness and intensity. Her breathing turned ragged as she touched my face, staring at me in disbelief and awe. "Is this real? Is this really happening?"

A short laugh escaped my throat. "Oh, this is really happening," I said and kissed her again.

I gave her everything I had to offer, loving her the best and only way I knew how. And when she came shuddering around me, I followed her down into the unknown without any hesitation.

[seventeen]

"Why are you reading that?" Joss asked in her bed a short while later.

I gathered her closer into the crook of my arm, resting the tattered copy of Jane Eyre on her shoulder. "Because it's your favorite book."

"But right now?"

I read aloud, "I have for the first time found what I can truly love—I have found you. You are my sympathy—my better self—my good Angel—I am bound to you by a strong attachment. I think you good, gifted, lovely; a fervent, solemn passion is conceived in my heart; it leans to you, draws you to my center and spring of life, wraps my existence about you— and kindling in pure, powerful flames, fuses you and me in one."

She sighed. "One of my favorite parts."

"It's a long-winded way of saying I love you." I kissed the

top of her head, feeling a sense of rightness blanketing around us. I would have happily stayed like that forever, naked in bed with Joss, reading a book. It was my version of heaven.

She turned around and fit her back into my chest so that I spooned her. "Mmm. Read to me some more," she murmured, kissing the arm supporting her head.

"How about I tell you another story?"

She looked over her shoulder. "Oh? Who's the author?"

"Jake Mitchell and Jocelyn Blake." I set the book down and wrapped both arms around her, drawing her close. With my lips grazing the shell of her ear, I whispered, "Once upon a time there was man who fell in love with a woman he could never have."

"Ooh, a forbidden love story. My favorite trope," she said with a smile in her voice.

"Despite their circumstances, the two were inexplicably drawn together. They fought the attraction, tried to deny it even existed, until—"

"Can we get to the end of the story already?" she asked, rubbing her backside along my erection.

"So impatient." I parted her folds and slid inside in one strong thrust.

She gasped. "I'm not impatient. I just want to make sure there's a happy ending."

"Oh, there's definitely going to be a happy ending." To punctuate, I reached around and began to play with her clit as I dragged my cock in and out.

She pulled away and turned around, her eyebrows wrinkled with worry. "Jake, I need to know that you and I will be together at the end of all this."

"You're co-author, Joss. You get to decide the ending."

She mulled over my words, a smile forming on her lips. She hooked her leg over my hip and slid my cock back inside her sex. "Well then, spoiler alert," she said, clutching at my ass and urging me to thrust harder. "The boy gets the girl and they lived happily ever after."

She stopped then, the smile fading away, reality seeping back into our fairytale. "Even though I don't think we deserve it," she added with a quiver in her voice.

I held her by the back of the head and kissed her hard, reminding her of what we had between us. "I don't know how, but your mom can have a happily ever after too, Joss. Her story doesn't have to end in tragedy."

A tear slid down the side of her face and soaked into the pillow. "It already has."

Jocelyn and I stayed awake into the early hours of the morning. In between making love, we talked about books, school, work, about anything and everything that popped into our heads. It was as if we'd been mute all our lives and now we were finally free to speak.

When her alarm went off in the morning, I planted soft kisses all over her face, excited at the prospect of waking up with her every morning from here on out.

She giggled and cracked open her eyes. "Morning."

"Morning." I nuzzled her neck, my hand straying down south.

"We don't have time," she said, grabbing my wrist. "I have to get to work."

I groaned. "I was hoping we could spend the whole

morning in bed together."

"You can take a shower with me, if you'd like?"

She didn't have to ask twice. I practically carried her out of bed and into the shower. Once under the hot spray of water, Joss stood back and eyed my naked body with open appreciation.

I set my hands on my hips and let her look her fill.

She bit her lower lip. "I've daydreamed about this—you—in the shower." She reached out and touched her fingers to my stomach. I flexed, my abdominals popping up.

"Since when?"

"My friend Ashley put the idea in my head that night you picked us up," she said tentatively, looking so adorably shy I wanted to pinch both sets of cheeks.

I wrapped an arm around her back instead and pulled her flush against my naked, wet body. "Is that why you faked that illness and pulled my towel off?" I asked with a grin.

Her cheeks flushed. "No! I was legitimately sick."

"Sick in lust with me," I teased, sliding a finger down her spine and into the crevice of her ass.

She gasped when my fingers found her cleft, gliding through her slippery folds.

I was too caught up in Joss, wholly absorbed by the look of unadulterated pleasure on her face, to notice the bathroom door opening. To see the woman walking inside.

"Jake?" Amanda stood a few feet from us, separated only by the foggy glass shower door. Her eyes flicked from me to the woman in my arms, her mouth falling open when she finally discovered her identity. "Joss?"

[part three]

jocelyn

June Gray

[eighteen]

"Mom?" I turned to stone in Jake's arms, too shocked to move.

My mother, too, was frozen in place. "What is going on here?" she asked, her voice barely audible over the running water.

Jake reached behind him and turned off the shower, then grabbed a towel from the hook. "Joss," he whispered, wrapping the towel around my shoulders even as I dug my nails in his back. "We have to get out."

I managed to move my head side to side. "I... I can't."

"You two have to come out of there some time," Mom said, the anger in her voice a gathering storm.

Jake gave my arm a squeeze and exited the shower. After wrapping a towel around his waist, he turned to my mother.

"Don't you dare tell me this is not what it looks like," Mom said, her chin lifted, her lips taut.

"I wasn't going to say that," Jake replied.

The danger in Mom's gaze was unmistakable; I had never seen her look so furious. She tried to look over Jake's shoulder but he tried his best to shield me.

"My own daughter, Jake?" she asked. "She's nine years younger than you, you fucking asshole!" She slipped off one shoe and hurled it at Jake, catching him hard in the chest.

He didn't even flinch. He only picked up her shoe and set it up on the counter. "I'm sorry," he said, approaching her with his palms up. "I didn't want you to find out this way."

Mom bit her lips together, her nostrils flaring. "How long?" she demanded. "How long have you been fucking my daughter behind my back?"

It was then I realized I was acting like a frightened child, huddled in that shower while Jake fought for the both of us. Only then did it occur to me to do the same.

I wrapped the towel around me and straightened, and even if it was one of the hardest things I'd ever done, I opened the glass door and stepped out. I pressed a hand to Jake's back, letting him know I was there with him, that I was ready to stand beside him even if it meant going against my own mother.

I hoped to hell I was making the right choice.

"Right after my birthday," I said, forcing the words out.

Mom looked at me and the hurt in her eyes shredded me into ribbons.

"I didn't expect it to happen. It just developed. He wanted to break up with you first but you didn't answer the phone," I said quickly, throwing out reasons and excuses in hopes that one stuck.

"And what? If I'd answered the phone, he wouldn't have put his dick inside you?"

Beside me, I felt Jake's breath catch.

"He would have broken up with you before he and I did anything," I added.

Jake leaned the slightest so that his arm was touching mine in a small show of solidarity. Or maybe he was asking me to stop.

Mom tried to keep her composure but her face crumbled. And so did mine. "So what, that's supposed to be better? That instead of cheating on me, my boyfriend breaks up with me to be with you?" she asked, a tear streaking down her face. "My own daughter?"

I took a step forward as my own tears fell. "I never wanted to hurt you, Mom. I love you more than anything in the world."

"Not more than Jake."

"Mom..." I watched helplessly as she turned and stalked out of the room, eventually kicking off the second shoe down the hall.

Jake placed a hand on my shoulder and I spun into him, pressing my face into his chest and letting the flood of tears loose.

I went to work. I probably should have called in sick and stayed to talk to my mom, but the truth was I didn't want another confrontation. I was afraid of what she would say, afraid that it would guilt me into breaking it off with Jake.

And, God, after all this heartache, the last thing I wanted was to end it with him. Not after I'd finally had a taste of what real passion felt like.

When my shift ended a few hours later, I walked around the outdoor mall to procrastinate. But eventually I made my way back home.

As soon as I walked in the front door I heard my mom's voice from her office. I peeked around the corner and saw Jake standing in the middle of the room, my mom in front of him with her arms folded.

"You never even told her, did you?" she asked.

"No," he said with a defeated sigh. "I didn't tell her you were never pregnant."

I bit back a gasp.

Mom shook her head. "Why?"

"Because I didn't want her to think that you wanted me to stay so badly, you convinced yourself you were pregnant."

My mother's hand flew up to his face, the slap loud and sharp. "You really are an asshole, Jake, you know that? You with all your big talk about doing the right thing."

"I meant every word," he said, ignoring the red welt on his cheek.

"Until you didn't."

"Despite what you may think, I really did love you."

"*Did*," she said.

There was a long, terrible silence, when I was sure everyone in the house could hear my heart thudding.

Jake was first to break the silence. "So what now?"

"What now? You get your stuff and leave me and my daughter the hell alone. What did you think? That you could stay here and move into her room?"

"Of course not."

"Did you really think you two could be together?" Mom asked, the anger in her voice now laced with curiosity. "That there'd be a chance I would ever be okay with your relationship?"

"I had hoped—"

"Then you're a complete idiot," she broke in. "You want to do the right thing, Jake? Then leave Joss alone. She doesn't need someone like you in her life."

"Someone like me?"

"An opportunist who only thinks with his dick."

"If that were the case, I wouldn't still be here, trying to make things right."

"Really? That's what this is? How?"

"I don't know. But I love Joss. I want..." He paused, blinking fast. "I want to be with her. To give her the life she deserves."

"She deserves a life without complications," Mom said with resignation in her voice. "She deserves to graduate from school, start her first job, move out on her own. She has so much more living to do, free from you. If you were being completely honest with yourself, you'd know I'm right."

I left right then, too scared to hear Jake's answer because, in my hearts of hearts, I knew he'd agree.

I stayed in my room and read a book with headphones on, waiting for Jake to knock on my door, sit on my bed, and say the inevitable goodbye. But he never came.

It was near midnight by the time I gathered enough courage to venture outside. The house already dark by then, all the doors locked and curtains pulled close. Listening out for my mother, I passed through the dark hallway to the garage but Jake was not in there. And I realized with dread that some of his larger tools were missing, the space they once occupied outlined by sawdust. I took a deep breath and hit the garage door button, holding my breath as the metal doors squeaked to life, rising, climbing, and ultimately revealing the empty spot on the driveway where his truck used to sit.

——————

The garage was empty by the time I got back from classes the next day, the floors swept clean. With a thundering heart, I ran into the house, dropping my book bag somewhere along the way. I ran to the master bedroom and straight in to the closet, finding nothing but bare hangers and half-opened drawers on Jake's side.

Tears stung my eyes. Last night I'd known he was leaving. Now I knew he meant to do it without saying goodbye.

"Jocelyn?"

I spun on a heel at the sound of the voice, smacking my arm into a bunch of hangers and sending them spilling to the floor. I kicked them aside and ran out, colliding with a tall, hard body.

Jake grabbed my arms and steadied me like only he could. His warm breath fanned across my face as he said my name.

"I thought you left without saying goodbye."

"I almost did," he said, his words bringing tears to my eyes. "But I couldn't."

The air rushed out of me in relief and I leaned into him before I could even think.

"Joss," he said, pulling me away. "We have to talk." He walked me to the bed and sat me down, tipping his head down at me.

"I know what you're going to say," I said, swallowing back the tears. "You're leaving, both this house and my life."

He crossed his arms across his chest, his jaw hardening. "I'm sorry. It has to be this way."

"Does it?"

He kept up with the hard façade, but even I could see how much it hurt. "You know it does."

"So that's it? You come in here, wreak havoc in our lives, and then leave? You're not even going to stick around to help clean up the mess?"

"Joss..."

"No, I know. You want me to live a normal life, one where I spend my life wading through bad relationships, looking for the right guy," I said. "Only..."

"Don't say it," he pleaded through his teeth.

"Only I've already found the right guy," I said anyway. "So you're just condemning me to a life of disappointment and heartache?"

He dropped down to his knees before me, hanging his head. When next he looked up, his eyes were dark and dismal. "I *know* you, know how much you love your mom. If you chose me over her, you'd never forgive yourself."

My shoulders sagged as all the air seeped out of me. I stared into his blue eyes and realized with heartbreaking clarity that this was it. This was the end for us.

My voice was quiet, almost unrecognizable in its despair, when I said, "I guess we don't get that happily ever after."

He let out a breath, setting his hands on my knees. "This

doesn't change the fact that I love you."

"But you love me enough to let me go," I whispered.

"Please try to understand."

I nodded. I understood it all too well. I knew why he was choosing to leave me now, to give me the life he thought I needed to live. But understanding it didn't make it hurt any less.

I bent down and touched my forehead to his, squeezing my eyes shut. "I love you too, Jake. So fucking much it hurts."

He crushed his lips to mine, grabbing the back of my head and deepening the kiss before I could get my words out. He kissed me hard, almost desperately, ripping every thought out of my head. I didn't know how I could do it, how I could live without another kiss like this, but one thing was for certain: I would wait my whole life until I could taste it again.

"Bye, Jocelyn Blake. I wish we could have met at a different time in our lives."

After Jake left, I wandered around the house and tried to find a place to catch my breath but every room, every corner, held a memory that tightened my chest. First of my mom and the happy little life we'd led before Jake had come into our lives. Then there were the memories of Jake, of our easy banter, of the casual way he'd thrown a dimpled smile my way, never realizing that he was slowly stealing under my skin.

The memories split me in half, asking me to make a choice. Staying with my mom should have been a no-brainer. Why then did my heart break at the thought of never seeing Jake again?

[nineteen]

Our lives went back to normal, or as close to normal as it could be after Hurricane Jake. Mom worked a lot and I found myself alone at home again. The nights were the worst, so quiet and lonely.

Mom refused to talk to me beyond the necessary, addressing me as if I were nothing but a stranger. And I suppose, after what she found out about me, that was true. All this time she thought she could trust her own daughter and all this time I was betraying her.

One night, I sat in the living room and waited for her to come home. I fell asleep on the couch and only awoke when I felt a blanket sliding over my shoulders.

"I'm sorry," I said right away. I grasped her hand before she could run away. "I'm really sorry, Mom."

She refused to look at me. "I don't want to talk about it, Joss."

"I don't blame you for hating me."

She pursed her lips and turned away, her chin beginning to tremble. But I held onto her, needing to speak my peace. I couldn't live in this silent house anymore.

I sat up, still holding her hand. "I didn't do it to hurt you, Mom. I tried to stop it from happening, but I couldn't."

Her eyes grew wide. "You mean Jake forced—"

"No," I said quickly. "He tried to stop it from happening too. But it just..." My words died at the sight of my mom's falling face. "Didn't. We fell in love."

She pulled her hand away from my grasp, her eyes shuttering. "I've had a long day. I'm going to go to bed."

"Mom," I said before she could go. I stood up and grabbed the computer printouts from the coffee table. "I found an apartment. It's east of here, in Hollywood. Not too far from Fort Lauderdale. Ashley's rooming with me."

Mom looked down at the printed map and details of the apartment, then at the contract Ashley and I had already signed. "When do you move?" she asked in a dull voice.

"As soon as next week, if I want." *If you want.*

Her lips pursed as she handed back the papers. "I'll buy the boxes," she said and left.

I held a fist to my cramping chest and turned in place as my vision blurred. What now? Somehow I had lost everyone I loved, and worst of all: it had been my fault from the very beginning.

My eyes landed on the bookcase and skirted along the uneven edges of my books, trying to avoid looking at the blank space that Jake left behind. It was then I noticed a book with a brown spine that I hadn't seen before. I walked over and pulled it out, realizing it was a leather notebook with a strap that tied it shut.

My skin tingled as I untied the strap, opening the book to the first page and finding Jake's handwriting. The next pages were his sketches of furniture, of things he'd made and things still in the planning stages. There were two pages dedicated to sketches of my bookcase, of how the ladder would fit, down to how many books it would hold. In the corner of the page was a circle and inside were words that brought a tiny smile to my face: *How many books does she have?*

Several pages later was a fully-rendered drawing of a crib, complete with details on the rails and drawers underneath. I shut the book just as a sob bubbled up from my throat at the thought of Jake wanting that baby. Even if it had never existed, to know that Jake had wanted a child was like a boulder on my chest.

He was ready to take that next step and become a parent, and I... I was only beginning to discover the meaning of love and sacrifice.

———————

Ashley and I moved out five days later with the help of her brother and his truck. Our apartment was in an aqua blue building in Hollywood, Florida, that wasn't exactly the safest or most beautiful part of town, but it wasn't the worst either. The upside was that it was only a ten minute walk away from Downtown Hollywood, a six-block long area consisting of cafes, stores, galleries, and restaurants.

"I can't believe you brought this behemoth," Ashley said, staring up at the bookcase that was taking up the entire living room wall.

"Me either," Ryan said, dropping dramatically onto the tile floor. Even though the bookcase had come apart in three pieces, Ryan had still done most of the heavy lifting. It was a miracle we got it up here at all. "You can thank CrossFit," he said, flexing his biceps for effect.

Ryan was older than Ashley by a good five years and owned his own landscaping business, but sometimes he struck me as younger. Or maybe it just felt like I'd aged a lot in the past year.

"Dinner's on me," I told him, sinking down into the new IKEA couch. It had taken nearly half of my savings to buy new (but still relatively inexpensive) furniture, but it was a small price to pay for my adulthood.

"I'm surprised your mom's not here, banging on our door right now, begging you to move back home," Ashley said from the corner of the room where she slipped new curtains onto a metal rod.

I shrugged, trying to ignore the tightness in my chest. "She's on a business trip right now. Ohio." I conveniently left out the fact that she had scheduled the trip to coincide with my moving date.

Ashley paused, frowning. "That's weird. Are you guys fighting or something?"

I considered telling her everything but a) Ryan was around and b) I didn't even want to speak Jake's name in our new apartment. As far as I was concerned, this place was going to be as Jake-free as possible.

We walked down to Hollywood Boulevard that night, the heart of Downtown Hollywood, which was a little more than a ten minute walk through a few shady-looking areas but nothing Ashley and I couldn't handle on our own.

While waiting for our food at a Cuban restaurant, Ryan regaled us with stories of strange things he'd found in people's yards while on the job. "Once, I found what I could swear was a human bone," he said with comically large eyes.

Ashley snorted. "No way."

"It looked like a femur of someone small, like a kid. Even the homeowner agreed."

"And you didn't call the cops *why*?" Ashley asked.

Ryan shrugged. "What if we were wrong and it turned out to be from a dog or horse or something? I mean, it was on a ranch."

Ashley smacked him upside the head while I laughed. "You're so full of shit," she said.

After dinner, Ryan decided he wanted to go out dancing.

"Um, don't you have a wife and a kid to get back to?" Ashley asked.

He shrugged with a sheepish look on his face. "Yeah. But they're probably asleep by now. A few more hours won't hurt."

I didn't even want to know what that was about; I had enough drama in my life to last me a good long while. "I think I'm just going to head home and do homework," I said as we emerged from the restaurant.

"You want us to walk you back?" Ryan asked at the sidewalk.

I looked around. "No, I think I'll be okay."

Ashley frowned. "You sure?"

"Yeah, I'll be fine. Go," I said, waving them away. I started back to our apartment, keeping my purse tucked under my arm, trying to keep my gait casual even as I vigilantly scanned my surroundings.

Halfway home, I noticed a stout man across the street smoking by a parked car. As I walked by, I felt his eyes following me.

"Hey, baby," he called out but I pretended not to hear him. As I passed, he threw his cigarette down and ground it with his boot before crossing the street.

My heart rate picked up to the same beat as my steps. I lengthened my stride, still trying my best to appear casual even after I heard him gaining ground. I took hold of my keys and slid them between my fingers, ready to Wolverine the hell out of his face if he attacked.

The footsteps became louder, closer. Then voices.

I chanced a look over my shoulder and saw that another guy in a hooded sweatshirt had stopped the man to ask him a question. Taking advantage of this minor miracle, I turned the corner and ran the rest of the way home.

Once inside my apartment, I locked the doors and ran to the window. When I peered through the blinds, I saw a dark hooded figure standing across the street, looking up at me. I dropped below the window, hoping he hadn't seen me. I almost peed myself when my phone chimed with a text message.

You made it home okay? Ashley asked.

With trembling fingers, I replied: *Yes, I'm here.*

K. Goodnight.

I turned off all the lights and peeked through the blinds again but, thankfully, the man across the street was gone. With a sigh, I went into my room and surveyed the sea of boxes surrounding my bed and desk. I dropped to my knees beside the closest box, resigned to unpacking for the rest of the night.

"The glamorous life of Jocelyn Blake," I muttered under my breath as I pulled out several books and set them on the floor. Under a few hardbacks, I unearthed Jake's brown leather sketchbook. Afraid that my mom would have thrown it into a lake full of alligators, I had taken it with me in hopes I could give it back to its rightful owner. At the very least, it would give me reason to see him again.

I opened the sketchbook, once again going through every page and poring over every drawing. For the first time in a while, I felt almost close to him.

Once again my breath caught on the drawing of the crib but I forced myself to move on. I turned to the next page and saw a pencil sketch of a woman's face. At first I thought Jake had drawn my mother, but I noticed the small cleft on the woman's chin. With a gasp, I realized the woman in the picture was me.

After staring at myself for a long time, wondering what he must have been thinking, I turned to a fresh page and allowed the words to tumble out the end of my pen...

Dear Jake,

I officially moved in to my apartment today. I don't think you'd approve of the location entirely, but maybe that's what made me want to live here. If I were a cliché, I'd be "cutting off your nose to spite your face." But it's too late. I've signed a six-month lease. I should probably buy a taser though.

To tell you the truth, I'm not sure I can do this whole adulting thing. I feel like I've just been faking it this whole time and now I actually have to grow up. Now I have bills to pay, a place to take care of.

I'm sure it'll be fine. I'll be fine. Everything will be fine.

(If I keep saying it, eventually it'll come true, right?)

Mom and I aren't talking right now. She told me before she left that we were okay, but I feel like she said that to make sure I go. Like maybe my guilt will prevent me from moving out (which is likely, actually). I just hate the thought of her coming home tomorrow to an empty house. It makes my heart hurt to imagine her walking in and finding my things gone. If it's anywhere near the same as the way I felt after you left then I'm sure it'll hurt like a bitch. I'd really rather not do that to her. I've hurt her enough.

There's so much I want to tell you. Everyday, when something funny or weird happens, my instinct is to call you. And like tonight, when something really scared me, I wanted to call you for help. But I can't pick up my phone and dial your number. Not anymore.

I wonder where you are, what you're doing. I hope you're taking care of yourself, not slicing your meat on that table saw. And, selfishly, I hope you're missing me as much as I'm missing you.

June Gray

[twenty]

The next day I headed to Pembroke Pines, unable to stomach the idea of my mom coming home to an empty house. I cooked, vacuumed, dusted, and cleaned the toilets, doing everything short of wiping down the baseboards. I doubted some housekeeping would absolve me of my sins but it was worth a try.

I took the casserole out of the oven and ran to the living room just as the front door opened.

Mom saw me and froze.

"Hi," I said in a small, breathless voice. I suddenly got the feeling my surprise presence wasn't really appreciated.

"What are you doing here?" she asked, finally setting her luggage down. She sniffed the air and gave me a questioning look.

"I cooked your favorite."

Her eyebrows drew together just the tiniest amount. She

looked like she wanted to say something but I couldn't tell what. I hoped it was something reconciliatory, but who knew anymore.

"So, you hungry?" I asked with a lift to my eyebrows.

She looked at me for the longest time until, finally, she shook her head. "No. I think I'm just going to take a shower and go to bed. Just take the food home."

With tears in my eyes, I put the casserole in the fridge hoping my mom would eat it anyway. She definitely needed it more than me. She was looking thinner and thinner these days, no doubt forgetting to eat when she gets home at night.

I vowed then that, no matter how much she hated me right now, I would come by and cook for her as often as I could. If only to make sure she was taken care of.

The day started off well enough. When I woke up to one of those wicked Florida rainstorms, my first thought was that I'd accidentally left the sunroof to my car open last night. After the rain, I went downstairs armed with a roll of paper towels but discovered that someone had draped a black trash bag over the sunroof and taped it down.

I turned in place as if I'd somehow spot the good Samaritan. But there was nobody around.

The run of good fortune continued when the hot water actually lasted the entirety of my shower, when the coffeemaker worked the first time round, and I checked online and found I'd done well on my last Comm test.

But nothing good ever lasts, at least, not in my life. My

luck ran out a few hours later when my tire blew out on my way to school.

"Shit, shit!" I kicked at the busted tire of my Honda, wishing I'd followed Jake's advice from a while ago, back when things were still good.

He'd come in one day after a run and said, "Your tires are bald."

"Excuse me?" I'd asked with sass. "What did you just say to me?"

He'd chuckled, his face shiny with sweat. "The tires on your car need replacing."

I'd waved him away, saying I didn't have the money to spend on frivolous things.

"This isn't frivolous. It's a real hazard, Joss. If you're driving on the turnpike and it starts raining you could—" He'd stopped and taken a deep breath. "I could front you the money."

I had waved off his offer with a promise to get new tires but the days had turned to weeks and then to months and, here I was, stuck on the side of the road, late for my one o'clock class.

I moved to the sidewalk and looked through the contact list on my phone. Calling Ashley was no use as she was at Disney World with her brother and his family for a few days. I called Mom's phone but it went straight to voicemail. Then there was Eli…

I snorted. There was no way he'd come out to help me after how things had ended between us. He'd just as likely drive out just to watch me suffer under the searing midday Florida sun.

I stared at Jake's number for the longest time, searching for the courage to press the Call button. Around me, cars zipped by without slowing down, without even a second's glance at the stranded, reminding me that I was well and truly alone.

So this was what being an adult was all about it. I had to admit, it sucked.

I was looking up the number to a local tow service when an open-top Jeep parked behind my car.

"Do you need help?" came a deep, masculine voice.

I held my breath, afraid to look up. Was it possible Jake read my thoughts and came to my rescue? Did that kind of magic really exist?

"Miss?"

I was both disappointed and relieved when I looked up. The man, though also tall with dark features, was not the one I was expecting to see.

"Yeah," I said, pushing all thoughts of Jake to the back of my mind. "I had a tire blowout. Front passenger side."

He nodded, his expression hidden behind a pair of sunglasses. I looked him over as he crouched down and inspected the offending tire. He wore a thin v-neck shirt in a bright turquoise color and white shorts, flip flops on his feet, looking every bit like a guy on his way to the beach. "Do you have a spare?"

I bit my lip. "I'm not sure."

He stood and looked over at my car. "Usually it's in the trunk." I popped open the trunk and he pulled at the false bottom, revealing a hidden compartment with the spare tire.

"I had no idea that was there," I said, feeling ridiculous. I'd had this car for five years and never once had I gone looking for the spare tire. I was every bit the helpless damsel right now and I hated it. "In my defense, I didn't have a father to teach me these kinds of things."

He raised an eyebrow, one corner of his mouth tilting up. "You were immaculately conceived?"

"Yes, I'm something of a miracle," I joked.

He hooked his hands on the open trunk of my car and openly ogled me in my white sundress. "Yes, you are."

If my face wasn't already red from the sun, I'm sure I would have flushed even more. "Well, if you can walk me through it, I'm sure I can change the tire myself."

"No, I got this," he said, pulling the tire out along with the jack and wrench. "Wouldn't want you to get that dress dirty."

It didn't take him more than fifteen minutes to lift the car up on the jack and change out the tires.

"Thank you," I said after he'd set everything back in the trunk, including the busted tire. "I don't know how to repay you."

He reached into his Jeep and grabbed a rag from the back and used it to wipe the grease off his hands. "You can come with me."

I was immediately on high alert. South Florida was infamous for its crazies. "Um, no thanks. But I have twenty dollars if you'd like?"

He shook his head, chuckling. "No. I meant to say I know of a tire place just south of here. You really need these tires replaced. You might not be so lucky next time you have a blow out."

"Um. Hold on." I checked my phone, logging into my bank account to see if I could afford four brand new tires. I would have to pick up a few more shifts at work, but I could probably swing it. "Do you think I can drive with the spare tire for about a week?"

He looked at the tire—which was obviously way smaller than the other three—then shook his head.

"Okay," I said with a sigh. "Lead the way."

I followed the guy to a strip mall in Aventura, stopping at a place called T's Garage. We parked our cars and went inside to the bright reception area.

He took off his sunglasses before greeting the older man sitting behind the desk. "Hey, Joe, do we have any open bays?"

"Bay 3 is open for another hour."

"Perfect." The guy turned to me with hand held out. "Keys please."

"Wait, don't we need to talk about tires and prices and stuff first?" I asked, looking around at the different tires mounted on the wall.

He winked, his brown eyes bright with mischief. "Don't worry about it."

"Sorry, I can't do that. I have a finite amount of money. I can't just spend a bunch of it on tires, not when I need to eat and pay my bills."

He took hold of my elbow and led me out of Joe's earshot. "Okay, how about a deal."

I crossed my arms over my chest. "What deal?"

"Four tires for a date." The grin on his face was one of self-satisfaction, like I'd already said yes.

"No."

One dark eyebrow rose. I got the feeling he didn't hear that word very often.

"That's too much," I said.

"How about this: You pay wholesale prices. I'll get labor."

"I don't think your boss would like that."

He grinned. "Oh, I think he'd be okay with it. Especially if it gets him a date with a beautiful woman."

"Wait, you own this place?"

He held out his arms. "I'm T of T's Garage. And you are?"

I studied his face again, finding it hard to look away. There was something so familiar about him, something that made me feel like he could be trusted. "I'm Joss," I said as I held out my car key. "So what does the T stand for?"

He folded his hands over mine. "Tristan."

[twenty-one]

On my first day off without school or work in two weeks, I decided to enjoy the sunshine and walk to Downtown Hollywood to window shop. After spending almost four hundred dollars on tires the other day (which would have been twice that if Tristan hadn't gotten involved), all I could buy at the moment was food, of the cheap ramen noodles kind.

On the way there I passed by an old-style garage, the kind with tall doors that rolled up on both sides of the building, except now it appeared to be a furniture showroom. On the window was a vinyl sign that said Rochester Furniture. My thoughts immediately flew to Jake, but I pushed the thought away and continued my way down the sidewalk.

Walking along the busy street, the sun warm on my skin, I didn't feel like a broke college student. Today I felt more like myself than I had in a while, free from anxiety and the heartache that had plagued me the past several weeks.

I looked in the stores, taking photos of things I liked but could never afford with the thought of *someday*. The one word was my mantra these days: Someday I'll graduate and get a better job. Someday my mom and I would get back to good. Someday I won't wake up in the middle of night aching for Jake anymore. Someday.

My thoughts turned back to *now*, to the date I had tonight. Turned out, not only was Tristan kind enough to give me a significant discount, he also changed out the tires himself. He was charming and helpful and funny. If anyone could break me free of Jake, Tristan could certainly try.

As I ate lunch at a sidewalk café, a pick-up truck passed by, the same model and color of Jake's truck. My eyes followed the vehicle until it turned the corner, trying to get a glimpse of the driver, hoping against hope it was Jake.

I turned away, disgusted with myself. Even after all that's happened, I was still waiting for him to come back.

"Hey, Creepy McCreeperson is outside again," Ashley said to me that night. She entered my room and sat on my bed, motioning toward the window.

"Who?" I asked from inside the closet.

"You know, the guy who stands at the street at night?"

I walked over to the window and peered between the blinds. Sure enough, the man in the hoodie was out there again. Only this time, he promptly turned away and walked off down the street. "He probably lives around here," I said with a shrug, trying to ignore the strange feeling of being watched.

"He's a drug dealer for sure," Ashley said and promptly turned her attention to the clothes on the bed. "Ooh, which top are you wearing?" she asked, looking at the two shirts I'd laid out, one in aqua and the other in coral. She scrunched up her mouth, considering the choices. "The blue looks better with your skin tone but the other one makes your boobs look like *whoah*."

A nervous laugh escaped my lips. "Do I want my boobs to look like *whoah*?" I asked, turning to the mirror and holding the shirt up to my body.

"On a date? Definitely."

I put on the coral shirt and held my hands out to the sides. "So?"

Her smiling nod should've made me feel better; instead it made me even more nervous. "I don't know why I'm so freaked out right now," I said, looking at myself in the mirror. The v-neck of the top did make my cleavage look really nice, but did I want them to be that appealing?

Then it struck me that I was nervous because, in some sick way, I didn't want Tristan to be attracted to me, that some part of me didn't want anyone but Jake to be attracted to me.

"Stupid," I muttered, shaking my head. "I'm turning into a basketcase."

I went into the closet and paired the top with a formal shorts and tall heels. When I was done, Ashley actually whistled. "Oh yes. You're going to have Tire Boy spinning in circles."

I snorted. "I see what you did there."

"What? Is the joke too tire-d?" she asked with a wink.

I threw a pillow at her, laughing. We traded a few more lame puns while I finished getting ready. By the time the doorbell rang, my nerves were nothing but a distant memory.

Tristan took me to a bookstore in Coral Gables called Books & Books. I'd been to the store before during the day, but I had no idea that it transformed into something hip and lively at night. The store itself was shaped like a square with an outdoor patio in its center. During the day, the courtyard was populated with round tables and white umbrellas, a lovely outdoor place to eat lunch surrounded by books. Tonight, however, it looked different with a small bar set up under an arched breezeway, people milling around with alcoholic beverages in hand.

Tristan led the way through the courtyard's iron gates with one hand on the small of my back. "What would you like to drink?"

My head turned as we passed by the one of the entrances to the interior, my eyes automatically drawn to the books.

"Joss?"

I turned back to my date with a sheepish smile. "Sorry. Distracted."

"I take it you like the place?" he asked, handing me a glass of white wine.

I forced my attention back on Tristan in his simple v-neck tee and dark wash jeans, looking so effortless and cool, his smile toeing the line between confidence and cockiness. But there was something about him that drew me to him, made me want to know more.

"You couldn't have picked a better place," I said with a smile, taking a sip of wine. "Do you like to read?"

"Mostly magazines and manuals. I don't really get a lot of free time to read." He flashed me a charming smile that almost eclipsed the fact that he wasn't a reader. "It was actually my brother's idea to take you here."

"Oh?"

"Yeah. He said, "Any girl worth dating would be thrilled to be around books.""

"Your brother sounds like a wise man."

"Yeah, but sometimes he makes the stupidest mistakes."

"Don't we all," I murmured into my glass.

When next I looked up, I found him quietly studying me. "There's a story there," he said with a curious look.

"There is, but it's not first date material."

"I expect to hear it on our second date then," he said with a confident nod.

"This date just started. You don't even know if we get along yet."

He leaned in. "We have chemistry, that much I know." He held out his hand. "So, should we go inside and take a look around?"

Tristan and I talked as we looked through the book displays. Occasionally he'd pick up a book to take a closer look while I fought the urge to read through all the blurbs. One book in particular caught my eye, one about furniture design. I slid it off the shelf and took it to a nearby chair.

"You into woodworking?" Tristan asked, standing over me as I paged through the book.

"I was just looking for a friend." I stood, hugging the book against my chest before setting it back on the shelf.

"What about you? Is there one you'd like to get?"

I looked around, my eyes spinning in my head. I always come down with a little Attention Deficit Disorder when I'm around books. "I want to get them all."

"So hey," he said with an apologetic look. "My brother just called me. The alarm is going off at his shop but he can't get there right now. Do you mind if we go check it out? It's not too far from your apartment, actually."

I held up the book. "Let me pay for this first."

Tristan drove us to Hollywood, directly to the old-timey garage I'd passed the other day. Even before we parked, I could hear the sharp chirp of the alarm. He unlocked one garage bay door and slid it up, revealing the dark interior intermittently lit up by a red flashing light from somewhere on the ceiling.

"I think the alarm's faulty. This is the third time it's gone off this week for absolutely no reason. Probably mice chewing on the wiring."

I grabbed his hand as we walked inside the dark interior. By the crimson light of the alarm, I could make out tables, chairs, armoires, and various other pieces of furniture set around the large space.

"This is the showroom," Tristan said. "My brother's been working hard, getting ready for the opening next week."

"Did he make all of this?" I asked, thinking Jake would really appreciate a place like this. It was just his style.

I caught myself and rolled my eyes. I needed to stop thinking of Jake every time I saw furniture. Otherwise, I'd never stop.

"He made most of it. There's also a few commission pieces from other craftsmen around the area." He squeezed my hand. "Wait here. I'm going to check the workshop in the back."

I wandered around after he left, trying to spot any of Jake's pieces, running my fingers along the surface of the wood. In the dim light, I could almost imagine they were all his designs.

And then the alarm stopped and the flashing light turned off, leaving me in complete darkness. A second later, slow music started filtering in through the darkness.

I jumped when a hand went around my waist.

"Dance with me?" Tristan whispered.

I clutched my chest, my heart still beating fast. "You scared me."

He spun me around and hooked his hands around my hips. "Sorry. I just wanted to dance with the prettiest woman in the place."

"I'm the only woman in the place," I pointed out.

"Still a true statement." He started swaying to the sensual beat of the song, taking me along for the ride. "You're amazing, you know that?" he said close to my ear.

I got the feeling that this was Tristan's strength, his ability to charm the ladies. But I gave in to the moment anyway, enjoying this process of being wooed. Even if I wasn't the first, at least I knew I was the only one right here, right now.

I wrapped my arms around his neck and a moment later, our lips met in the dark. Tristan was tender and seeking, his tongue dancing with mine. In that kiss I felt a stirring.

I pulled away, fighting to catch my breath.

"What is it?" he asked.

I touched a finger to his lips, my heart pounding in my chest. "Nothing," I said and kissed him again.

Tristan took me home a little over an hour later, walking me up the concrete steps to my apartment door. "Is your roommate home?" he asked, the hint as subtle as an anvil to the head.

"No. She's out with this guy she just started dating." I looked up at him, hoping he didn't think I'd invite him inside. I'd never been that kind of girl and, as much as I liked Tristan, I wasn't about to become her now. "Well, I had a great time."

He set a hand on the wall and leaned in, kissing me again. "Invite me in, Joss," he whispered against my lips.

I pulled away with a nervous laugh. "What are you, a vampire?"

"I *vant* to suck your blood." He leaned down and nuzzled into my neck, sucking gently on my skin. "And anything else you want me to do."

I put a hand on his chest, torn between anxiety and just giving in. "Let's take it slow, okay?"

"Sure." He straightened, a rueful smile on his face. "Are you sure, though? I mean, I can go slow. Veeeery slow," he added with a flirtatious lift of an eyebrow.

I chuckled. He was nothing if not persistent. "I had a good time tonight," I said, giving him a kiss on the cheek.

He let out a resigned breath. "Goodnight, Joss."

I locked up and practically floated to my bedroom, my lips curling into a smile. I set my bags on my bed and sat down, flipping through the furniture book once again. Then I remembered the sketch book and I looked through it, seeing if any of Jake's designs matched those in Tristan's brother's showroom. I almost convinced myself it did. But honestly, I'd been too distracted by my handsome date to focus on woodworking details.

And I realized then, as I hummed while getting ready for bed, that maybe I could do it. Maybe I could move on from Jake.

It was that thought that finally wiped the stupid smile off my face.

June Gray

[twenty-two]

On the night my mom returned from Indiana, I went over to the house bearing a gift in the form of her favorite selection of sushi. I rang the doorbell and waited, holding my breath until she finally answered the door.

"Joss," she said with a smile that almost appeared relieved. She stepped out and threw her arms around me.

I held her tighter and longer than was comfortable. "Welcome back."

She laughed softly as she let go. "I was only gone a week."

"Felt like a million years."

She took hold of my hand and pulled me inside. "Why didn't you just come in? Did you lose your key?"

I shrugged as tears stung my eyes at the friendly reception I most certainly didn't deserve.

We sat down for dinner, and it was almost like old times. But even though she was talkative, I could still sense her holding back. Still, I was grateful we were here at this point at all.

After we cleaned up the dishes, we sat on opposite ends of the couch with a cup of tea each and talked some more. She told me about her latest trip, the difficult clients, and the man she met on the plane.

"Did you get his number?" I asked, spreading the blanket so that it was covering both our laps.

"No. I'm not ready to be dating again." She watched me for a long, tense moment, a thousand questions in her eyes. And I was ready to answer them all. But she said instead, "So, how are you?"

I let out a breath. "Busy but good. Getting As in all my classes, and I'm looking at an internship at a small publishing house this summer." I waited a beat, weighing my words. "I met someone," I said in a soft voice.

An emotion flashed in her eyes before she blinked it away. "A boy?"

"His name's Tristan," I said and told her about the date, feeling lighter with every word.

"He took you to a bookstore for a date?" she asked with a smile. "Sounds like the perfect guy."

"I don't know about that," I said, sipping my tea. "He's too smooth for me. One of those guys who knows how to charm the ladies."

"But you like him," she said with a knowing nod. "I can see it in your eyes."

And I saw in hers that she really wanted to believe that, because it meant I was over Jake. "We do have a lot of chemistry. I wouldn't say no to another date."

Her mood shifted then, the smile fading along with the light in her eyes. "Joss, we have to talk."

I steeled my nerves, preparing for the long-overdue conversation. "I'm sorry, Mom," I said, tears stinging my eyes already. "I didn't do it to hurt you."

Her lips thinned. "But you did."

"I tried to fight it. We both tried to fight it."

She took a deep breath, her face hard as stone. "Who initiated it?"

"Me." I cleared my throat in lieu of looking her in the eye. "I developed a crush on him and stupidly acted on it. I'm sorry."

"Did he flirt with you before then? Did he make any advances?"

"No," I said, finally looking up. "It was all me. He was just being his usual self."

"And you couldn't help but fall in love," she added, sarcasm lacing her voice.

I picked at imaginary lint on the blanket. "I really couldn't. I'm sorry."

"Joss, look at me." Her stern voice had me cringing but I met her eyes eventually. "Stop saying sorry."

"Why? I am."

"It's not your fault. It's mine."

Her words knocked me back. "No, it's not. Not even close."

"I should have been around more. You two asked me to slow down and stop working so much, but I didn't listen. I practically pushed the two of you together."

"No…"

She let out a hollow laugh, shaking her head. "I even made that stupid wish for you on your birthday, not realizing the

great love of your life was going to be my own boyfriend."
She wiped at the corners of her eyes but gamely went on. "But
a man like that has no honor. Coming into our house, taking
advantage of both of us."

I wish it had been that simple. Then maybe it would be
easier to get over him. "Before he and I… before anything, he
wanted to break up with you. He didn't want to cheat. He
didn't want to do anything behind your back. He was going to
tell you. But then the baby…"

Mom said nothing, but I could tell she was trying her best
to keep from falling apart.

My own face crumbled. "I'm sorry. For everything."

"Come here, honey," she said, patting the space beside her.

I went to her, snuggling under her arm like I used to and
wrapping my arms around her waist. "He and I are through,
Mom. He doesn't want anything to do with me." My voice
cracked at the last word, betraying my emotions.

"You love him, don't you?" she asked quietly.

I pressed my cheek to her chest. "I don't want to."

She kissed the side of my head with a sigh. "I guess he
broke both our hearts."

That night, I came home to find that some douchebag had
parked in my designated parking spot. I had to drive around
the block and park my car at the street. I was then faced with
two choices: Walk around the entire block or take a shortcut
through the narrow alleyway between the apartment building
and the grocery store.

I chose the stupid route. Story of my life.

Even as I walked through the dark alley, I knew I was making a huge mistake. But I kept going, pure pig-headedness propelling my feet forward.

My breath caught in my throat when I heard someone call out behind me but I chose to ignore it. I had almost convinced myself that I'd imagined the noise when it came again, louder this time and more clear. "Hey!"

I looked over my shoulder and saw a tall man following me, his eyes gaunt and cheeks hollowed out.

He leered, giving me an all-body look that made me prickle with disgust. "Hello there, pretty lady."

I walked faster. "Leave me alone," I said, reaching into my purse and feeling around for my can of mace.

"Come on, I'm just being friendly. I just want to talk," he said, sounding closer and closer.

"I don't want to talk." I didn't stick around. I broke out into a run, cursing myself for being so stupid. If this were a horror movie, I'd be the first to die.

The man followed, calling out to me and laughing even as he gained ground on me.

When I rounded the corner, I ran smack dab into something or someone, I couldn't tell. Before I could figure it out, two large hands clamped around my arms, trapping me in place.

I screamed. I threw my fists around, fighting for my life. I channeled Mia Hamm and kicked like hell.

"Stop! Hey!" The man held me at arm's length to minimize the damage.

I looked up and realized I was face to face with the man in the black hoodie. "You!"

"Hey, that one's mine!" my assailant yelled. I twisted around and saw he had stopped several yards away, balling his hands into fists.

The man in the hood let out a snarl before letting me go and giving chase. They ran half a block before the hooded guy caught up to him and tackled him to the ground. I watched, frozen in terror, as the two men struggled back to their feet, grabbing each other and throwing punches. When taller man grabbed at the black hood, the face underneath was suddenly thrown into sharp focus.

The breath rushed out of me. "Jake."

As if he heard, he turned around and looked me right in the eye. A moment later, the other man's fist hammered the side of his face.

I ran. I had no idea what I'd do when I reached them, but I had to protect Jake. I felt like I was underwater, moving in slow motion while the two men continued fighting in real time. Jake eventually gained the upper hand, delivering blows that sent the guy crumpling to the ground.

By the time I reached them, my assailant had run off down the street.

Jake huffed when he faced me, his lip cut and bleeding, the right side of his face already starting to swell. But he didn't say anything. He just shook his head and pulled out his phone, dialing 911.

Overcome with emotion, I wrapped my arms around his waist and pressed my face into his chest. Tears burned my eyes as I breathed in his familiar scent, felt his familiar warm body.

But he pushed me away, turning his back as he reported the attack. After he hung up, he let out a big breath before facing me.

"Are you purposefully trying to get killed?" he demanded, his face contorted with anger.

I panted, feeling like I couldn't draw in enough breath. I could only shake my head and say, "No."

"So why is it that every time I turn around, I have to save your ass?"

The coarseness of his voice made me flinch. I could almost see the anger radiating off him. "Nobody asked you to do that!"

"Well somebody needs to!" He took a deep breath, his voice losing its edge. "I was trying to take care of you the only way I knew how."

"Have you been watching me?" I asked.

His hands clenched into fists at his sides as he stared at an indistinct point over my shoulder. "Watching over you. Making sure nobody harms you." His eyes finally met mine, a million emotions running through them. "I almost didn't come out tonight. I don't know what would have happened if—"

I pressed my hand to his mouth. "No. Don't."

His eyes were full of fear and longing as he stared at me, saying nothing, only pressing his lips to my hand.

"Do you want to come back to my apartment?" I found myself asking then added lamely, "to put ice on your face, I mean."

Gently he tugged my hand away from his face. "I can't, Joss."

"I miss you," I blurted out. "I still don't get why we're not together."

He sighed, folding his hand over mine. "Joss, there are ten thousand other guys like me, but you only have one mother. I

can't let you destroy that relationship. Not for me."

I could barely see past the tears, even when he gathered me in his arms. How could something feel so good and yet hurt so much at the same time?

"I want you to move on, Joss," he whispered, brushing hair away from my face. "And I swear I'll do the same."

I pressed my face into his chest, my tears bleeding onto the damned black sweatshirt. "I think... I think I finally met someone who can help me get over you." I didn't know why I said it. Maybe I wanted to hurt him as much as he was hurting me.

He stopped breathing, stopped moving altogether. "Who?" His voice was so faint, I almost didn't hear him.

"His name is—"

"No, never mind. I don't want to know."

He pulled away, his eyes averted. Taking hold of my hand, he walked me back down the street to my apartment building and up the stairs. "Promise me you'll take care of yourself, okay? Don't do anything stupid."

"You mean stupider than falling for my mom's boyfriend?"

The corner of his mouth tilted up, his eyes full of warmth. "Yeah. Stupider than that."

With my arms wrapped around myself, I watched Jake make his way down the concrete stairs. "You're wrong, you know," I called out just as he'd reached the bottom step.

He looked up. "About?"

"There aren't ten thousand other guys like you," I said with a sad smile. "There's only you."

[twenty-three]

A few days later, Tristan walked in to the bookstore and headed straight for the information desk. "Miss, can you help me please?" He set his elbows on the counter, a charming grin on his face. He reminded me of someone right then, someone I'd promised to forget, so I pushed the thoughts to the very back of my mind and returned Tristan's smile.

"Hi." I ran a hand through my hair. "What are you doing here?"

"I'd like some information, please."

Despite the lousy day I was having, the sight of him lifted my spirits. "What can I look up for you?" I asked, my fingers poised over the keyboard. "Something in the self-help department, perhaps?"

He raised an eyebrow. "Believe me, for what I have planned, I don't need a self-help anything."

"Oh? What did you have planned?"

"I was thinking of inviting this awesome woman over to my place and cooking her dinner."

I narrowed my eyes at him and said playfully, "So you need a cookbook?"

"Nope. The information I need is whether this woman is interested in coming over or not." He straightened. "What do you say? Saturday? I can pick you up around six."

I bit my bottom lip, considering his invitation. "Okay. But I'll just drive to your place instead."

"Okay, now that that's settled," he said, rubbing his hands together. "I need to find a cookbook."

I laughed and walked out from around the counter. "Come on, I'll show you where they are."

With a grin, he took my outstretched hand. "The service here is exceptional."

The drive to Aventura that night took longer than expected due to typical Miami traffic. Drivers wove in and out of traffic without using blinkers, random cars stopping in the middle of the road for no clear reason.

On the upside, the anxiety of being late afforded me no time to stress over the date itself.

"Sorry I'm late," I said when Tristan answered the door of his tenth floor apartment. "There was an accident on the expressway. Some guy stopped on the shoulder to text and was struck by a semi."

Tristan shook his head. "Gotta love South Florida." He ushered me in with a hand to my back, kissing my cheek. "I'm glad you made it in one piece."

His apartment was typical Miami modern, with white couches and sleek, modern furniture. On one side was a bay of windows with a panorama of the city lights. "Nice view." It was then I noticed the table on the balcony, all set up with napkins, wine glasses, and of course, a lit candle in the center.

Tristan came up behind me, his hands on my waist. "You're just in time. I just finished setting the table."

"So," he began after we sat down to eat. "Now that we're on our second date, will you tell me about the stupid mistake you made? The one that got your heart broken?"

"I never said my heart got broken."

"You didn't have to. I saw it on your face."

I took a bite of chicken and chewed. For a long time. "Why do you want to know?" I finally asked.

He flashed me a lopsided grin. "So I know what to avoid from becoming just another mistake."

I turned to the view of the city, drinking my wine while considering how much to say. I wasn't a big dater but it didn't take a genius to know that it wasn't appropriate to talk about failed relationships with a potential new one. Still, something about Tristan's open expression made me want to trust him.

"I fell in love with a man who was already taken. He was with someone I really cared about but I still pursued him." My eyes dropped down to the table as a fresh wave of shame washed over me. "It ended... badly."

"Do you still love him?"

My eyes flicked up to Tristan's face, at the lines creasing his forehead, wishing I could tell him no. When I said nothing, he nodded and turned his attention back to the food.

"I guess I should have warned you beforehand that I have some baggage," I said.

He shrugged. "None of us are perfect."

"Really? Tell me about your flaws," I said, embracing the shift in subject matter.

"Well, for one, I'm terrible with names," he said with a chuckle. "I may have botched a few relationships because of it."

"Oh no."

He laughed. "Oh yes. It might be the reason why I can't do relationships."

"You do remember my name, right?"

He narrowed his eyes. "Joni, right?" he said with a grin.

"One point for getting the first letter correct."

He lifted his glass and with a wink. "How about a toast then?"

I followed suit. "For?"

"For hope, however misguided sometimes."

"I don't know what you mean."

"Without hope, we wouldn't be here, trying again even though our past relationships left us scarred."

I clinked my glass to his. "Here's to moving on."

"So who is he?"

I shook my head. "No way. I'm having too good a time to talk about him right now."

An almost bashful smile curled his lips. "Yeah, I am too."

After dinner, we put the dishes in the sink and sat down to watch a movie. The couch, despite its spartan appearance, was surprisingly comfortable.

"More?" Tristan asked, holding up the wine bottle.

I shook my head, already riding the sparkly wave of a buzz. "I'm good, thanks. I still need to drive home, remember?"

He set down the bottle on the glass coffee table and settled in beside me. "You're more than welcome to spend the night," he murmured, moving closer so that our thighs touched. "But you'd have to stay in my bed since my brother is currently using the guest room."

"How convenient."

"Very." He stretched his arms out, draping one over my shoulders.

"Oh, smooth," I teased, poking him in the side.

He brushed hair away from my ear and leaned close. "Do you want me to show you just how smooth I can be?"

I turned my head just as he leaned down. "Maybe..." I said, suddenly entranced by his lips.

I heard the jangle of keys behind me but was too distracted by Tristan's nearness to notice that someone was about to enter the apartment. The door opened just as Tristan's lips touched mine.

"Hey, T," came a voice behind us.

I buried my face in the crook of Tristan's neck, my face burning from embarrassment at being caught necking.

"Dude, knock," Tristan said over my shoulder, his palm smoothing over my back. "I'm kind of on a date here."

"Sorry. I just forgot something." Heavy footsteps crossed the room and from somewhere further into the apartment Tristan's brother asked, "Hey, you haven't seen my sketchbook around, have you? The leather one with the strap?"

I should have recognized the voice as soon as I heard it;

I'd certainly dreamed about it enough. But when Tristan's brother came back to the living room and said, "I haven't seen it since—" I lifted my head and found Jake standing right behind me, the area around his right eye black and purple.

The words fell from his lips like a gasp. "What the hell?"

[part four]

June Gray

[twenty-four]

"What the hell are you doing here?"

Joss flinched at the outrage in my voice but, at that moment, I couldn't bring myself to regret it. I had just caught her making out with my brother. How the hell else was I supposed to react?

Tristan wisely withdrew his arms from around Joss's shoulders and jumped up. "She's my date," he said, like he had any right to be angry. The fucker.

"Your date?" A roaring sound filled my ears as I turned back to Joss, who sat there with a dumbfounded look on her face. I fought the urge to jump over the back of the couch, torn between wanting to kiss her and shake her shoulders.

Joss stood. When she touched Tristan's arms, I almost went postal. "I think I'd better go," she whispered.

"I'll walk you down," Tristan said.

My hands clenched into fists. "Like hell."

"No. Stay." She threw a quick glance my way before retrieving her purse and heading to the door.

I glared at my traitor of a brother. "You and I are going to have words," I spat out before rushing out the door.

"Joss!" I ran down the stairs after her. "Stop."

She spun around, a myriad of expressions crossing over her face. "I'm sorry, I didn't know." She paused. "Did you?"

"Of course not!" I took in deep breaths, trying to reign in my temper. Then I remembered the things he'd told me about her—how beautiful, how amazing she was—and my face flamed. "You think I'd be okay with my brother dating you?"

She shook her head, a helpless look on her face. "I don't know. I..."

Then something occurred to me, something she'd said the last time we saw each other. "Wait, was he—was Tristan the guy you thought could help you get over me?" I didn't know how I got the words out. All I knew was that it felt like chewing on glass.

"Yes," she whispered, looking at her feet.

I shook my head in disbelief, letting out a humorless laugh. "He took you to the bookstore on my suggestion. I'm such an idiot."

"I loved it," she said in a quiet voice.

I felt so stupid. I'd even been thinking of her while suggesting the place to Tristan. "Do you love him?" I didn't know why I asked; I sure as hell didn't want to hear the answer.

"That's none of your business."

I stuck my hands in my pockets and took a step back.

"You're right. It's not."

"Don't worry. You won't see me again. I'm not going to see your brother anymore."

My shoulders sagged. I'd be a complete asshole if I deprived her of someone she cared about. Again. "If you really want to be with him," I began, questioning my sanity with every word. "Then I won't stop you."

"You'd do that?"

"If that's what you really want."

She shook her head, tears glistening in her eyes. "You'd still be in my life, torturing me."

"You know that's not my intention." My head hurt, my heart hurt, my everything hurt.

"We can't keep doing this," she said with a quiver in her voice. "I can't keep saying goodbye to you. It hurts too much."

I nodded, a lump stuck in my throat.

"I don't want to do it anymore." With that, she turned and left.

"Why did you let her go?" Tristan asked as soon I came back in to the apartment, closing the balcony door behind him. No doubt he had eavesdropped.

I slammed the front door. "Because I'm the last person she wanted to see." I paced the room with hands on my waist, chest heaving up and down, while my brother leaned against the back of the couch, casually drinking beer. I stopped as it all dawned on me. "You fucking knew. You knew who she was."

When Tristan shrugged as if it was no big deal, I lost it. I lunged forward and grabbed hold of his shirt. "Do you think this is a fucking joke? She's not one of those brain dead Barbie dolls you play around with."

Finally, his cool façade broke. "You think I'd do that to you?"

I pushed him back so hard, he fell over onto the couch. "Well you just did, you asshole."

He scrambled back to his feet, huffing. "I was trying to help you."

"By dating her?"

"I didn't know who she was when I first met her, but yes, after I figured out who she was, I thought I'd date her and get her to open up about you."

I looked at him incredulously. "And what would that have done?"

"To make her miss you. To make everyone else pale in comparison."

My hands squeezed into fists. "So you two making out on the couch—that's supposed to make her miss me?"

He held up his hands and chuckled. "I'm sorry. That was... unexpected."

I tackled him back into the couch, holding my forearm against his throat. "Did you sleep with her too?"

"No." He pushed me off him and picked up the beer bottle off the rug. "You spilled my beer, you fucker."

"You kissed my girl," I huffed, sinking down on the coffee table.

"Your girl? I thought you broke up?"

"We did." I set my elbows on my knees and buried my face in my hands. Regardless of the situation, of distance and relationship status, I still considered Joss mine. Probably always would. "Do me a favor: Don't ever try to fix a relationship for me ever again."

Tristan threw a beer-stained rag at my head. "She still loves you, you know."

"Well that doesn't change the fact that we can't be together."

"Now why is that again?"

"Because of her mother."

Tristan grinned. "You want me to date her mom instead?" he asked with a raised eyebrow.

I threw the rag at his face, laughing despite myself. "Asshole," I mumbled and rose to my feet.

"Come on, bro," he called as I headed to the guest room. "Just one word and I can make this a whole family affair. Let's go all Days of Our Lives on this shit."

"You're sick."

His laughter followed me down the hall.

A few days later, I finally closed on a two-bedroom Spanish-style house within a mile of my store. The down payment had damn near emptied my savings account, but getting my own place was a necessity. I was closing on thirty-one years old. I couldn't live with my little brother forever.

It took longer to move out of Amanda's house than it did to move into my new place. But then again, extracting myself from that life was like pulling out a bad tooth—hard but necessary. And it had hurt like hell.

"Tell me again why I'm doing this for free?" Tristan asked after we'd brought in the last of my furniture that had been sitting in storage. He went to the fridge and got out two beers, holding one out to me.

"Blood is thicker than water or something." I sagged onto the couch, taking a deep breath. "And you owe me."

He sat on the arm of the leather couch, eyeing me as he drank his beer. "I think you did the right thing," he said, sounding so serious, so unlike him, that it made me look up. "Opening the store store, buying this house."

"It was definitely way past time."

He clinked his bottle to mine. "So I guess this means you're staying in Florida."

I sighed through my nose. "Guess so. I mean, I've lived here long enough. It was probably time to commit."

Tristan snickered. "I never took you for a guy who had trouble committing."

We were lost in our thoughts for a moment when Tristan said, "I talked to Joss yesterday."

I glared at him. "What?"

He held up his hands. "Just to set things straight."

"She called you?" I asked, bristling.

"Yeah. To ask me if I was playing her all along. I had a lot to explain."

"And?"

"And what? She thinks I'm an asshole. Called me as much."

"She's not wrong." I took a long pull of beer then shook my head. "I don't know what the hell you were thinking."

"I had good intentions, brother."

"Haven't you heard that saying about the road to hell being paved with good intentions?"

"Yeah, so I hear." He paused, studying me. "So you two are definitely over?"

"Yes. But don't even think for a second you can ask her on a date again."

"No, I was just thinking I know someone you might really click with."

"No, thanks. I'm good."

"So you're just going to be a celibate monk forever?"

"No. But the next woman I date will be someone I picked for myself. Someone without any ties to you or anyone else I know. I need a completely clean slate," I said, even if I didn't completely mean it. Because, no matter how many times I wipe that slate clean, the surface will always be scuffed by the memory of Joss.

June Gray

[twenty-five]

I made an honest attempt at avoiding Joss, even if we lived within five miles of each other. Still, that didn't mean I wouldn't occasionally drive past her house after I was done at my workshop late at night. Even if I never caught a glimpse of her, it was soothing to know I was somehow still watched over her like her secret protector.

"Secret protector," Tristan sniggered after I relayed the thought to him one late night as I closed up the store. "You've been reading way too many fantasy novels."

I shrugged. "So I'm protective of her. Sue me."

"I think it's more than that. I think you've got some sort of knight in shining armor complex," my brother said. "You always act like you have to save everybody."

"It's better than the person who only thinks about himself," I shot back.

Tristan took the jab in stride. He knew what kind of man he

was and was more than okay with it. "If I'm so self-centered, how come I tried to get you and your ladylove back together?"

"By kissing her?"

"That was part of the plan." He grinned, rubbing his jaw and looking off into space. I'd seen that look on his face before, but now I didn't like it one bit.

"Wipe that smile off your face," I said, pushing him out the front door and locking it.

He chuckled. "Sorry. I can't help it if she kisses like a champ."

"Tristan, you're about to get beat the fuck up."

He held up his palms in surrender. "Relax. I'm just playing. So you want to get some beers?"

"Sure." My phone rang then, the name flashing on the screen freezing me in place. "Hang on, I have to get this," I said, turning away. "Joss?"

"Jake." In that one word I heard the panic in her voice.

"What's wrong?"

"I'm at Miramar Memorial Hospital."

Those four words sent a spiral of fear down my spine. I was already in my truck, waving a hasty goodbye to my brother, before she could speak again.

"Please come," she added in a tiny voice.

I pulled out of the parking spot and threw the gear into Drive. "I'm on my way."

Please let her be okay. She's got to be okay.

The drive to the hospital felt like forever. I seemed to hit every stoplight and fell behind every slow person in all of South Florida so that by the time I pulled into the hospital lot, my knuckles were white on the steering wheel and I had practically ground my molars down to dust.

I jumped out and ran to the entrance, berating myself for lapsing in my responsibilities. I should have kept a better eye on Joss, should have continued watching over her. I should have been around to prevent this.

At the reception desk, the woman looked up Joss's name then shook her head. "There's no Jocelyn Blake checked into the hospital."

I turned around, pissed that I'd gone to the wrong hospital, when a thought struck me. I turned on a heel and marched back to the front desk with dread. "What about Amanda Blake?"

Sure enough, a minute later, the receptionist said, "Third floor, room thirty four."

After exiting the elevator, I ran down the hallway. When I passed by a waiting area, I caught sight of a lone figure hunched over, blonde hair hanging down as she held her face in her hands.

I stopped. "Joss?"

She brushed the hair away from her face as she tilted her head up and fixed her red-rimmed eyes on me. She didn't say anything. Without a sound, she stood up, crossed the distance between us, and wrapped her arms around me.

I held her as she fought to keep her composure. I kissed the top of her head and rubbed circles on her back, hoping my presence was enough for the time being.

"It's my mom," she said, her voice muffled by my shirt. "She's... sick."

"What happened?"

She pulled away and wiped at the tears I didn't even realize had fallen. "I went over to the house to cook her dinner and I found her laying on the floor, clutching her stomach. She was in so much pain, she couldn't even move." She stopped, tucking a lock of hair behind her ears. "So I called the ambulance and they took her here."

"What is it? What's wrong with her?"

She took in a deep breath. "Ovarian cancer. Stage five."

I staggered backwards, the news slugging me right in the chest. "Cancer?"

Big fat teardrops rolled down Joss's cheeks as she looked at me with woeful green eyes. "It's why her period stopped, why she always felt so exhausted."

Why she thought she was pregnant.

I turned to continue to Amanda's room but Joss grabbed my wrist.

"She's in surgery right now. They're going to try and take out the tumors."

I sagged, forcing myself to focus on what I could fix. "She'll be okay, Joss," I said, wiping at her cheeks.

Her lips stiffened, her jaw becoming rock. "I know she will."

I wanted to take her in my arms and tell her that she didn't need to act brave, at least not around me, but I let her be. Maybe she was braver than I gave her credit for. Maybe she didn't really need me for comfort. But she had called me in her time of need, and that had to count for something.

For several hours, Joss and I sat in the waiting room, our stomachs tied in knots, our eyes glued to those green double doors for the doctor. We took turns pacing, going to the bathroom, buying coffee, but more often than not, we sat together in silence, only speaking in hushed tones.

"I should have taken better care of her," Joss whispered, twisting her fingers together. "I should have seen the signs."

"How the hell could you have known?"

"I don't know," she said, shaking her head. " I could have forced her to see a doctor. Made her take her yearly pap smears. Something."

"There's no way you could have prevented this."

She fixed me with a steady look. "I should have been a better daughter. I shouldn't have...." Her voice filtered away, but the unsaid words hung in the air between us.

"Don't do that, Joss," I said, my face growing hot. "We didn't do this to her."

Her eyebrows knitted together as she asked softly, "Didn't we?"

I jumped to my feet. "That's ridiculous. We didn't give her cancer."

"No, we didn't," she said. "But did we take away her will to care?"

I spun around with a huff. Anger coursed through my veins, but I didn't know if I was angry because Joss was wrong... or because she was right. Had our betrayal done this to Amanda? Had she simply stopped taking care of herself?

"I'm going to get more coffee." As I walked away, the double doors whooshed open and a doctor walked through in his scrubs, the white mask still hanging around his neck.

I looked over my shoulder in time to see Joss jumping to her feet. "Is she okay?" she immediately asked.

The doctor glanced at me as I came closer. "She's out of the OR and stable. You should be able to see her soon."

"And the cancer? Did you get it?"

I took hold of Joss's hand, lending her my strength.

The doctor—Dr. Pointer, PhD—shook his head. "We took out what we could but the cancer has spread."

Joss squeezed my hand as her breathing turned ragged. "What does that mean?"

The look in Dr. Pointer's eyes didn't lend much hope. "There are still some avenues we can try."

"Such as?" I asked.

"At this stage of the cancer, I suggest an aggressive approach. Radiation and chemotherapy."

"Will that work?" Joss asked, nodding her head as if urging the doc to do the same.

He looked down at his hands a moment before looking her in the eye. "There's a chance. But I don't want to raise false hopes, Miss Blake. The truth is that your mother's cancer is at a very advanced stage. If it doesn't respond to the radiation and chemo…" He trailed off, unwilling to speak the dire possibility.

Joss straightened her spine. "How long?"

"Conservatively speaking, about a month. Maybe two."

I felt the breath leave Joss's lungs, felt her deflate beside me. I slipped my arm around her waist to support her should she fall, but she pushed me away.

"I'm sorry," Dr. Pointer said. "I'll let a nurse come and get you when you can see her."

After the doctor left, I turned to Joss. I opened my mouth to speak but she cut me off, holding up a palm. "Just don't," she said and walked off.

The nurse came out a half hour later but Joss still hadn't returned. "I'll go find her," I said and went in search. I checked bathrooms and stairwells, but finally found her in another waiting area on the other side of the building, sitting in the far corner with her head on her knees. The sight of her on the floor almost broke me.

I sank down on my knees in front of her, touching her hand. "You can go see her now," I said gently.

She looked all of sixteen when she lifted her head, so young and so lost. "I don't know how I got here," she began, glancing at her surroundings. "I was just walking. Then I didn't want to walk anymore so I sat down."

I took hold of her hand and helped her up. We walked down the hallway in silence, our steps sluggish, dread wrapped around us like an invisible cloak.

It seemed only a few seconds passed before we were faced with Amanda's door.

A nurse hurried over and stopped us. "Family members only please."

I took a step back, letting Joss's hand fall away. Her head swung around to me, eyes wide, but whatever it was she wanted to say would not come out. "I'll be right here," I told her.

She swallowed hard and gave a slight nod. Then she took a deep breath and opened the door. Over her shoulder, I caught a glimpse of a woman on the bed, her eyes closed, tubes in her nose. But before my brain could recognize the face, the door swung shut.

[twenty-six]

Joss and I went home a few hours later, after the nurses urged Joss to get some rest. She drove her car and I followed close behind to make sure she made it home safe.

I stayed in the truck as Joss parked and walked up the stairs to her apartment. But instead of going in, she just stood in front of the door, staring at its brown surface with hunched shoulders. I watched her, my heart quietly breaking. Then she turned her head and looked at me and next thing I knew, I was jumping out of the truck, taking three steps at a time, and gathering her in my arms. "Ssh, I've got you."

She held onto me like her life depended on it. "I can't lose her."

"You won't," I said, knowing there was a good chance it was a lie.

Gently, I took the keys from her hand and unlocked the door, ushering her inside. I left her standing in the living room, looking lost, and went in search of the bathroom. I turned on the water in the tub and set the plug in the drain.

"What are you doing?" Joss asked at the doorway.

"Drawing you a bath." I stood up and wiped my hands on my jeans. "Why do they call it that anyway? There's no actual drawing involved. Unless you want an actual sketch of a bathtub."

But the smile I was trying to coax out of her never appeared. "You don't have to do that," she said, her voice hoarse from crying.

"What? Taking care of you or cracking jokes?"

"All of it," she said. "I'm fine, Jake. Really."

I turned off the faucet, suddenly at a loss. I stared at this young woman before me, taking note of how much she'd aged since we first met. Gone was the innocence and joy in her eyes. "Did I do that?" I whispered.

Her eyebrows furrowed. "Do what?"

"Did I take away your light?"

She blinked up at me for the longest time, neither one of us daring to move. A million silent words passed between us, things we badly wanted to say but couldn't. When she broke the connection and looked away, I got my answer.

Nodding in resignation, I came towards her and kissed her forehead. "Goodnight, Joss."

———————

I halfway expected Joss to ask me to come to the hospital again, but she didn't call. I spent the afternoon in my workshop at the back of the store, my phone kept in my back pocket just in case. I tried to focus on the task at hand but my mind was elsewhere, at the hospital miles away and the two women inside who were fighting battles together and apart.

It wasn't fair that Amanda would get cancer. She, who worked so hard, who loved with her whole heart.

She and I had met through a blind date. A client of mine had told me about her single friend. "She's a little older but gorgeous. She's settled, her kid's grown. She's a real catch."

I had never dated an older woman before, but I'd agreed to be set up anyway. It had been some time since my last relationship—one that I'd unwittingly sabotaged by thinking she was cheating on me at every turn, the remnants of my relationship with Eleanor still coloring my every thought.

But when I met Amanda Blake, when I saw the kind of person she truly was, I decided I was ready to give love another chance. I no longer wanted to be held back by the fear of infidelity.

My love for her had come slow and steady, like a rowboat drifting to shore with the tide. The first few times she'd traveled out of town, I had to tamp down the inner demons that demanded to know where she was and whom she was with. But Amanda taught me to have faith in someone once again, to know that my trust was not misguided or abused.

And in return, I had destroyed it all by upending the boat and drowning in her daughter.

I closed up shop at six. After tidying up, I got in my truck and hurried to the hospital, hoping I hadn't missed visiting hours.

I knocked on the door and listened for the soft "come in" before entering Amanda's room. She was alone, lying in the bed with a television remote control in her hand.

"Hey," I said, hesitating at the door. To see her so pale and so weak desiccated my mouth.

"Jake." She turned off the TV and set aside the remote control. "What are you doing here?"

I stuck my hands in my pockets. "I, uh… Joss told me. She called me after you were admitted."

Her expression shuttered, trying to hide the hurt that her daughter would turn to me in her time of need.

"She didn't know who else to call. She was freaking out."

Amanda shook her head gently. "You don't have to rationalize her actions. I'm not surprised she called you."

"You're not?"

Her green eyes flashed with some emotion I couldn't decode. "No. You're the closest thing she has to a father."

Ouch.

Now that the first shot had been fired, I took a few steps closer. "How are you?"

A smile touched her lips. "Dying."

Her reply, said so boldly, brought tears to my eyes. I crossed the space between us and took hold of her hand. "I'm sorry."

"Why? You didn't give me cancer," she said, staring down at our hands. "Though I'm surprised you didn't give me an STD after all your sleeping around."

"Amanda…"

She dug her nails into my skin, her lips tight with anger. "Why her? Why my own daughter?"

I bore the pain, gritting my teeth as she started to draw blood. I deserved every possible punishment she could mete out.

After several moments, she finally loosened her hold.

"I'm sorry," I said again. "I don't know if I can be sorry enough for what I did to you."

A sob escaped her throat. "You never even thought about the baby. You just went straight for Joss."

I dragged a chair to the bed and sat down. "You're right, I did go straight to Joss." I sighed. "But I did—do—think about that baby, Amanda. I think about what could have been, what our lives would have been like if that baby had been real."

"You wouldn't have married me," she said, her gaze direct and searing. "You would have still left me eventually."

"You don't know that."

"What makes you think you would have made a good father anyway?" she asked, her face starting to flush. "You're a thirty year old man with nothing to your name, no home, no real job."

"I have a store now, in Hollywood. And I just closed on a house a few days ago. I've mostly got my act in order."

She turned her head away. "Joss lives in Hollywood."

It dawned on me what brought about the chill in the room. "Joss and I broke it off when I moved out. She's not the reason why I moved to Hollywood." I hadn't even known she'd moved out until I caught sight of her walking alone in the dark one night, the same night a man had started to follow her home and I'd distracted him by bumming a smoke.

"I don't believe you," Amanda said.

"You really think I'd lie to you here, right now, while you're lying in a hospital bed?"

I saw the glistening of a tear as it slid down the side of her face. "Why not? You've lied before."

"Amanda—"

She reached for the nurse call button. "I think you'd better leave now, Jake."

"Look, I get you're still angry with me and that I have no business asking you to forgive me. All I came to say is that I'm sorry. I'm sorry I did what I did, and I'm sorry that you've got cancer." I stood up and walked to the door. "I know you hate me, but I'm here. Even if you just need a burger in the middle of the night, call me and I'll get it with extra pickles like you like. Because despite what it seems like right now, I do care about you. Very much."

She kept her head turned. "Just go. I don't need anything from you."

————————

Amanda didn't ask anything of me but I went over to her house in Pembroke Pines anyway to at least bring in her mail and set the trash bin at the curb. But when I arrived, I found Joss's car in the driveway.

I did what I came to do, then rang the doorbell. Joss answered a few seconds later, wearing the khaki skirt and collared shirt she normally wore to work.

"What are you doing here?"

I handed over the stack of mail in my hands. "Just getting your mom's mail and taking the trash out."

"I forgot about trash day," she said. "Do you want to come in?"

I followed her to the kitchen, taking note of the changes in the house. The wall where Joss's bookcase once stood was bare, its absence leaving a gaping hole in the room. "Does she have anymore trash that needs to go out?" I asked, taking note of the several tools on the counter by the sink. "What's going on here?"

"Her faucet was leaking so I was trying to fix it."

"May I?" I checked the likely culprit. "It'll just need a new o-ring. Easy fix."

"Oh." She looked down at her watch. "It'll have to wait until after work. I don't have time to stop at Home Depot."

"Wait here." I jogged to my truck and rifled through the plastic bag in the passenger seat. When I found the package, I went back inside and fixed the leak.

"You just happened to have a spare o-ring in your truck?" Joss asked, folding her arms across her chest. "Like that's something you always travel with for damsels in distress?"

I couldn't help it; I chuckled. "As luck would have it, I just went there yesterday because I had a leaky faucet in my laundry room. I bought a few just in case there were a few more in the house."

"You have a laundry room?"

I nodded. "I own a house now. I no longer live with my little brother."

"Congrats." She watched me quietly as I put the faucet back together. "Mom told me you visited her."

I leaned against the counter, wiping my hands on my jeans. "Yeah. She wasn't too happy to see me."

"No, she wasn't." She picked up her purse and keys off the table. "Could you maybe not visit her anymore? I don't want to upset her more, you know?"

"I didn't go there to upset her."

"I know. But seeing you is the last thing she wants, especially when she's vulnerable like that." Her breathing sped up as she blinked fast. "Just promise me you won't visit her again."

"I won't. Unless she asks for me."

"You don't have to worry about that," Joss said with certainty.

"And what about you?"

She swallowed, staring down at the keys in her hand. "I'm good, Jake. Really. You don't have to worry about either of us anymore."

"Sure?"

She lifted her chin and met my gaze, her jaw set tight. "I'm sure." And with those two words, she ejected me out of her life.

[twenty-seven]

The first week I didn't receive a call, I figured they were dealing with the cancer in their own way. But after the second week, it started to sink in that maybe they really no longer wanted me in their lives. And why should they? I was just the man who had almost successfully ripped apart their little family.

Still, this man wanted to be useful in some way, *any* way.

After I called the hospital and was informed that Amanda had been released, I was able to breathe a little sigh of relief. I wasn't naïve enough to think she'd beat the cancer in a month, but at least I knew she was no longer at death's door. There was still hope.

And I foolishly held onto mine.

I didn't keep my promise to Joss, however. A few times after I closed up shop, I found myself driving through her street. The first night I only drove through at a slow pace. The second night, I parked but kept the truck running. The third night, I got out and stood on the sidewalk across the street, looking up at the dark window of Joss's room. But no more than a few minutes passed when a silhouette appeared at the window to the right. The blinds slid up and Ashley, Joss's friend, stuck her head out the window.

"She doesn't live here anymore," she called out, stopping me dead in my tracks. "She moved back home."

Caught red-handed, I spun away and headed back for the truck.

———————

"Jake, you have to meet Mig," Tristan said at my house the next night.

I took the pot of macaroni off the stove and poured cheese sauce over the steaming pasta. "I told you, I'm not interested in being set up," I said as I stirred the concoction before taking a spoonful and shoveling it into my mouth, succeeding in burning the roof of my mouth.

"Dude, that's sad," Tristan said, watching me with something like disgust on his face. "How many times have you had mac and cheese this week?"

I shrugged. "Last night I went out for a burger."

Tristan shook his head. "How about this: I'll spring for dinner at Palme d'Or if you take her out for dinner?"

"I'm really not in the French food *or* dating frame of mind right now." I didn't bother with a bowl; I started eating straight out of the pot. Less dishes to wash this way.

"God, you're so pitiful."

I shrugged. Maybe guys my age who had their shit together ate dinner using real plates, but I never claimed to have my shit together.

"How about Fogo de Chao?" Tristan asked, going straight for the jugular. He knew my weakness was the Brazilian steakhouse.

I paused with the spoon halfway into my mouth, actually considering his offer. "How about you just give me her number and I'll call her when I get the chance?"

He pulled out his cell phone and texted me the woman's number. My phone chimed, letting me know I'd received the woman's information. "Just make sure you call her," he said. "And try to wait till the third date before sleeping with any of her family members, okay?"

"Shut up," I said through a mouthful of pasta. A few moments later, I asked, "What's wrong with her? Why is it so important that I meet her?"

"Because she's money. You don't want a woman like that getting away."

I cocked my head, one eyebrow raised. "You still feel guilty about dating Joss, don't you?" Tristan rolled his eyes, but I knew better. I reached out and punched his shoulder.

"Just go meet this girl, okay?" he said, heading for the front door. "Thank me later by naming your firstborn after me."

Two weeks later, I took out Tristan's friend—a woman named Migdalia. Half Puerto Rican, half Swede, she had curly blonde hair, an easy smile, and a no-bullshit attitude. I liked her immediately.

"I don't like to beat around the bush," she said early on in the date at the Brazilian steakhouse in Miami Beach. "I say what I mean and I mean what I say."

"I'll toast to that." I lifted my beer and she tapped it with her wine glass, smiling as she did.

"So your brother has been trying to fix us up for a few weeks now," she said just as a man with a large skewer of meat arrived at our table. He cut us both a slice of filet mignon before moving on to another table. "Why is that?"

"Because I'm pathetic, is my guess."

Mig tilted her head down and raised an eyebrow, letting me know she didn't believe my bullshit.

"Pretty sure he just wants me to get over someone," I said with a little more honesty.

"Funny. I'm trying to get over someone myself."

We toasted again. "Well here's to our exes. May they find the happiness they're seeking."

I watched as she cut into the meat on her plate, her movements relaxed but precise. "Why are you still single?" I asked.

Her eyes flicked up in surprise. "Didn't Tristan tell you?"

"No."

"I just ended a long term relationship. With a younger man."

I shook my head, chuckling. "My brother's a jackhole."

"Why?"

"Because the girl I'm trying to forget?" Mig nodded and I went on, "She was nine years younger than me."

She threw her head back and laughed, a reaction I was completely unprepared for. I had to admit, it was a little disarming. "Well, if nothing else, he has a sense of humor."

After dinner, went out for a walk along the beach, though it was windy and a little chilly by Miami's standards. Migdalia's hair kept getting blown in her face and she had to hold her skirt together to keep from flashing her panties, but didn't utter one complaint.

"You're not enjoying this, are you?" I asked, reaching out and removing a strand of curly hair stuck to her lips.

"I'm not really a fan of windy, sandy things."

"And you live in Miami?"

She laughed. "My entire family is here. I can't move away."

I took her home. We talked all the way back to her house in Kendall, the conversation flowing easily as if we'd known each other a long time. I walked her to her doorstep, and for the first time in a long time, Joss was far away in the back of my mind. I almost didn't miss her.

"I had a lot of fun," Mig asked, touching my chest. "I'd like to do this again."

I didn't know how to tell her that this would be our first and last date without sounding like a pompous jackass, so I said nothing.

Sensing my hesitation, she grabbed fistfuls of my shirt and pulled me in. Her kissing style was, much like her, honest and bold. She wanted me and she wasn't afraid to show it. "What about now?" she asked after pulling away.

I took a deep breath, trying to clear my thoughts. "Believe me, if circumstances were different, I would."

She nodded, her gaze direct, thoughtful. "I get it. But if things ever change, call me."

"They probably won't. I'm kind of locked in on this one."

"Okay." Her hand slid off my chest. "Good luck with everything, Jake."

I bent down and kissed her cheek. "Same to you, Mig."

[twenty-eight]

In the third week of December, I headed to the Broward campus of Florida International University for Joss's commencement ceremony. With a formal invitation and a wrapped package in hand, I walked into the auditorium and found a seat in the back, all the while searching for that one face in the sea of thousands.

But I didn't see Joss until an hour into the ceremony, when they finally called her name and she walked up on the stage. I found myself rising to my feet, mesmerized by the sight of her, as she shook the dean's hand. Then she turned to smile for the photographer and, somehow, her eyes flicked across the room and met mine. In this packed auditorium, she found me. I had to believe that meant something.

I lifted my hand in a wave but she just turned away and walked off the stage.

Feeling stupid, I sat my ass back down.

After the ceremony, I moved through the crowd, my height an advantage as I searched the room for that familiar head of blonde hair. I spotted Joss rushing to the side of the room, trying to make a hasty exit, but someone stopped her with a hug. I made my way over, taking hold of her arm before she could escape.

"Congratulations," I said, beaming at her.

"I didn't know you'd be here," she said.

"I wouldn't have missed it."

She stared at the invitation in my hand, her eyebrows furrowed. "I didn't send you an invitation."

"You didn't?"

She shook her head. "Why? Why would I want you here?"

I took a deep breath, trying to quell the burning in my chest. Wow, that hurt more than expected. "Okay, well," I said when the pain had subsided to a muted stabbing in the gut. "Congratulations." I handed her the gift, turned on a heel, and left.

I stomped to my truck, ripping the tie away from my throat. Why the hell had I bothered?

"Jake."

Joss's voice floated over the parking lot, gluing my shoes to the asphalt. But I kept my back turned, trying to catch my breath. "What?" I called over my shoulder.

Her heels clicked as she came closer. Then her hand touched my shoulder. "I'm sorry." She stepped around in front of me, looking like a vision. Her blonde hair glowed in the sunlight, like a wavy halo around her beautiful face. "I didn't mean that."

I folded my arms across my chest. "What? That you didn't invite me or that you didn't want me here?"

"I wasn't the one who sent you the invitation. But it's good to see you." Her green eyes flew all over my face before venturing down, taking in my slacks and button-down shirt. Hell, I was even wearing my good shoes. "You look nice," she said.

I tried to keep my cool in this muggy heat, pretending the spike in my body temperature had nothing to do with the woman before me. "Where's your mom?" I asked, sounding grumpier than I felt.

The light in her eyes dimmed. "She was too weak so she stayed home."

"What about your dad? Did you invite him?"

She nodded. "He didn't RSVP either."

I let out a breath. I would have given anything to hold her right then, to let her know I would always try to be there for her. Instead, I jerked my head toward the gift in her hand. "I hope you like it."

She started to tear at the wrapping. "Thank you. You didn't have to get me anything."

"Of course I did," I said, a warm glow radiating in my chest. "I'm proud of you."

Her eyes flicked up to mine. "Careful, Jake. That sounded almost paternal," she teased before unwrapping the gift. "Oh," she breathed, turning the dark brown leather notebook over in her hands, her fingers tracing over her embossed name on the front.

"It's similar to a sketchbook I once had, except this is a journal."

She blinked up at me with a strange look but said nothing.

"What?" I asked, peering into her face.

"Thank you," she said. "It's beautiful."

"I figured you could write our story." I took a step closer, tucking a strand of hair behind her ear. "Or rewrite it, maybe."

She tipped her head back to look at me, a wistful grin on her face. Before she could say anything, her phone rang. "Hey, Mom," she said, turning away from me. The phone call was short and in no time, Joss faced me again, but the spell was broken. Reality had once again seeped back in. "I'd better go. Mom has to go to the hospital for chemo."

"Do you want some help?" I offered automatically, not wanting to be separated again.

"No. I got it." She stared at me for the longest time, like she wanted to say something but couldn't gather the courage. Finally, she said, "I'm happy you came today." When she stood on her toes and pressed a soft but lingering kiss on my cheek, I closed my eyes and breathed her in. "Thank you," she whispered before pulling away.

As I watched her walk away, I felt a shift in the wind, a sure sign that things were about to change. Little did I know just how much.

———————

The next day I received a text message while I was helping a customer at the store.

Jake, it's Amanda. Can you come over to the house?
I'll be right there.

I finished up with the customer, helping her load the armchair into the back of her SUV before closing up the shop a few hours early. Then I rushed to Pembroke Pines, and into the subdivision that was once so familiar to me.

I went in through the unlocked front door. "Hello?" I called out, half expecting to find Joss reading on the couch. The bookcase was back in its original place, completing the room once more.

I found Amanda in the bedroom, sitting up in bed. The sight of her looking so frail and thin took my breath away. "How are you?" I asked, approaching slowly.

"Still dying." She touched the scarf wrapped around her head. "Chemo's doing a number on my hair."

"Did you send me that invitation to Joss's graduation?" I blurted out.

"No beating around the bush with you," she said with a grin. "Yes. I sent it. I just couldn't bear the thought of Joss walking on that stage without anyone to see her."

Neither of us spoke for a long time, both lost in our thoughts. I kept my gaze direct and open.

"I knew about the cancer for a long time," Amanda finally said.

Her words took a few moments to sink in. "You did? When?"

"After our visit to the OB, I got a call saying my pap smear was abnormal. I went back in for a biopsy and they found... something."

"Why didn't you say anything?"

"You and I were already over by then."

"I meant to Joss."

Amanda broke eye contact. "I couldn't." She began to pick at the tape covering the IV needle in her hand. "I couldn't put that on her shoulders too. She already blames herself for so much."

I reached out and touched her hand, knowing she wasn't just talking about Joss. "None of this was your fault either," I said gently.

She looked up with a spark of the old Amanda in her eyes. "I know. It's yours."

I nodded, taking shallow breaths.

Her fingers wrapped around my hand, squeezing. "I'm kidding, Jake. I don't blame you, not for the cancer at least. But for the rest..." I opened my mouth to apologize when she shook her head. "Do you think you would have still let yourself fall for Joss if you'd known about the cancer?"

It took me a few minutes to wrap my mind around the theoretical scenario, but my head was already shaking before I could come up with a response that wouldn't hurt. "It wasn't a choice. Falling for Joss was—"

"Inevitable," she finished for me, her eyes shining with tears.

"Yeah." I let out a breath. The truth was that my feelings for Joss were completely independent of my relationship with Amanda. "You couldn't have done anything to prevent it."

"Jake, I need you to do me a favor."

"Anything," I said without hesitation. "What do you need?"

"I need you to take care of Joss," she said, her voice raw with emotion. "She'll need you when I'm gone."

"Don't even talk like that. You're going to get better." I let out a breath, sure that the room had gotten ten degrees hotter in the last few seconds.

Amanda shook her head, a tear sliding down her pale cheek. "And if I can't?"

"You will."

"But in case I don't…"

"You will." I sat on the edge of the bed, her hand still in mine. "You're the great Amanda Blake. There's nothing you can't conquer."

"Except love." She let out a humorless laugh. "And also, cancer."

I stared at her, unable to speak. Sweat beaded on my forehead.

"Dying has a way of putting things in perspective. I've had a lot of time to think these past few months, between the hospital visits and the chemo and basically being too sick to get out of bed. It helped me see what I couldn't—or wouldn't—before." She licked her chapped lips. I handed her the cup of water from the nightstand and she took a grateful sip. "You feel something for her in a way you never did for me."

"Amanda…"

She leveled me with a look. "We're way past false denials here."

I pressed my lips together, my nostrils flaring.

"I just need to know someone's going to look out for her," she continued. "To do what's right by her, for her, with her, whatever. I just need to know someone's going to be there for my daughter after I'm gone."

Tears stung my eyes but I shook my head. "You're not going anywhere."

"Please." She was crying now, tears running freely down her face. "Promise me."

I leaned over and pressed my lips to her forehead, sadness washing over me in waves. "Okay. I'll do it."

We looked at each other for long moments, an unfathomable sadness passing between us. And, despite it all, there was still love there and maybe, hopefully, forgiveness.

"Thanks," she whispered.

We both turned at the sound of the doorbell. "I'll get it," I said, gathering my wits as I headed out of the bedroom. When I opened the front door, I came face to face with an older man with silver hair. "Can I help you?"

"Yes, I'd like to come in," he said, looking over my shoulder.

"Who are you?"

"I'm Patrick Blake. Amanda's ex-husband."

[twenty-nine]

The man raised an eyebrow and tipped his head. "And you are?"

"Jake."

"Nice to meet you." He held out a hand. "I didn't realize Joss had a boyfriend."

I shook his hand and stepped aside, letting him inside the house. It occurred to me to correct the misconception, but decided it didn't matter.

He regarded me through narrow eyes. "How old did you say you were?"

"I didn't."

He bristled, regarding me through narrowed eyes. He didn't like me, and the sentiment was returned twofold. Before neither of us could speak, Amanda called out, "Who is it?"

Patrick turned at the sound of voice, moving past me and heading to the bedroom without hesitation.

A second later, I heard Amanda gasp.

I didn't stay. I went back home and tried to make sense of it all, tried to predict the fallout of Patrick's arrival. How would Joss react knowing her dad was back?

A knock at the front door pulled me from my thoughts. I unlocked it to find Joss standing outside in the rain.

"My dad is back," Joss breathed, her lips trembling.

I grabbed her hand and pulled her in from the downpour. She stood in the foyer, hair plastered to her head, water collecting at her feet.

"I know. I met him." I grabbed a sweatshirt from the coat rack and held it out.

She ignored it, her green eyes fixed on me. "How?"

"Your mom asked me to come over to talk. Then your dad knocked on the door."

"She asked you to come over? Why?"

I moved closer and dried her face, her arms. "She just wanted to talk. To clear the air between us."

Her chin trembled, the air shuddering out of her. "So it's true. It's almost time," she said on a whisper. "That's why he's here."

"He probably came here for your graduation."

She shook her head, swiping at the new moisture on her cheeks. "My mom thinks she's protecting me by not telling me the truth. Is that what you're doing?"

"No."

She came to me, wrapping her arms around me and pressing her face into my chest. And I held her, smoothing her hair back and taking comfort in the giving, even as I got soaked in the process. "Your mom is a fighter, Joss. Don't give up on her just yet."

"My dad wants to stay and nurse my mom back to health. Like his presence is suddenly going to cure her of cancer," she said, her voice laced with bitterness. "He told her he loved her, that he always had."

"Do you believe him?"

"Would you?" she asked. "If you loved someone, would you be able to stay away that long?"

I stared down at her, imagining myself in his situation. "If I thought I was doing the right thing." I held her face in my hands. "Even if it felt like my insides were getting ripped out of me, I would suffer through it all if it meant she'd have a better life."

"He'll leave her again," she said through her teeth. "And me..." She pressed her face to my chest and began to sob. I wrapped my arms around her and tried to absorb the pain, imagining it drawing away from her and soaking into me. If only such a thing was possible.

Behind me I felt Joss's hands gather fistfuls of my shirt, her body vibrating with anger. "Why would he come now? So he could watch her die?"

"Jocelyn..." I pulled back and tilted her face up. "Maybe he means to stay."

"And what happens when she's gone? He'll go back to Houston and I'll have nobody."

I let out a soft breath. "You'll have me."

She blinked up at me for a long time. Finally, she reached up and touched her fingers to my lips, her features softening. "Can we be friends again?"

I blinked. "Friends?"

"We were friends before everything, remember? I miss that," she said. "After all that's happened, I could use a friend."

With a sigh, I pressed my lips to her forehead. "I've never not been your friend." Then I took a step back and gave her space.

She gave me one last look before pivoting around, turning her attention to my house. "It's nice," she said.

I looked around at the sparse space, and wondered if we were looking at the same thing. "I still need to get furniture."

"Not like you know any furniture makers or anything," she said with a hint of a grin. She walked over to the couch and picked up the book I'd left there, flipping it over to read the blurb. "Do you like it so far? I've heard it's good but mired with a bunch of science-y mumbo jumbo."

"It's not too bad. Here—" I held out my hand and parked my ass down, flipping to the first page of the story and reading the hilarious first line.

Joss chuckled and sat down beside me. "Go on."

So I did. When I was done with the first page, I looked up and found Joss leaning back with her eyes closed. "Keep reading," she said. "I love the sound of your voice. It's deep and soothing."

"Get comfortable and I'll read as long as you like."

Shoe toed off her shoes and reclined on the couch, hesitating before setting her head on my lap. I knew we were steering into dangerous territory but having her so near felt too good to turn back.

But unlike the last time we were in this position, Joss seemed more relaxed, even content. I continued to read out loud, turning page after page, losing myself in the story. It was only much later I realized I'd been combing my fingers through her hair.

"Want me to go to the next chapter?" I asked and belatedly realized she had fallen asleep.

I ran the back of my fingers along her cheek, watching her peaceful face as she slept. I set the book down and leaned my head on the back of the couch, intending to close my eyes for only a few minutes.

I jerked awake hours later, finding Joss still asleep on my lap. My watch said it was a little before two in the morning, way past time for her to go home. But, for the life of me, I couldn't bring myself to wake her up.

Instead I gently slid out from under her, laying her head on a pillow. Then I went to the closet and grabbed a blanket, draping it across her body.

I squatted by the couch, my heart squeezing painfully in my chest as I watched her sleep. How was it possible to miss someone when they were right in front of you?

I stood up to leave when I heard her say, "Stay with me, Jake." Her eyes blinked open, a dreamy expression on her face. "I don't want to sleep alone."

Without another word, I bent down and picked her up in my arms, carrying her across the house toward the bedroom. I placed her gently on the bed then lay down on the other end of the mattress.

"Why are you so far away?" she asked with eyebrows raised.

I swiped a palm down my face, tuning out the definitely *un-friendly* thoughts running through my head.

She shifted closer, curling up against my chest. "This feels better."

I ground my teeth together, hoping she couldn't feel the rock hard thing in my pants.

But this was Joss after all, the same girl who had pulled my towel off while deliriously sick. "You seem uncomfortable, Jake," she said with a soft chuckle. I jumped when she pressed her hand to my erection.

"Joss…" It wasn't a plea so much as a warning. I was very nearly past the point of no return. "If you keep doing that, we're not going to be friends much longer."

She tilted her head back and touched the pad of her fingers to my lips, tracing them back and around. "Friendships can have benefits too, right?"

My cock twitched, painfully hard and desperate for release, but I reached up and grabbed hold of her wrist. "I don't want you to regret anything in the morning." I leaned my forehead against hers, breathing through the bittersweet ache.

She took in a ragged breath, her cheeks flushed. "I could never regret you."

I gathered in my arms, fitting her against my body. "Good night, Jocelyn," I murmured into her hair.

She pressed a soft kiss to the base of my throat and finally—thankfully—settled down.

[thirty]

Being friends with Joss was a double-edged sword. As friends, we were free to enjoy each other's company without all the accompanying guilt. But having the invisible barrier between us was the sweetest form of torture, keeping me from touching her like I wanted.

I didn't regret a thing.

———————

One late night, Joss came by the workshop carrying a brown paper sack. She waited at the doorway, watching as I turned on the circular saw and cut through a large board. When I was done, I set aside the saw and took off my earmuffs.

"Hey," I said, shaking sawdust off my head.

She came closer, holding a large paper sack in her arms. "I thought I'd find you here." She looked around the room at the various tools and pieces of wood lying around. "Always working late."

"What can I say? I have no life."

"I figured. So I brought nourishment."

I cleaned off some space on the workbench, blowing sawdust off its surface before grabbing two old metal stools. "Sorry about the mess."

Joss set down the paper sack and handed me a little white box and a pair of chopsticks. She sat down and pulled apart her own chopsticks. "So what are you working on today?" she asked, rubbing the wood sticks together.

I went to the small fridge in the corner of my workshop and grabbed two beers. "A dresser for a hotel on South Beach."

"That's a big deal," she said, her eyes going wide.

I took a bite of food. "It's just a small boutique hotel."

"Do you think they'll ask you to fill the whole hotel with your designs?"

"I hope they will but I seriously doubt it," I said with a shrug.

We were quiet for some time, both of us swallowed up in our own thoughts as we ate.

After a while, I asked, "So what are your plans for the future? Career-wise."

She frowned into her fried rice. "Work at the bookstore until I find the perfect job."

"What happened to that internship you told me about? The one at the publisher?"

"I couldn't do it. I didn't have time to do that, work a real paying job, *and* take care of Mom."

"Oh." I studied her for a few moments. "What would you rather be doing?"

"I'm not sure." When she finally looked up at me, her eyes were dim with uncertainty. "I wish I have even an ounce of your passion, your drive."

"It wasn't always this way. I slowly fell in love with my job. Like the best things, it kind of sneaks up on you when you least expect it."

She eyed me, her expression too serious for Chinese food and beer.

"So what about a book blogger? You can read books and then review them."

"It sounds like heaven but I doubt it'd pay my bills." She shook her head. "I should've majored in something more practical, like my mom."

"That's not your passion."

"Passion?" she scoffed. "I only have two things I'm passionate about: books and—" She stopped abruptly, her cheeks immediately flushing. She took a sip of beer, avoiding eye contact.

"And?"

She chewed on her lip. "Doesn't matter. Neither one is a career."

"Is it me?" I pressed, enjoying her discomfort. "Am I the second?"

She rolled her eyes. "Get over yourself."

I wiggled my chopsticks in her face. "That's not a no."

She laughed, smacking my hand away. "How do you like that Honey Chicken?"

I leaned closer, crowding her space. "You're my passion too, Jocelyn," I whispered. Before she could respond, I added, "And the Sesame Beef is delicious."

"Friends?" Tristan asked as we made our way to South Beach with the finished dresser in the back of the truck. "You seriously agreed to that?"

"Look, that's all she can handle right now."

"Whose idea was it again? Let me guess: Not yours."

"It was a mutual agreement."

"So how mutually agreeable you think you're going to be once she tells you about a guy she's dating?" I opened my mouth to retort when he said, "And you know she will. Any guy with eyes can see that Joss is Grade A."

I took a hand off the steering wheel and smacked his shoulder. "Shut up. She's not a piece of steak."

"Speaking of, let's eat lunch at Texas de Brazil."

"Fuck you, fucker."

Tristan chuckled and held up his hands in surrender. "Okay, okay. Still, I bring up a valid question. The moment she starts dating, you're going to go apeshit-caveman-possessive and punch any guy who comes near her."

"I won't."

"You have."

I took a deep breath and tried to loosen my grip on the steering wheel. He was right, of course. Just the thought of Joss dating made me want to punch a hole through the windshield. "Damn it, Tristan," I yelled. "I was fine being in the friendzone until you said that."

"Sorry, brother. Just looking out for you."

I stewed in my thoughts the rest of the drive. Tristan, thankfully, left me alone, busying himself with his phone instead.

Once we reached the hotel, we unloaded the dresser and carried it up to a second floor room. After, I took my brother to lunch to show my gratitude. It wasn't steak though.

That night I decided to go see Joss at work. I waited in the parking lot until the store closed and met her outside.

"Hey, what are you doing here?" she asked as she walked through the double doors.

"Just wanted to make sure you made it to your car safely."

She looked at me unconvinced. "And?"

"And I wanted to talk to you about this whole friend thing."

"Oh," she said as if she'd been expecting it. But before neither one of us could say another word, her phone rang. "Hang on, it's my dad."

She turned away and answered the phone. Her normal voice quickly gave way to panic. "What? When? Okay, I'll be right there." When she faced me again, her eyes were wide, lips parted.

"Is Amanda okay?" I asked as soon as she hung up.

She stared off into space. "My dad took her to the hospital. She's in bad shape."

"Come on. I'll take you," I said, taking hold of her hand.

She resisted. "I'm scared," she whispered. "What if this is it?"

My heart squeezed in my chest. "Then you need to be there to say goodbye."

"I'm not ready to say goodbye." Her chin trembled at the last word.

"I don't think any of us is ever ready for that."

At the hospital, I held back in the waiting area, allowing the family to have their time together. I sat among strangers, all of us fearing the worst even as we hoped for the best.

No more than fifteen minutes passed before Patrick turned the corner and came marching towards me.

"Why are you still here?" he asked, wasting no time for fake pleasantries.

I stood up, finding myself a few inches taller. "I came here with Joss."

"She's with her family now. You're free to leave."

I stared at him, unmoved by this man who had abandoned his family. I wondered what Amanda had seen in him—still continued to see in him. He had a certain Richard Gere look about him with his gray hair and distinguished face, but he didn't seem like anybody outstanding. But then again, Amanda had seen something in me too, and I wasn't exactly a prize.

Not for the first time I wondered why the universe binds us to a person and connects us through time. Why it was that I fell for Joss at the worst possible time and why it was I couldn't recover.

I clenched my jaw. "I'll leave when Joss tells me to leave."

"Amanda told me everything," Patrick said, his jaw muscles working. "You're a despicable human being."

That, I couldn't refute. "And you left Amanda alone to raise a daughter. Let's not throw stones here."

His face reddened. "You are a grown man. You have no business fucking around with a girl."

I glanced around, realizing people could hear our conversation. "I know you haven't been around for a while, but look around. Your daughter is a woman now. And she's free to make choices," I said between my teeth.

He nodded, still glaring. "Free to sleep with assholes, sure," he said, crossing his arms over his barrel chest. "She's also free to leave."

I mimicked his pose. "Yes, so ask yourself why she keeps coming back."

"She's leaving," he said, leaning forward. "For good."

"What?"

He lifted his chin and smiled. "I've secured a private jet and am flying Amanda to Houston for better care," he said. "I've asked Jocelyn to come with us."

June Gray

[thirty-one]

Joss avoided me for the next few days. I wanted to call and ask if her father was telling the truth, but knew she'd come around eventually when she was ready. So I gave her space, even if it killed me.

Finally, after four long days, she came to me in the middle of the night.

"Joss," I said as I answered the door in only my boxers. I yawned, taking in her work attire. "What are you doing here?"

She gave me a tight smile. "I'm sorry. I know it's late."

"It's okay. Come in," I said, leading her inside. "Hang on, let me put on a shirt."

She looked me over, biting back a smile. "No, you're fine."

I grinned. "You think I'm *fine*?"

She leaned into me, biting her lower lip. And just when I thought she'd kiss me, she reached out and twisted my nipple.

"Hey." I reared back, folding my arms over my chest. "Friends don't purple nurple each other."

She laughed and for that one moment it was like we were back to normal. Still, an annoying voice in the back of my head reminded me that things weren't the same. That they never would be.

I decided it was time to rip off the bandage and get to the fresh wound beneath. "So your dad told me about Houston, said he was taking your mom there for care."

The laughter slid off her face. "Yeah," she said, her eyes drawing away. "He wants to leave Saturday morning."

"As in a four days from now?"

"Yes."

"Are you going with them?"

She looked up and, without a word, gave me the answer.

"You're going with them," I said with a sigh.

"I have no choice."

"You do. You can stay."

"You know why I can't do that," she said. "I don't know how much time my mom has left."

I had known it was coming, but to hear the confirmation from Joss's own mouth was a punch to the gut. Somehow a part of me was still holding onto the hope that she would choose me. "God, I'm such a selfish prick," I said, running a palm down my face.

"You're not."

I turned to her, all my hopes and expectations laid out on my face. "We both know I am, because I wanted you even though you were off limits. Because even though your mom's sick, I still want to be with you. Because despite everything, I want you to stay."

She didn't speak for a gut-wrenchingly long time. "Why?" she finally asked. "What do you think is going to happen in Texas?"

"I'll tell you what's going to happen—" I stopped and forced myself to take deep breaths. "I think you'll go over there and you'll forget what it's like between us. And you'll meet somebody and fool yourself into thinking you could be happy with him."

"That's not going to happen." She stared up at me, pain etched across her features. All of a sudden she grabbed the back of my head and dragged me down for a kiss.

I parted my lips and devoured her, not bothering to question this gift. If, in a second, she decided she was making a mistake, I'd gracefully draw away. But for now, I kissed her back, and would continue to do so until she told me to stop.

Hey, I never said I was a saint.

I backed her into the front door, tugging her shirt upwards. Her fingers hooked into the waistband of my boxer shorts, dragging them down over my ass and down my legs. In very little time, we faced each other, completely naked and panting with desire. Her chest heaved, the curves of her breasts glistening, taunting me. I didn't—couldn't—resist. My bare knees hit the tile floor and I took a breast in my mouth, sucking on it greedily while massaging the other with my hand.

She gripped my hair and arched her back into me, a pained moan escaping her lips. The sound energized me, spurred me to keep going. My lips moved lower, my tongue tracing a wet trail down her stomach. I lifted her leg over my shoulder, giving me access to her most wet spot.

"Jake, please." She shivered, staring at me, and I understood then what she was asking for.

Her entire body bowed off the door when I touched my tongue to her clit and slid it through her folds. I groaned at the taste of her and reached down between my legs to stroke myself. With my free hand, I gripped her fleshy ass and brought her closer, drilling her with my tongue. In response, she ground onto my face, seeking more and finding it when I thrust two fingers inside her.

"I want you inside me," she moaned.

I paused, my fingers still embedded in her heat. "Is that what you want?" I asked, watching her face contort in pleasure when I massaged that special spot.

"Please."

I rose to my feet and carried her to the couch, laying her on her back on the dark leather. I hooked her legs over my arms and crouched over, rubbing my hard cock along her wet folds, teasing, tormenting.

With a glint in her eyes, she reached down between us and positioned my tip at her hot entrance. "Just screw me already."

"Yes, ma'am." I shoved inside her in one swift, solid motion, making her gasp. "I intend on fucking you—" I withdrew slowly. "Until you scream my name— " I paused before driving back in. "Make sure you never forget me."

I repeated the process over and over, drawing out each stroke until she was practically begging before slamming back in. We moved in unison, two bodies fused by love and heartache. I couldn't take my eyes off her face, couldn't stop wishing for a day when we could leave all the bullshit behind us and just be together.

For now, I tried to reach her with my body, my cock, trying to give her all of me.

"Jake," she whispered, her eyes filling with tears.

I stopped, bowing over and taking her face in my hands. "Did I hurt you?" I asked, our lips a whisper apart.

"No," she said just as a tear slid down the side of her face. "I just... I love you."

I stared at her, chest heaving, my entire body coiled to fight for this woman beneath me. Right then, faced with the reality of what I would lose, did I realize that Joss was *It*. Nobody else could or would come close.

I dipped my head and she met me halfway, our tongues colliding, lips sucking, breaths exchanging.

I didn't ask her to stay; I couldn't do that to her. Instead I rocked my hips into hers, making love to her the best I could so maybe, one day in the future, she might remember this night and return to me.

———

"Anybody home?"

Tristan's voice echoed through the front of the store and into the workshop, but I ignored it and focused all my energy into not breaking the thin cherry board as I ran it through a scroll saw.

"You in here?" Tristan's voice came closer and before he long, he stood at the doorway that separated my workspace from the rest of the store. "Dude, it's Friday night. Why are you here?"

I finished cutting the design and turned off the machine. "Why are *you* here?" I shot back before blowing sawdust off the piece of wood inlay. "Don't you have other friends you can annoy?"

"I do but I came here to annoy you," he said with a grin.

"Like you always do," I muttered, turning back to the wood inlay design I had laid out on the table like puzzle pieces. "Feels like you're here all the time, sticking your nose in my business."

He folded his arms across his chest, one eyebrow raised. "So it's a crime to look out for your big brother?"

"I don't need you to look out for me."

"Clearly I do because you're still mooning over some chick who's no good for you. I mean, Joss is hot and all, but she is not worth all this trouble."

"She's leaving tomorrow. For Houston. For the foreseeable future," I ground out. "Feel like an asshole now?"

"Huh." He looked at me, deep in thought. "Guess she doesn't love you as much as she thought."

I gripped the edge of the table, my knuckles turning white. "Is there a reason why you're tormenting me? Do I owe you money or something?"

Tristan shook his head and fixed disapproving eyes on me. "What happened to you, Jake? When we were younger, you were the shit. You were this cool ass guy who could have any girl he wanted. I looked up to you. I wanted to *be* you." He motioned to me. "And now..."

I faced him, anger squaring my shoulders. "Now what?"

"You know what," Tristan said on a sigh.

I ground my teeth together. Maybe my little brother had a point, but hell if I'd ever admit it. "Someday, Tristan, some girl is going to come along and kneecap you and you'll spend the rest of your life on the ground. Maybe then you'll understand."

He shook his head and chuckled. The jackass. "If that woman ever comes along—if she even exists—I sure as hell would fight for her. I wouldn't just let her leave."

"You think I didn't fight for her?" I asked, rounding on him. He was two seconds from getting a knuckle-shaped bruise on his face. "You think I'm just letting her go because I'm such a good guy?"

Tristan stood his ground, his head bobbing up and down. "Yup."

I spun away from him. "What is your angle, T? Are you for me or Joss or against it?" I demanded. "One minute you're telling me she's not worth the breath, the next you're saying I'm not doing enough to prove my love. Get to your point because I'm brewing a migraine."

Tristan shook his head. "I don't know my own point. I don't know anything about love, remember?"

At that moment, I wondered if maybe I didn't either.

June Gray

[thirty-two]

I woke up early the next morning and rushed over to Pembroke Pines before the sun had even broken the horizon. I drove into the neighborhood and parked my car across the street from the orange stucco house I'd once called home, filled with renewed purpose.

I would fight for her. Nothing less would do.

It took fifteen steps to cross the street and make it to the front door. I lifted my fist, ready to rap on the door, but hesitated long enough for my conscience to slip in and make a last appeal.

She needs to be there for Amanda.

I leaned forward and ground my fist to the door, trying to breathe through the fireball in my throat. I tried to tell myself I could be selfish, that I could make it difficult for Joss to leave, but I wasn't that guy. I'd been selfish once, had allowed my emotions to dictate my actions and, as a result, had almost ruined their lives. I refused to do that again.

My hand fell to my side, the air seeping out of me.

The memory of Joss from our last night together flashed before my eyes, of the way her fingers had gripped me as if never intending to let go, of the absolute anguish on her face as she came trembling around me. And later, the tears rolling down her cheeks as she'd said goodbye.

God knows it wasn't easy for her to make this choice. I'd only be hurting her more if I asked her to stay.

Unable to bring more pain to her doorstep, I turned on a heel and walked away, hoping like hell I was doing the right thing this time.

[part five]

jocelyn

[thirty-three]

"Are you ready for tomorrow?" Emerson asked, pressing his hand into the small of my back as we made our way up the walkway.

I slid the key into the front door and entered our house. "Why wouldn't I be?" I asked as he followed me inside, straight into our bedroom. I sat on the bench at the foot of the bed and slid the heels off my feet with a sigh.

Emerson disappeared into the walk-in closet and came out a few minutes later in pajama pants. He'd undoubtedly already hung up his slacks and put his dirty clothes into the hamper, his shoes in their rightful place, and watch nestled in its dark wood holder.

He walked up to me and touched my cheek, his green eyes tender as he took me in. "I just wanted to make sure you don't have any last minute reservations."

I smiled up at him, turning my cheek into his palm. "I have

no reservations about it. None."

He bent down and pressed a quick kiss to my lips. "Good." He walked over to his side of the bed and piled pillows against the metal headboard. The bed was my first purchase when I'd first moved to Houston three years ago but it wasn't comfortable, especially for a man who liked to sit up in bed and read medical journals.

Once I was in my sleep clothes, I slid under the covers and reached for my leather notebook. I opened up to where I'd left the story, intending on writing at least two pages, but no matter how long I stared at the page, I couldn't make my brain think. I'd been stuck at this part of the story—the inciting incident, that moment when the heroine decides she couldn't live without the hero—for several weeks now and it looked as if it would remain incomplete for several weeks more.

I shut the book with a sigh and looked up to find Emerson observing me. He leaned down and kissed my cheek. "It'll come, sweetheart. Don't force it."

I put away the notebook and snuggled into Emerson's side, this man who was hard and soft in just the right places. "Can you read to me?" I asked, threading my fingers through the blond hairs on his chest, the facets of the diamond on my finger catching the light.

"You sure? This is boring stuff for you."

I nodded. "I just want to hear your voice." I closed my eyes and leaned my cheek on his chest as he began to read. His voice was low and pleasant, just what you'd expect from an intern doctor at the MD Anderson Cancer Center.

Right then I decided the life I had chosen was good enough.

The next day found me in a fancy dress, standing at the front of a church with a bouquet in my hands.

"If anyone here can show just cause why these people should not be joined in holy matrimony, speak now or forever hold your peace."

I turned to the guests sitting in pews, halfway expecting someone to speak up. But it had been three years since I last saw Jake; I should have long stopped searching for his face in every crowd by now.

I turned my attention back to the priest as he continued the ceremony.

Finally: "With the power vested in me by God and the state of Texas, I now pronounce you man and wife. You may kiss the bride."

With breath held, I watched as my father leaned down and kissed my mother for the world to see. It was then I finally accepted that my father really loved Mom, that he meant it when he said he'd never leave her side again.

And my family was whole once more.

"Emerson is looking very handsome today," Mom whispered to me at the reception a little while later.

My eyes traveled across the room until they found the man in question. He caught me looking and grinned. "Yeah, he is," I said.

She took hold of my left hand and smiled down at the ring on my finger. "Did you send out the invitations yet?"

"Last week." I pulled my hand away. "Hey, no wedding planning talk during your reception, remember?"

She laughed, a carefree, joyous sound. It wasn't that long

ago I thought I'd never hear it again. "I'm so happy, Joss. I'm just so excited for you to feel this way."

"I will. On my day," I said, threading my arm through hers and leading her back across the dance floor to my father. "For now, dance. Drink. Live it up."

"Were you two gossiping about me?" a deep voice whispered behind me.

I spun around to Emerson. "Possibly."

He wound his arms around my waist and pulled me close. "You happy?" Emerson asked as we began to sway together to the music.

I looked over at my parents—Mom in an off-white cocktail dress that accented her fuller figure and dad in a black suit—as they flirted and laughed on the dance floor. I had never seen her like this, not even with Jake. It was as if someone had turned on a light inside her. My father was probably a small part of the change, but beating cancer had a way of bringing light back into a person's smile. It was as if the old Amanda had died and the woman that survived was happier, more carefree.

I smiled up at my handsome date. "Yes. Very much." I leaned my head on his shoulder and breathed him in, this man who came into my life at just the right time. When it had seemed my mother wouldn't last much longer, Emerson had suggested a new, experimental procedure to his resident. My father and I had been desperate to save Mom and had agreed to try.

Now here she was, healthy and glowing on her wedding day. And here I was, ready to marry the man who had saved her.

———————

A week later, after all of the wedding excitement had died down, Mom came over to the house to help plan my wedding though, honestly, I suspected she just wanted to talk about what she and Dad did on their honeymoon.

"Snorkeling in the Bahamas has always been on my bucket list," Mom said as she flipped through the new wedding magazine she'd bought. "I can now check that off. And also—" She paused, flashing me a sheepish smile. "Having sex on the beach."

"Mom!" I crumpled an RSVP envelope and threw it at her.

She ducked, laughing. "What? Too much information?"

"Way, way too much." I shook my head, smiling to myself as I ripped open the second RSVP envelope that came in the mail. "I don't need to know that you and D—" I froze, my eyes catching on the name printed on the card.

"What is it?" Mom plucked the card from the fingers and looked it over. "Joss, what is this?"

I met her eyes with a sick feeling in my stomach.

"This is an RSVP to your wedding," she said with knotted eyebrows. "From Jake."

I covered my face with my hands, trying to breathe through the tightness in my chest.

"Oh, honey." She sighed. "Why?"

With my eyes fixed on the table's surface, I said, "I was writing out the invitations one night and Emerson was working late and I was drinking. And I thought it might be a good idea to invite him."

Mom slipped the card towards me. "He doesn't share that same sentiment."

I stared at that card, at the angry slashes indicating that he,

Jake Mitchell, would not be attending my wedding. I wasn't surprised to see that X, which was not to say it didn't hurt.

Mom reached across the table and patted my arm. "I thought you already closed that chapter of your life?"

"I did." I held up the envelope. "This is the final nail in the coffin."

Mom didn't look convinced. Honestly, I wasn't sure if I believed my words either but Jake was not coming and that was that.

"What were you expecting?" she asked gently. "Did you really think he was going to come here and watch you get married? He didn't even see you off when you left Florida."

I look down, blinking fast. When I finally looked up, I found her watching me intently.

"Or did you want him to come and stop the wedding?"

I pushed away from the kitchen table and walked over to the cabinet, taking my time to get a glass and fill it with water.

"Joss..."

"Mom, can we just drop it? Please?" I gulped down the contents of the glass but my throat was still a desert.

"Why are you really marrying Emerson, Joss?"

I shook my head, tears stinging my eyes. "Because he loves me."

"And you? Do you love him?"

I slammed the glass onto the granite counter. "Of course." I set my back against the counter, hugging my arms around me. "He and I make sense. And you like him. You get along with him."

Mom sighed. "Joss, I forgave you and Jake a long time ago. You know that, right?"

"Yeah."

"In fact, if it weren't for you two, your father and I wouldn't be where we are today." She stood up and walked over to me. "So please let go of the guilt."

I tried to smile through the tears.

"Don't let the guilt ruin your life," she said, leaning forward and wrapping her arms around me. "If it's Jake you really want, you should tell him."

I didn't give myself the chance to even consider it. If I did, who knew where my thoughts would take me. "That ship has sailed. We've both moved on."

He didn't even bother to say goodbye.

"Don't be that girl, Joss."

"What girl?"

"The kind who settles." She hugged me again, patting my back. "You always have a choice, honey."

"Do I?"

June Gray

[thirty-four]

I couldn't sleep that night. Every time I closed my eyes, all I could see was Jake opening the mailbox and finding the invitation inside. I couldn't stop imagining the emotions he felt when he opened that envelope and saw the name of the man I was planning to marry. Was he angry? Sad? Or was he, like I hoped, happy for me, glad that I'd finally found a stable relationship?

Mom was right: I had sent the invitation with the secret hope that Jake would come and sweep me away. But why, when I was already happy with Emerson?

The answer, I knew, could only be found in one place.

As soon as Emerson arrived home from the hospital early the next morning, I said ,"I think I need to go back to Florida."

Emerson just nodded as he took off his scrubs. "When?"

"After my shift today," I said. My boss at the bookstore where I worked had been gracious, allowing me to take leave on such short notice.

"All right."

I followed him into the bathroom and sat on the edge of the tub as he turned on the shower. "That's it? You're not going to ask why?"

He turned to me, his eyes lined and weary from many hours at the hospital, and shook his head. "I already know why. You have unfinished business you have to take care of before we get married."

I opened my mouth to—I didn't know, deny? Confirm?—but shut it again when I couldn't figure out what to say.

Emerson stood in front of me, completely bare, and laid a hand on my cheek. "I trust you, Joss. I'm confident that, when you come upon that door to the past, you'll do the right thing and close it."

Tears stung my eyes. "You're too good to me."

He pulled me to my feet and held my face in his hands. "I love you, Joss. I want you to walk down that aisle towards me without doubt or reservation."

I bit my lips together, hoping for the same. At that moment, as I undressed and led the way into the shower, I couldn't think of a single reason why I wouldn't want to marry this man.

I almost cancelled the trip to Florida. But in the end, I knew there would always be a "what if" if I didn't go, if I didn't ask Jake the questions burning inside me.

After work, I took a taxi to Bush Intercontinental Airport with my purse and a rolling luggage full of memories.

An hour and a half later, as I settled into my seat in coach, it finally dawned on me that I was actually going home, back to the place I'd been avoiding for over three years. I leaned back and closed my eyes, taking in deep breaths to calm my racing heart. What if it was no longer the place I remembered? Or worse, what if it stayed exactly the same?

"Excuse me, is this seat taken?"

I looked up and found Emerson smiling down at me. He took the seat beside me and leaned in for a kiss on the cheek. "Surprised?"

"What are you doing here?" I asked, unable to hide the hint of panic in my voice.

"I was able to convince Dr. Pataki to take my shifts for a few days. Provided I work her graveyard shifts for the next two weeks." He leaned his elbow on the armrest and took hold of my hand. "But it'd be worth it to see your old stomping grounds. I would love to get to know the younger Joss."

I leaned back in my seat, the smile frozen on my face. I hoped I was a convincing enough actress, otherwise Emerson would be able to see just how much I suddenly dreaded this trip.

It was late by the time we arrived in Miami. As soon as we exited the airport, the humidity wrapped around my skin, reminding me of my former life. Yet despite the familiarity, I couldn't relax, couldn't get past the fear that Emerson would discover my secrets.

We decided to skip dinner, taking a taxi directly to my pre-booked hotel in downtown Miami. In true Emerson style, he upgraded my room to the executive suite.

"You didn't have to do that," I said when we entered the room. I walked through, my mouth falling open as I took in the huge foyer, separate office, living room, and the enormous bedroom that overlooked the Miami bay. Even the overly spacious bathroom had a television. "This must have cost a fortune," I said, looking out the floor-to-ceiling window of the bathroom.

He came up behind me and wrapped his arms around my waist. "This is our first vacation together. I want it to be nice," he said. "Besides this is the only room that has a separate office, in case you get inspired to write."

"With a view like this, I doubt I'd get any writing done."

He nuzzled my neck and murmured, "Then I'm sure we can find other ways to utilize the room."

I closed my eyes, focusing on the feel of his lips against my skin, but part of me couldn't help but imagine Jake standing at the sidewalk below. I twisted away from Emerson, my heart inexplicably pounding. "I'm kind of hungry. Maybe we should go to a restaurant."

He checked his watch. "It's late. How about we just order room service?"

I latched onto the reprieve. "Okay," I said and put some safe distance between us.

After breakfast the next day, we drove over to South Beach and took a walk on the water's edge. I took it all in, my eyes no longer accustomed to the half-naked beachgoers, to the veritable meat-market atmosphere of the entire area. All around us, people were preening, showing off their goods.

"Wow," Emerson said as a heavyset man walked by wearing only a red thong. "I am not mentally prepared for this place."

I grinned, watching a group of women in bikinis playing volleyball, their breasts always just a spike away from popping free. "I guess I'd forgotten how different Miami is. It's like a country all its own."

He took hold of my hand when two men walked by giving me the eye. "I'm not so sure I like it," he said, taking me by surprise. In our year and a half together, Emerson had never displayed any form of jealousy before.

I tugged him down onto the sand. "Let's sit for a bit."

As soon as he sat down, his cell phone began to ring. "I have to take this," he said, getting right back up. "Excuse me a moment."

Finding myself alone, I hooked my arms over my knees and inhaled the ocean air. For the first time since we landed, I felt free to finally take a breath.

People moved around me, enjoying the sunshine and warm water, but in that moment, I felt nothing but regret. This used to be my home. Why had I stayed away for so long?

When Emerson came back minutes later, he wore the look of the troubled.

"What's wrong?"

"Seems one of my patients is having complications after surgery," he said as he settled back down in the sand.

"Do you need to go home then?" I asked, hoping my voice didn't betray my eagerness for him to leave.

He stared at the phone in his hands for a few seconds then shook his head. "No. Pataki has it under control." He turned his attention back to me. "So, should we go drive around your old neighborhood?"

I looked at him, trying to come up with a valid reason not to go. I always meant to go back to my old stomping grounds, I just didn't want Emerson with me.

He stood up and held out a hand. "Come on. I want to see where you grew up."

Forty minutes later, we exited the interstate and drove towards the gated subdivision where I used to live. At the gate, I punched in the code, hoping it no longer worked.

But the gates swung open, allowing us entry to my old life.

We drove slowly through the neighborhood as I pointed out our former neighbors. Finally we came to a rolling stop in front of a stucco house that had once been orange but had since been painted pale green.

"They changed it," I said under my breath. The new owners had also changed the landscaping out front, taking out the palm trees and replacing them with various other plants. They had also added pretty planters on either side of the garage and added a bench by the front door.

I jumped when I felt Emerson take my hand, a reassuring smile on his face.

"Hey, do you want to see my first apartment in Hollywood?" I asked, knowing the danger of running into Jake was high but no longer caring. I had already set off down memory lane; might as well go the rest of the way.

Emerson squeezed my hand and started the car. "I'd love to."

We drove east towards the ocean and I showed him the apartment I'd once shared with Ashley, even pointed out the alley where I'd almost been assaulted.

His forehead wrinkled. "What were you doing out there at night anyway?"

"I had to park one street over and just took a shortcut." When he gave me an incredulous look, I added, "It wasn't my brightest moment."

"I'm glad you weren't hurt," he said, tucking a strand of hair behind my ear.

We coasted through Hollywood Boulevard as I pointed out my favorite stores and restaurants. When we passed by the old garage-turned-furniture store, I held my breath. Surprisingly— or not—the store was still there. Only now it was twice as big as before, appearing to have expanded to the building next door.

Good for you, Jake, I thought with a smile.

It took me entirely too long to realize that Emerson had turned into the store lot and had parked the car.

"What are you doing?" I asked in a high-pitched voice. I caught myself and forced the panic out of my voice. "Why are we stopping here?"

He turned and grinned at me. "I know you like this brand of furniture. You're always looking for it when we go into hotels and stores."

I swallowed, wishing for the first time that Emerson wasn't so observant. "And?"

"I just thought of what I could get you as a wedding present." He jumped out of the car and opened my car. "Come on. I'll tell you inside."

I didn't move. Behind the relative safety of the windshield, I stared at the huge garage doors, feeling completely unprepared. My hair was a wind blown mess, my dress all kinds of wrinkled, and I had put on very little makeup. I had imagined this reunion with Jake so many times over the years and looking a hot mess with my fiancé in tow was definitely not it.

Emerson bent down and peered at me through the open door. "You okay? You're kind of pale."

I held my hand to my stomach. "I'm not feeling well. Can we just go back to the hotel?"

He glanced at the store then back at me. "All right."

At that moment, the front door opened and a woman walked through. She held the door open as a tall man with dark hair passed through, carrying a side table in his arms.

I sucked in a breath and watched as Jake carried the table to the woman's car, taking the time to set it in the trunk with care. Then they shook hands and she drove away.

He would have gone back into the store, completely oblivious to my presence, but suddenly Emerson was in front of him, shaking his hand. They spoke a few seconds before Emerson pointed to the car. To me.

Time slowed as Jake turned his head, his blue eyes finding me.

[thirty-five]

Jake's eyebrows drew together as he looked at me, his mouth falling open. He looked different now, a dark brown beard covering the lower half of his handsome face. He wore a button-down shirt with its sleeves rolled up and dark jeans, looking sexier than anyone had any right to be.

"Joss?"

I looked up and realized Emerson had opened my door. "Come on. Come meet the craftsman who makes the furniture you love," he said, holding out a hand.

I stepped out of the car, brushing my fingers through my hair. Jake never took his eyes off me, quietly taking me in as I approached, no doubt taking stock of what had changed and what was the same.

I held out my hand and, surprising even myself, I said, "Nice to meet you."

He looked confused for a second then shook my hand.

"Hi," he said in a soft rasp. He blinked a few times, coming back to his senses. "So your boyfriend—"

"Fiancé, actually," Emerson said, slinging an arm over my shoulder.

I spied a muscle in Jake's jaw tic. "My mistake. He says he'd like to commission a bed."

Emerson squeezed my shoulders. "As a wedding present for my beautiful bride." Oblivious to Jake's discomfort, he continued, "A king, don't you think, sweetheart? Nice and big so the kids can snuggle up with us on Sunday morning."

Jake's face darkened. "Kids?"

"No," I said quickly. "We don't have any."

Emerson laughed. "Sorry. Projecting too far into the future."

Jake tried to keep a poker face, but I could see the storm brewing in his eyes.

"Would you have time to discuss this project?" Emerson asked.

Jake looked at his watch then up at me. "Sure. Come to my office," he said and held the door open. As I passed, I felt his hand brush against my arm and I jerked back like I'd been electrocuted. Jake only snickered.

The store was completely different now. Whereas it once retained the rough garage interior, now the cement floors had been stained a dark color, the walls and ceilings done in exposed brick. The furniture, once haphazardly placed, were now grouped together in room scenes.

"It looks amazing in here," I said and caught the look of surprise on Jake's face.

"Thank you," he said curtly.

We entered his office, a spacious area with an urban rustic feel.

"Please," he said, motioning to the two leather armchairs in front of a massive wood and metal desk.

Emerson and I sat down, while Jake grabbed a sketchbook, similar to the one I had in my possession. He flipped to a blank page and clicked his pen. "What kind of bed were you looking for?"

I wanted him to look at me but his gaze was fixed firmly on Emerson. I said, "We weren't really looking for a b—"

"I'd like something rustic modern, exactly your style here," Emerson interrupted, running his hand along Jake's desk.

"And you?"

My stomach flip-flopped when I looked up and found Jake raising an eyebrow at me. Three years apart and one look from him still reduces me to mush.

Emerson tapped my arm. "Joss?"

"I'm not sure. Whichever you like, I guess," I said with a shrug, dragging my eyes away from Jake, stopping at the bookshelves taking up one side of the room. My eyes flew to Jake and I bit my lips together to keep from asking how he managed to get a hold of it when I'd sold it three years prior.

Jake gave only the smallest shake of the head before turning back to Emerson as the two continued to discuss the design of the bed. I sat wordlessly, trying but failing to calm my nerves. How could I when only a desk separated me from the man who had haunted my dreams for so long?

After the two came up with a design, Jake stood up.

"Thank you for your time," Emerson said, shaking Jake's

hand. "How long do you think it will take to build?"

The skin between Jake's eyebrows wrinkled as he looked down at the sketch.

"This won't work," I blurted out, rising to my feet. I turned to Emerson. "There's no way he'd be willing to drive a king-sized bed all the way to Houston."

Jake's eyes flicked up to mine, his blue gaze boring into my brain. "You'd be surprised how far I'd be willing to go." When he blinked, the connection broke and his expression once again shuttered. "I do have the means to ship furniture all over the country."

Emerson smiled at me. "See? The man has it all worked out."

Jake folded his arms across his chest and raised an eyebrow, looking both sexy and intimidating at once. "It's very nice to meet you, Emerson. Jocelyn."

I said nothing. I only flashed him one last meaningful look before leaving.

I tossed and turned in bed that night, unable to get the image of Jake's glare out of my mind. I didn't blame him for being angry. Hell, I'd showed up at his place of business—however unintentionally—with a fiancé. He had every right to be pissed.

But I had come back to Florida to get answers and I was determined to get them.

After Emerson took his melatonin pill and went to sleep, I got dressed and called down to valet. Ten minutes later, I was on my way to Hollywood, Florida.

It was nearly midnight by the time I parked in the driveway of Jake's house. I stood at his doorstep for an inordinately long amount of time, wondering if I was doing the right thing, if I'd even be welcome. Would he even open the door to the stranger I'd become?

My question was answered a moment later when the swung open and Jake stood at the door shirtless and barefoot, holding a bottle of beer. He didn't let me in immediately. He simply set one arm on the doorframe and stared at me through hooded eyes. "What are you doing here so late?" he asked, taking a casual sip of his beer.

"Can I come in?" I asked, trying to pretend his nearness, his very scent, didn't do things to my insides. It was infuriating that, after all this time, he still had that effect on me.

"Where is *he*?" he asked, motioning to the car behind me.

"He's back at the hotel."

He reached out and took hold of my left hand, lifting it up to the light. "Beautiful ring, Joss. Huge rock. Well done."

I yanked my hand back. "Are you going to let me in or not?"

He didn't say a thing, acting as though he had no intention of letting me in. After a long, tense moment, he finally stepped aside.

"Your place looks... different." All around the room were brown boxes, areas that normally held furniture now bare.

"That happens. Things change in three or so years."

I spun around to him, my anger simmering to the surface, the question that had been tormenting me for over three years finally boiling over. "Why didn't you say goodbye?" I swallowed, fighting to keep my voice from wavering. "I called but you never answered. And, believe me, I waited. Even at the airport I held back, hoping you'd run in at the last minute. But you never did."

His eyes flashed and jaw hardened. "I was trying to do the right thing."

"By making me think it was over?"

"By making it easier for you to leave."

Tears stung my eyes at the memory of the day I'd left, my entire heart breaking as I'd looked around one last time before boarding the plane. "Well you failed. Miserably."

His jaw clenched as he blinked down at me. It was wrong but part of me wanted him to just apologize and kiss me, sure that one gesture had the power to erase the heartache that had accumulated all these years.

"So you stayed away for three years," he began, his voice raw with emotion. "And then show up at my place of business with a fiancé and a rock the size of my fist?"

I stepped away, unable to stand the heat of his anger any longer. "I'm sorry. I didn't mean to come to your store. Emers—"

"Don't you fucking say his name to me," he bit out.

I lifted my chin. "Stop acting like you have any claim to me. Because you don't."

"Oh, I don't?" He slammed the beer down and closed the distance between us again. His arm snaked around my waist, keeping me from taking another step. "Then what the hell are you doing here?"

"I..." I blinked up at him, finding it hard to breathe. "I needed to talk to you."

"You needed to see me," he said in a low, raspy voice that I felt down my spine. "You couldn't stay away. You never could."

"I managed to stay away for three years, didn't I?"

The fire in his eyes raged. He lowered his head until our noses were only inches apart. "If you think I'm making a bed for you and another man, you have lost your fucking mind," he growled.

The fight in me died. "I'm sorry. I never meant for any of this to happen." I tried to step away but he tightened his hold on me.

"It's not over between us, Joss," he said in a low rumble that I felt in my bones. His blue eyes flew all over my face, the anger gone, only now the emotion that replaced it was equally daunting. "Tell me, Joss: Have you found your passion?"

"I..." I considered telling him about the novel but had no wind left in my lungs to speak. "Yes," I managed to say.

He said nothing, only blinked down at me.

"And your passion... it looks like you're doing really well," I said to ease the tension.

"I am. I'm moving to Boston to open another store."

"When?"

His eyes flicked around the room. "Soon."

"Is that why you're not coming to the wedding?"

"You know why I'm not coming."

I couldn't stand the expression on his face, so I changed the subject. "How did you get my bookshelf?"

"A client contacted me, telling me they'd seen one of my pieces listed on Craigslist like some trash piece of furniture," he said through stiff lips.

"It broke my heart to have to sell it, but I couldn't take it to Texas with me." I added in a whisper, "Believe me, I wanted to."

"It's yours again, if you want it."

I looked at him for a long time, trying to read the expression there. "Just the bookcase?"

"Joss..." He leaned closer until his lips touched the shell of my ear. "You know exactly what I'm offering."

I couldn't breathe, couldn't think past the thought that less than an inch separated us at that moment. There was no mistaking his intention and I'd be a freaking liar if I said I didn't want it as well. Even now, every particle in my body stood on end, reaching out to him.

I couldn't not touch him anymore. I reached up and pressed my hand on his bare chest, feeling the rapid thumping of his heart. He took another step closer and crushed our bodies together, his heat searing me inside and out.

"Do you feel that?" he asked, pressing his hard length against my stomach. "That's three years of frustration and want."

"I feel it." And, led by my base instinct, I slid my hand from his chest down to his crotch, curling my fingers around his erection. "You have no idea how many times I've dreamed of wrapping my lips around you, hearing you groan when I take you in my mouth..."

His lips fell open. And just when I thought he'd kiss me, he loosened his hold around my waist and took a step back. "No. We're not doing this again."

"But..." I couldn't breathe. Everything in me cried out for him.

"If you want me, you have me." He swallowed hard. "But I'm not sharing you with anyone. Not anymore."

I shook my head, fisting my hands at my sides to keep from reaching out for him. "Forget about everyone else right now. It's just you and me."

"We tried that once, remember?" he asked with a hard edge to his voice. "This time I want you without strings or conditions. No more lying or hiding."

I fought to catch my breath. "Was that an ultimatum?"

"Take it how you want it. If you say no again, I'm done. I'm moving on. I've had enough of this… this…" He clawed at his chest. "This torture."

Tears blurred my vision. I couldn't find the words to convey how sorry I was for putting him through the agony. "But you're moving," was all I could say.

He didn't hesitate. "So come with me."

[thirty-six]

Emerson was still asleep when I tiptoed into the hotel room at almost three in the morning. I sat on the edge of the bed and watched him sleep, this wonderful man who was counting on me to close the book on my past.

I had intended to do just that, only the visit with Jake had thrown me back into the story, and again I found myself having to choose between two people I loved. Jake had always been the wrong choice, the person I should never have reached for. And yet he was the only person I could not let go.

Filled with a need to express my thoughts, I retrieved my laptop and took it to the office at the other side of the suite. I opened up an email and began to compose a letter.

Jake,

Three years ago we shared an extraordinary

night together. Even now I still think about it, still think about the way you shielded me with your body, holding me so tight like you never intended to let go. You always tried to do that, to protect me from pain.

But then you yourself hurt me by not saying goodbye. I didn't realize until today, until I saw you again, how much that really hurt. How much it still hurts.

I came back to Florida to get closure, to get that goodbye I never got. But seeing you again after all these years...

My fingers paused, hovering over the keys. For the life of me, I couldn't figure out what next to say. With a groan, I dropped my head on the desk while my heart and my head battled it out, fighting for my happiness and sanity.

Finally I shut the computer and climbed into bed, curling up inside Emerson's arms. Only when he stirred and kissed my hair did my warring sides call a ceasefire. At least for the time being.

"So I was thinking, we could go drive down to the Keys today," Emerson said during brunch. "I'd love nothing more than to kiss you at the southernmost point of the United States."

"Sounds good." I lifted the coffee mug up to my lips, my brain still turning, twisting, trying to figure out what to do.

"Or perhaps see that coral castle in Homestead?"

"How about you go to the castle and I'll catch up with you this afternoon? I need to take care of something first."

He blinked at me behind those glasses, trying to assess my mood. "What is it?"

"Just an errand."

He didn't believe me, that much was clear, but I could see the struggle going on behind his carefully expressionless facade. Despite it all, Emerson still wanted to give me the benefit of the doubt. "Sure you don't want me to come with you?"

"Yeah. I think I need to do this alone." I reached across the table and patted his hand, not knowing how to alleviate his worries when I myself didn't know how things would work out. "But hey, maybe we can go watch a Miami Heat game tonight? I think they're playing the Cavaliers."

He didn't reply for a long time. Finally, he shook his head. "No. They're playing the Celtics."

"Oh."

"I'll go ahead and buy the tickets," he said, dabbing at the corner of his mouth with a napkin. "You go do what you have to do and meet me back at the hotel."

I leaned over and kissed his cheek. "You're too good to me," I said, wondering if he understood my meaning, fearing one day he'd finally agree.

I drove back up to Hollywood an hour later, recalling the events of last night when Jake had asked me to come to Boston with him.

"I don't know," I'd told him. "I can't just leave Emerson

like that."

"It's simple: You either go back to your life in Texas, knowing exactly what awaits you, or you could come with me to Boston and start over."

"It's a little more complicated than that," I'd said.

He'd held his palm up to my cheek, shaking his head. "No, Joss. It's not."

My insides began to tremble the moment I drove into Rochester Furniture's parking lot, the nerves increasing, becoming an all out quake when I got out of the car and pushed the front doors open.

At the entrance, I scanned the showroom teeming with salespeople and customers. My heart twitched when, at the back of the store, I caught sight of a tall man with dark hair and warm blue eyes.

It was then I came to a crushing realization: Jake was the one. It had been him all along. I'd been fooling myself these past few years thinking I could be happy with anyone else. For the first time in a long time, I knew exactly what I wanted.

With tear-blurred eyes I watched him, willing him to turn around and see me.

I couldn't wait anymore. I took a step forward… and froze as a beautiful woman approached him, wrapping her arms around his neck. He bent down and gave her a kiss on the cheek, greeting her with intimate familiarity. I stood, transfixed, as he leaned into her, grinning as he told her something that made her laugh.

"Joss, is that you?"

I turned and found a familiar face smiling down at me. "Tristan," I said in surprise.

He bent down and air-kissed my cheek. "I thought you'd moved to Texas?"

"I did."

He frowned. "Are you back then?"

"No. I'm just visiting."

His eyes roamed all over me, catching on the ring on my finger. "Congrats," he said, motioning to my left hand.

"Thank you."

He followed my gaze and saw Jake and the woman still engaged in flirtatious conversation. "That's Migdalia," he said.

Migdalia, with the curly blonde hair and the sunny smile, who was familiar enough to touch his beard and rub her palm along his jaw. "She's pretty," I said, feeling the hope in me start to drain.

Tristan nodded. "And a really cool person too."

"How long?" I whispered, trying not to sound crushed. If Tristan knew I was jealous, who knew what he'd do.

"How long what?"

"Have they been together?"

Tristan glanced back towards the couple before turning back to me with eyebrows knotted. I held my breath, hoping he'd say they were just friends, but he dashed my hopes when he said, "A long time now."

"He never even told me," I said under my breath.

"Maybe he didn't want to hurt you."

I blinked rapidly, trying to keep my disappointment from spilling over onto my cheeks. "Is he happy?"

"Certainly looks it."

I turned away, my heart breaking in a million pieces. "Can you just tell him I came by?" I asked, taking a deep, fortifying breath.

"You're not going to talk to him?" he asked.

"No. I have to get going." I reached into my purse and pulled out a leather sketchbook. "And could you give this to him for me?"

"Sure." He flipped through the first few pages. "Isn't this the sketchbook he lost? He's been looking all over for this."

"He left it at the house when he moved out." I felt a clawing in my stomach at the idea of giving back this thing that had become a part of my life. I'd written many letters in there, things that I wanted to say over the years but couldn't. And now that it was going back to its original owner, I felt bereft, like I'd lost my last line of communication with Jake. "It's probably time I gave it back."

"Sure." Tristan bent down and hugged me. "Good to see you again"

"You too."

"Joss," Tristan said.

"Yes?"

He flashed me a sad sort of smile. "Good luck. You know, with the wedding and everything."

"Thank you."

I sat in the car for a long time, staring at the store through tear-blurred eyes. A part of me hoped for Jake to see me, to come out and tell me that it was all a misunderstanding. But the better part of me knew the right thing to do was give Jake his shot at a good life, one that wasn't complicated by me. I owed him that, at least.

With an aching heart, I started the car and drove away.

When I got back to the hotel, I found our luggage packed and ready in the foyer of the suite.

"Hello?" I called out. I walked around until I found Emerson in the office area with a laptop on the desk in front of him. *My* laptop.

"What are you doing?" I asked, fighting the urge to run over and slam my computer shut.

He looked up, a grave expression on his face. He took off his glasses and set them on the desk. "I was going online to buy basketball tickets but I found this instead." He turned the laptop around and showed me the email on the screen.

I walked over and shut it. "What are you doing looking through my things?"

"That Jake is the same one from Rochester Furniture, isn't it?" he asked in a carefully even voice. When I didn't answer, he said, "And please don't insult my intelligence. I saw the way you looked at him. At the time I thought maybe you were just seeing an attractive man but now that I've seen the email and I see you standing there trying to come up with an excuse, I realize it's not just a coincidence."

I swallowed, my heart racing. "Yes. That's him."

"And I am the idiot who drove you right back to him."

I took a step forward. "I went to see him today," I said, suddenly filled with the need to confess.

"You don't have to explain anything." He pushed away from the desk, rising to his feet. "I just want to know how you wanted to finish that letter. Are you leaving me for him?"

I shook my head, hot tears sliding down my cheeks. The vision of Jake with the other woman bore into my mind, a painful reminder that Jake was my past. It was time to leave him there.

"No," I whispered.

jake

June Gray

[thirty-seven]

"Damn you have a lot of books," Tristan said as he lifted the last box into the back of the U-haul truck. "Please tell me this is the last of it?"

"Let me check." I went back inside the house, going through every room to make sure I hadn't left anything behind. Finally, in the living room, I paused and said a silent goodbye to my home. I imagined the new owners moving in—a couple and their two young kids—making this space their own, filling the house with laughter and warmth. The image was a happy one yet I felt nothing but unbearable sadness.

"Good to go?" Tristan called from the front door. "We still got a freaking twenty-four hour drive ahead of us."

I followed him out, locking the door behind me one last time. Then we dropped by the store, ironing out any last minute issues with Alexis, my branch manager, before finally getting on I-95 heading north.

"So what's your plan while in Boston?" I asked, needing to fill the silence. Otherwise I'd end up thinking about Joss again, and that was something I'd vowed to stop doing. A week had passed since that night at my house, since I asked her to move to Boston with me and she promptly disappeared from my life once again.

"See the folks, get some beer with the buds, maybe see a honey or two."

I flashed him a dubious look. "You only have one full day before flying back."

"One full day is all I need," he said with a chuckle.

"I guess that's all you need when you only last five minutes," I said, punching his shoulder.

"Fucker," he said with a chuckle. "So hey, I have something to tell you."

Every suspicious bone in my body was immediately on high alert. "What the hell did you do now?"

"Actually, it's more like what I *didn't* do."

I ground my molars together, waiting for the blow. I'd noticed my brother acting strangely the past week but hadn't cared enough to ask. I'd assumed he was only being his usual prick self. "Just tell me."

"Okay, but remember that I only have your best interest at heart."

"Don't make me pull over, Tristan."

"Fine." He held up his hands in surrender. "Joss came by the store the other day."

The truck jerked a little on the road. "What? When?"

"Sunday morning."

"How come I didn't see her?" I turned to him. "What did you say to her?"

"I didn't say anything. She saw you with Mig and assumed you two were together."

"Let me guess: You didn't exactly clear up the misunderstanding?"

"It wasn't my place."

I ground my molars to keep from shouting. Even as mad as I was, a part of me wondered if maybe Tristan had done the right thing. True, I had asked Joss to come with me to Boston, but the fact that she'd hesitated was answer enough for me. She hadn't wanted me three years ago, and she certainly hadn't wanted me a week ago. A man's ego can only take so much. It was officially time to give up the ghost.

"Jake?" Tristan asked after some time. "I'm sorry, man. I really was trying to help you."

I sighed, though it came out halfway like a growl. "Forget it."

"You for real?"

"Yeah." I shook my head, glancing at the rearview mirror. "I've officially left Florida—and Joss—behind. I'm done."

"That... I'm..." In place of words, he gave a slow clap. "Good deal, brother. Proud of you."

"Fuck off."

He set a hand on my shoulder and gave it a shake. "No, really. I'm happy to hear that. I thought you were never going to get over your Joss obsession."

"She wasn't an obsession," I bit out.

"Okay then, your *love*," Tristan said. "Potato, potato."

I pressed the button to wash the windshield, my eyes following the water droplets before the wipers swept them away. "I'm done talking about her. In fact, I'm completely done with Jocelyn Blake. Period."

It was his turn to release a sigh. "I respect that. But there's one last thing." He bent over and rummaged in the backpack by his feet, coming up with a book. "She asked me to give this to you." I glanced at the leather-bound notebook, thinking at first it was the one I'd given Joss at her graduation. "It's your sketchbook. The one you lost a while back."

I swallowed down the disappointment. A part of me had hoped she had given me her journal. But then again, the last thing I needed was to be haunted by her words and thoughts.

"What's in there that's so important?" Tristan asked.

"Nothing. Just sketches," I said, taking hold of the book and throwing it onto the seat between us.

———————

Tristan and I took turns sleeping and driving, and twenty four hours later, we finally pulled into our parents' driveway.

After we caught up on sleep, we (including our parents) headed over to my new house.

Tristan was first to react to the rundown colonial-style house before us. It had once been an ocean blue color but the paint had since faded and chipped, some of the white shutters falling off its hinges. "You saw this house in person before you bought it, right?" he asked, approaching the overgrown bushes flanking the walkway.

"Yes. On my last visit," I said.

"And you still bought it?" Dad asked.

Tristan chuckled. "I thought you were loaded now? Is this all you could afford?"

Mom smacked my brother upside the head. "You two leave him alone. I'm sure Jake has a plan."

I stepped up to the creaky porch, adding it to the mental list of things that needed to be repaired. "This is a nice neighborhood and the house is in good shape. It just needs some updates." I stuck the key in the lock and opened the door, allowing my mother inside before heading in.

We walked through the empty house, left surprisingly clean by the previous owner. Everyone voiced opinions on things that needed remodeling, adding to my already-long list of renovations. But for now the most important part—the complete overhaul of my life—had officially begun.

Mom stayed behind, turning her attention to wiping down the cabinets in the kitchen while Dad, Tristan and I worked on unloading furniture. Several hours later, with an empty truck and a clean kitchen, we sat around the island and celebrated with pizza and beer.

"To Jake," Tristan said, raising his bottle. "To going back to your roots."

"I have to say, it's nice to have the whole gang back together," Mom said, smiling at the three men around the room. But her gaze caught and sharpened on my brother. "And when are you planning on moving back home?"

Tristan drained his beer and stood up. "Sorry, Ma. I just remembered we gotta get the truck back to the rental place before they close for the day."

Mom shook her head. "We're not done talking about this."

Tristan chuckled, bending over to drop a kiss on her head. "I don't doubt that for a second."

"Here, take my pickup," Dad said, throwing his keys my way.

I followed Tristan out, chuckling behind him. "You know she's not going to let this go. Might as well start planning on opening a T's Garage here in Boston."

"Boston is home and all," Tristan said, standing in the driveway. "But Miami is where my heart belongs right now."

"I give you a year, two tops." The thought of my brother helplessly bowing down to love brought a smile to my face. "Then you'll get married and move back here."

"Screw that. I'm a bachelor for life."

My amusement died down as reality sunk in. "Yeah, well, maybe you won't be the only one."

He slung an arm over my shoulder. "Won't be so bad, bro. We can go to clubs together. We'll be the two old geezers standing at the bar, bobbing our heads to the music like the SNL Roxbury Guys," he said. "It'll be epic."

"Shit, that's sad," I said before we got into separate vehicles and returned the U-haul back to the rental facility.

[thirty-eight]

Months passed quickly. Between house renovations and setting up a workshop in a warehouse, I had very little time for anything else.

"It's like you're back in Florida," Mom said during a Sunday dinner I was actually able to attend. "I've seen you a total of three times since you moved here."

"Sorry, Ma. It's been a hectic five months."

"You need to slow down a bit, son," Dad piped in, coming in with the bowl of vegetables and setting it on the table. "Working yourself to an early grave."

"Speaking of…" I grinned, my chest swelling wide pride. "I have some news."

Mom's eyes widened. "You're getting married?"

I nearly choked on my mashed potatoes. "No. No."

"Well why the heck not?"

"He hasn't even brought a girl over, Myra," Dad said. He

squinted at me thoughtfully. "Are you coming out of the closet?"

"No!" I set the napkin down on the table, intending to steer this conversation back to calm waters. "It's about my business."

"Oh," Mom said, the disappointment clear in her voice.

Dad chuckled. "Why didn't you say so?"

"When I got here I put in a bid to do restoration work at the Boston Public Library, never really thinking it would amount to anything. Well, they called me yesterday and told me I got the job. My crew and I start in a few weeks."

"Honey, that's wonderful!" Mom said.

Dad beamed. "'Atta boy."

"This means I'll have to put the furniture side of things on the back burner. The new showroom will just have to wait," I said. "But for now I get to work in a library, surrounded by books. It's the perfect job."

"Now all you need is a special person in your life," Mom said with a twinkle in her eye. "Just say the word. I already have a list of eligible bachelorettes."

I shook my head, willingly pushing away the thought that was trying to edge its way back in. "No thanks, Ma. The last thing I need right now is a relationship."

"Come on Jake, you're not getting any younger," Mom said.

I laughed, despite myself. "My ovaries are fine, I assure you."

Mom glared at me. She probably would have smacked me upside the head had she been hitting distance. "I'm ready for grandkids."

I shook my head, maintaining the carefree facade. "Might

have better luck with Tristan then. He probably already has a bunch of little T's running around Miami."

Now *that* comment was enough to bring my mother to her feet to clip her oldest son's ear.

That night I went home and stood in the middle of my bedroom, surveying the barely-made bed and the boxes lining the walls. I had been here months, had already renovated my bathroom and the kitchen, and yet I hadn't managed to finish unpacking my shit. What the hell was I waiting for?

I kicked off my boots and dropped to my knees, slicing open the tape on the box and pulling out its contents. After I had unpacked most of the boxes, I went to the kitchen to grab a beer. It was during my search for the bottle opener that I found my sketchbook in one of the drawers.

I set the leather book on the counter, its leather cords tied together neatly, and stared at it as I drank my beer. A small part of me wanted to open up to that page with Joss's face, to see if those feelings were still there, but the smarter part of me knew that doing so would open up old wounds. So I threw it back inside the drawer and did what I'd become good at these past several months: I forced it out of my mind.

One Saturday morning, after working a long night at the library, I awoke to the sound of a high-pitched alarm. I grabbed my phone and cracked open an eye, wondering why the hell my phone was screaming at me so early on a weekend.

The words *Wedding Day* flashed across the screen. It took

my drowsy brain a few seconds to catch up, but when it did, I was instantly wide awake.

Today, at five in the afternoon, one Jocelyn Blake was going to walk down the aisle towards her future husband.

I jabbed at my phone, erasing the alarm as fast as humanly possible, cursing my brother for setting it back in Florida, the same day I'd come home to find that invitation in my mailbox. After years without hearing from Joss, finding that invitation had been jarring. Unsettling.

And to see her name alongside another man's—Emerson *Fucking* Peterson—in that fancy-dancy calligraphic print had been like a knife to the chest.

For the life of me, I couldn't figure out why the hell she had sent me, of all people, a wedding invitation. Surely she'd known that I was still holding my breath, waiting for her return? Had Joss always been so ruthless and goddamned cruel?

It was Tristan who'd come up with the only logical explanation.

"Don't you see?" he'd said. "She wants you to come to the wedding and stand up when the priest asks if anyone has any objections or whatever the hell it is they say."

A part of me—the desperate, hopeless romantic that refused to die—had wanted to do just that. What could be more valiant than to go over there and make a ruckus and ride away from the church with the bride on the back of a motorcycle? But the sane part of me had sneered at that ridiculous notion.

"Fuck that," I'd said and scratched out an X on the rsvp card. "I'm done chasing after her."

Tristan had made a grab for my phone, playing around with it before handing it back. "I'm putting the wedding date in your calendar," he'd said.

"What the hell for?"

He'd flashed me a confident smile. "Because I know that when that day rolls around, you'll have moved on. And you'll need a reminder to celebrate your freedom."

Tristan was right about one thing: I had moved on. To be free of Joss was a victory, to be sure, but I wasn't so convinced it was something to celebrate.

I lay back in bed, folding an arm over my eyes with the intention of sinking back to sleep, but my stomach had other plans. With a sigh I forced myself to get up and go into the kitchen to make a sandwich. When I grabbed the orange juice bottle, I was suddenly reminded of that afternoon in Florida, when a delirious Joss had fallen in a puddle of juice. I had taken care of her that afternoon, listening to her nonsensical mumblings while I wiped her down, all the while trying to ignore the twinge in my chest. I'd told myself I loved her like a younger sister, but even then I'd known I was only lying to myself. I loved Joss in every way a man could love a woman, a red hot blaze that refused to be extinguished.

And now I loved her enough to let go, to find a way to be happy with her choices even if she hadn't chosen me.

As I bit into my sandwich, I remembered the sketchbook. With a burst of nostalgia, I pulled it out of the drawer and untied the cords that wrapped around its middle. I flipped through the first pages, going past my sketches, and to the face of the woman whose spirit I was never able to capture on paper. As I stared at the imperfect representation of Joss, I wondered what she was thinking at that moment in Texas, if she was excited or panicking.

It was then, as I looked in her pencil eyes, that I noticed the ink on the back of the paper. I turned the page and found Joss's handwriting. Page after page were entries from Joss, all beginning with *Dear Jake*.

I swallowed, my eyes stinging. Ignoring the knives embedded in my chest, I flipped back to the first entry and began to read.

I spent the next few hours turning page after page, poring over Joss's thoughts during the time we were apart. She told me about the feeling of helplessness as she tried to make amends with her mom, the desperation when her mom was diagnosed with cancer. She described her time in Houston, her job as a freelance writer, and the day she accepted a date with the doctor who saved her mother's life. But within those letters she revealed how much she missed me, how every day she thought of me and wished for a different outcome.

It was nearing three in the afternoon by the time I reached the last entry. By then I was physically and emotionally exhausted but there was no stopping now. I needed to see this through to the bitter end.

Dear Jake,

Last week Emerson dropped down to one knee and proposed. And you know the first thought that popped in my mind?

I wonder how Jake would have done it.

That's wrong on so many levels, mainly because Emerson has been a good, loyal boyfriend. He loves me so much and I know—I know—he will do everything in his power to give me a good, stable life.

But I couldn't give him an answer. Not yet. We've barely just moved in together. Marriage was the furthest thing from my mind. So I asked him for a few days to think it over. He, of course, gave me space. Said he wanted me to be sure when I agreed to marry him.

I thought about it for a long time. There might have been wine and tears involved. My heart was torn because, as much as I wanted the life he was offering, I wasn't ready to give up the possibility of a future with you.

But there was that little seed of a doubt, that you no longer wanted me, that you'd moved on. Surely after three years you've found someone easier to love. And why wouldn't you? You're an amazing guy.

So I said yes.

I owe it to Emerson to give our relationship a fair chance, and I owe it to myself to find a love that isn't mired in pain. But mostly I owe it to you to move on, to give you the chance to live your life like intended. I often look at your drawing of me, wondering what the hell you see, why it was that you fell in love with me. Whatever it is, I hope you find it

*in someone else, someone more worthy. You deserve
someone who can love you with their whole heart,
without fear or apprehension. I only hope I can love
Emerson like he deserves.*

*I love you, Jake. That will never change. And
when I walk down that aisle towards another man,
I'll try not to think of you. When I say those two
words, just know that in the deepest part of my heart,
I'll be hoping it was you.*

Joss

I swiped a palm down my face, my entire body weighted
down by regret. I set my elbows on the table and hung my
head, reading the last few lines over and over again until my
vision blurred.

And then it finally dawned on me what she was trying to
say. I jumped up from the stool and grabbed my phone, before
realizing I no longer knew Joss's number.

I hurried to the bedroom and got dressed. I would never
make it to Houston in time to stop the wedding but I couldn't
sit here twiddling my thumbs. I needed to do something.

I'll be hoping it was you.

The words swirled around in my mind while I grabbed my
wallet and phone and made a beeline for the door.

And then I bumped into Joss.

[thirty-nine]

The sight of Joss at my doorstep knocked me back a step. "You're not in Houston."

She smiled, shaking her head. "No, I'm not."

"You're supposed to be getting married in a few hours."

Her smile grew. "Guess I'll be late." She smiled up at me, taking a step closer. "Can I come in?"

I stared at her, afraid to buckle under the weight of this moment. I had spent almost half a year trying to shut out any and all thoughts of Joss, and now here she was again, asking to be let back in. I'd have to be monumentally stupid to let that happen again.

But then again, I had always been a bit of a dumbass.

I stepped aside and allowed her to step through the threshold. "What are you doing here?"

"You asked me to come to Boston. So I came."

I folded my arms across my chest. "What about

Emerson?"

"I broke off the engagement when we got back to Houston."

My eyebrows drew together. "Why?"

"I realized my heart was already taken." She grabbed my hand and pressed something hard into it. When I looked down I found the African Blackwood heart I'd made for her a long time ago.

I turned the wood carving over and over in my hands, trying to collect my thoughts, feeling the walls I'd spent months rebuilding starting to crumble at my feet.

"It's yours, if you still want it," she said in a small, hopeful voice.

I squeezed my hand around the heart and finally looked up. Then I nodded, the words lodged in my throat.

Tears glistened at the edge of her eyes and overflowed onto her cheeks. "It's always been yours," she said, her lips trembling.

Unable to hold back any longer, I spanned the distance between us and took hold of her face, crushing my lips to hers. I groaned as she opened up and let me in, the taste of her frying my brain. I didn't know until that moment how much I needed her, and now that she was back in my arms, I didn't think I could ever let go again.

We only broke away when we ran out of breath. I pressed my forehead to hers, breathing hard, my heart beating an erratic, hopeful beat in my chest. "Tell me you're here to stay," I whispered against her lips.

Her face split apart in a wide smile. "You're never going to get rid of me now."

Laughing in relief, I swept her into my arms and carried her to my bedroom. Instead of the bed, I carried her to the bathroom, setting her down on the counter and turning on the shower.

She leaned back on her hands, biting back a curious smile as I took off my clothes. I stood between her legs and slipped the sweater over her head. In place of words I dropped a kiss on her shoulder and hoped she'd understand that we needed a clean slate.

She pulled away and unclipped her bra, letting it fall to the floor. I held my breath, trailing a finger from her collarbone and down one breast, coming to a stop at the peak of her hard nipple. Then I slid her panties out from under her and took a step back to admire the view.

My eyes devoured her, took in every detail from the pulse ticking rapidly at her neck to the rise and fall of her breasts. "Damn, I've missed you." I held her face and ravaged her mouth, her neck, and all the soft skin in between.

She wrapped her legs around me and slid closer, pressing her heat against my painfully hard shaft. We kissed for what seemed like forever as steam gathered in the bathroom, enveloping us in a cloud. When I couldn't take it anymore, I cupped her ass with my hands and swung her off the counter straight to the walk-in shower, shielding her from the hot spray. I held her in my arms, staring at her in disbelief.

"I don't know why I ever thought I could be happy without you," she whispered.

"And are you? Happy?" I asked, reaching up to touch her lips.

She kissed my fingers. "More than."

When she lifted her hips, I positioned my cock at her entrance and lowered her onto me one torturous inch at a time until I filled her entirely. A groan escaped my lips, my legs almost buckling from the pleasure.

Joss's arms tightened around me as she buried her face in my neck. "I'm sorry I hurt you," she said in a strangled voice. "I'm sorry I kept trying to push you away. I thought I was doing the right thing."

I thrust upward. "You feel that?"

She bit her lip and nodded.

"This, right here, is the right thing." I ground into her, going as deep as our bodies would allow. "Just you and me with nothing between us."

And there, under the cleansing spray of the water, we washed away all that had come between us, all the hurt and deceit, until all that was left was Joss and Jake and the love that refused to be swept away.

After the shower, I dried her off, leisurely rubbing the towel over every inch of her body. Then I carried her back to my room, throwing her onto the bed in a fit of laughter.

"I missed you so much," she said as I stretched out beside her. "Every single day I thought about you, wondered what you were doing, if you were thinking of me." She reached up and brushed her fingers through my damp hair.

"Always," I said with a wry smile. "Even when I didn't want to."

We held hands and talked for hours. I told her about my work, how I'd managed to grow Rochester Furniture through word of mouth and hard work. And she told me about Houston, about her mother's recovery and marriage. A glow came over her face when she talked about her writing, about how she overcame writer's block after her trip from Miami.

"After Emerson moved out, I just started to write. The story just flowed out of me, like something got unstuck and there was this deluge of words. Before I knew it, I had finished the novel." Her hands flew around excitedly as she talked, her face glowing with excitement. "And best of all, I have a literary agent now. I don't know how I got so lucky, but she liked my manuscript and offered representation."

"You finally did it," I said, my chest swelling with pride. "You finally found your passion."

"Yes." The smile spread across the face, reaching all the way up to her eyes. "My third passion." She leaned forward and kissed the tip of my nose, a sweet gesture that had me instantly hard.

She noticed, looking down between us with a smile. I went to roll onto her but she pressed a palm on my chest and held me down, shaking her head. With mischief in her eyes, she started sliding down the bed, pressing her lips to my nipple, my stomach, hips, thighs. Finally, she set up camp between my legs, her lips so close but still so painfully far away.

I nudged her with one leg, flashing her a mischievous grin. "Just blow me already."

She chuckled. "You're so romantic."

I grinned at her, opening my mouth to make a joke, but the words dried in my throat when she wrapped her lips around the head of my cock and sealed it tight. Her mouth was warm and wet as it slid down my shaft, sucking me in. My hips bucked involuntarily, driving deeper into her mouth.

I closed my eyes, overwhelmed with the sensations. I had dreamed of this countless times over the years, never really expecting it to happen again. But here she was, the literal woman of my dreams, moaning in pleasure as she worked me over.

Before it was too late, I clamped my legs around her and flipped her over. I leapt on top, caging her in with my arms. "My turn," I growled and licked my way from the base of her throat to the swell between her breasts, down past her bellybutton. Finally, I slipped my tongue between her crease, finding her already wet and throbbing.

She grabbed hold of my hair as her hips rose up off the bed. Spurred on by her moans, I pushed her thighs apart and drew my tongue through the length of her folds, each stroke culminating at the top where I flicked at her clit.

I knew she was close when she held her breath, her entire body taut as she strained for release. Before she could come, I drew myself up over her and slid home in one solid stroke. That was all it took before she cried out, arms and legs trembling around me. I drew back and just as quickly thrust back in, closing my eyes against the exquisite pleasure of her tight sex quivering around my cock.

"God, Joss," I bit out as I continued rocking my hips. Leaning on my elbows, I held her face in my hands, our eyes locked for what seemed like hours. Then I slid my arms under her back and sat up, taking her with me. She linked her hands behind my neck and kissed me, taking long draws with her tongue and biting my bottom lip.

Over and over I thrust into her, crushing her against me as

we made love. When my body tensed, I buried my face in her neck and gripped her hips, my cock swelling and then surging.

"You came back," I said, my voice hoarse.

"I'm here, Jake," she said, squeezing me tight. "Without strings or conditions, I'm yours."

[epilogue]

"You must be Joss," Mom said as soon as she opened the door. Without missing a beat, she stepped forward and wrapped the girl beside me in her bosomy embrace.

"That's Myra. And I'm Peter," Dad said, flashing Joss an apologetic smile as he tried to pry Mom away. "Honey, I think you're cutting off her circulation."

Mom swatted him away and held Joss a few seconds longer before finally letting go. "I'm just so glad to finally meet you." She took hold of Joss's hand and pulled her inside. "It's been a month since Jake told me he was seeing someone. A month of keeping me in suspense!"

"I'm afraid that's my fault," Joss said, throwing me a quick smile. "I've been keeping him busy."

Mom's eyes widened as she glanced at the both of us. "Oh. I see."

"No," I cut in with a laugh. "I was helping her move from

Houston."

Dad raised an eyebrow. "To where?"

"To Boston," I said, unable to contain the smile on my face. "She moved in with me."

Joss sat across the table from me at the dinner table, occupying Tristan's seat. But though I grew up with my brother kicking my leg under the table, this time it was Joss's foot that nudged mine as she grinned at me.

"So Jake told me your mom is in remission from cancer?" Dad asked.

Joss nodded and began to tell the story, from the beginning of Amanda's illness to her near death and, eventually, to her slow but remarkable recovery.

"So what do you do for a living, Joss?" Mom asked after she served the meatloaf and mashed potatoes.

"She's a writer," I said, winking at her across the table.

"Oh? What genre?" Dad asked.

Joss gave a shy sort of smile. "Romance."

"Like the Fifty Shades book?" Dad asked. When my head whipped around to him in surprise, he added, "What? I can't read a book in my own home?"

Joss chuckled. "No. Not exactly."

"Oh. Have you had any books published?"

"Actually..." She fixed her eyes on me. Whatever news she had, it was something I hadn't heard before. "My agent just sold my book to a publishing house. They're looking at publication at the end of the year."

The news brought me to my feet. "What?" I asked, realizing belatedly that I still had my fork in my hand. I set it down and asked, "When?"

She nodded, beaming. "I just got the official word this morning."

"Congratulations. This is amazing." I walked around the table and swept her up in my arms, kissing her with abandon.

She pulled back a few seconds later, throwing a shy look around the table. "Thanks," she said, taking her seat.

I took my own seat, enjoying the blush in her cheeks. I couldn't stop smiling, couldn't take my eyes off the woman before me. "Marry me," I mouthed across the table.

Joss's eyes grew wide. She glanced at my parents for confirmation but both appeared to be busy with their food. She faced me again, her lips falling open, her eyebrows drawing together. "What did you say?" she mouthed back.

I did nothing but grin even though my heart was pounding double time. I hadn't meant to blurt those words out over Sunday dinner, but I wouldn't have taken them back for anything.

"Well this is perfect timing," Mom said, getting up. "I made my special blueberry and peach pie."

"Better just put their slices in a tupperware, Myra," Dad said, raising his eyebrows at me. "Looks like these two have some things to talk about."

"Okay, what did you say during dinner?" Joss asked as soon as we climbed into my truck.

"What? Oh, I said *many meats*. Mom gave me too much meatloaf," I said with a shrug and stuck the key in the ignition. I could feel Joss's eyes on me as I pulled out of the driveway, making it hard to keep a straight face. "What did you think I said?"

"I thought…" She shook her head. "Never mind."

I pursed my lips to keep from blurting out the words again, audibly this time. When I passed our turn and kept going toward Back Bay, Joss said, "Where are we going?"

"To the best place on earth."

"You're taking me to Disney World?" she asked incredulously.

I tickled her side. "No. Somewhere a little less crowded." I looked over at the clock—ten p.m. "In fact, we've got the whole place to ourselves right now."

I kept Joss guessing. When we drove past Copley Square and into the parking lot across the street from one of Boston's most famous buildings, she twisted in her seat and faced me with her mouth open. "The Boston Public Library? Really?"

I held up a camping lantern. "Are you up for a private tour?"

"Always."

We crossed the street and entered through a side door by the loading dock.

"Is this legal?" Joss whispered, keeping close as we walked through darkened halls. The lantern lit only so much; the rest of the place was still framed in shadows.

"Sure. Probably," I said, not disclosing that I'd already asked permission earlier in the day.

I led her through the front lobby with its stately columns and arched ceilings, and up the grand staircase. We stopped on the landing between the two marble lions, looking around.

"Wow, this is beautiful," Joss said, turning in place. She walked over to the banister, trying to read the inscription under the lion. "This is the most beautiful library I've ever seen."

I nodded, proud of my hometown and its rich history.

I led her upstairs and into the main reading room, showing her some of the shelves I had replaced or repaired. I lifted the lantern, trying to shine light up to the impressive ceiling. "It's hard to see, but this entire room has a barrel vaulted ceiling."

Joss broke away from me, walking around with her bottom lip trapped between her teeth. "This really is the best place on earth," she said, running her fingers along spines of books.

She moved towards the wall of shelves on the other end of the room that divided the alcove from the rest of the area. It was my favorite area of the library, with its doorway in the middle of the wall and the clock on top, like an entrance to another place and time.

I followed her inside without hesitation.

Despite all the grandeur and beauty around us, I couldn't take my eyes off Joss, couldn't stop the surge of my pulse. Taking a deep breath, I took her hand and led her over to a table where a pale green cloth-covered book lay on top.

I set the lantern on the tabletop and allowed Joss to examine the first pages of the book. "It's a first edition Jane Eyre," she said with wide eyes. "Look at the typesetting on this, it's so beautiful."

With great care, she lifted the book up to her nose and sniffed between its pages. "God, I love the smell of old books." As she did, a green silk ribbon slipped out from between the pages, and on its end dangled a sparkling object.

"What's th—" She froze, her lips forming an O as her eyes followed the gently swinging ring. Her hand flew up to her mouth when I took a step forward and unfastened the ribbon, holding the delicate diamond ring between my fingers.

"I bought this the day you came to Boston," I began, wishing I had written something down instead of winging it. I took a deep breath and forged on. "Because, despite all that's happened between us, I knew that this time was it."

She swallowed, her eyes twinkling like the diamond.

"And so, Jocelyn Blake, I ask you to pass through life at my side, to grow old with me in a house full of passion and books."

A grin tugged at her lips. "I'll write books and you'll build shelves to put them in."

I nodded, tipping my head down to hers. "And we can talk all night until we can't keep our eyes open anymore."

"That sounds absolutely perfect," she whispered as I took her hand and slipped the ring on her finger.

And there, surrounded by history and books, we began our happily ever after.

About the Author

June Gray is a daydreamer who was born in the Philippines, raised in Australia, and now calls the United States home. At the age of ten she penned a short story inspired by a Judy Blume novel and has been unable to stop writing since.

She has lived on four different continents and most recently inhabited a 240-year-old castle owned by a Graf in rural Germany. She now resides in Oklahoma with her husband, two daughters, and a mini schnauzer.

Her stories are drawn from dreams, fantasies, music, and trips through airports. Apart from her lifelong affair with words, she also loves graphic design, singing in the shower, Dunkin Donuts, and working out.

Also by June Gray

The Disarm Series
Disarm
Arrest
Surrender

The True North Series
Finding West
Heading East

The Origin Series
The Origin
The Forsaken

Taking Heart

Untamed: The Savage

Made in the USA
Middletown, DE
10 May 2021